> Jarod:
> Thanks man! (Sorry missing 'R'. hope you [?]
> it.)

PLOW THE BONES

Douglas F. Warrick

Douglas F. Warrick (signature)

APEX PUBLICATIONS
LEXINGTON, KY

APEX VOICES: BOOK 1

This collection is a work of fiction. All the characters and events portrayed in these stories are either fictitious or are used fictitiously.

Plow the Bones

Copyright © 2013 Douglas F. Warrick
Cover art © 2013 Saber Core
Cover design by Danni Kelly
Interior design by Jason Sizemore

"Behindeye: A History" © 2010, *The Drabblecast*; "Her Father's Collection" © 2009, Tales of the Mountain State 3 (Woodland Press); "Zen and the Art of Gordon Dratch's Damnation" © 2010, *Dark Faith* (Apex Publications); "The Itaewon Eschatology Show" © 2011, *Apex Magazine*; "Come to My Arms, My Beamish Boy" © 2009, *Murky Depths*; "Funeral Song for a Ventriloquist" © 2010, *The Drabblecast*; "Ballad of a Hot Air Balloon-Headed Girl" © 2012, DailyScienceFiction.com; "Rattenkönig" © 2013, *Vampires Don't Sparkle* (Seventh Star Press); "Stickhead (Or… In the Dark, in the Wet, We Are Collected)" © 2006, *MudRock*; "I Inhale the City, the City Exhales Me" © 2012, *Dark Faith: Invocations* (Apex Publications); "Inhuman Zones: An Oral History of Jan Landau's Golem Band," "Drag," "Old Roses," and "Across the Dead Station Desert, Television Girl" are original to this edition.

"Introduction" © 2013, Gary A. Braunbeck

"Apex Voices: What Do You Hear" © 2013, Jason Sizemore

All rights reserved, including the right to reproduce the book, or portions thereof, in any form.

Published by Apex Publications, LLC
PO Box 24323
Lexington, KY 40524

www.apexbookcompany.com

First Edition: May 2013
ISBN Trade Paperback: 978-1-937009-15-1

To Gene Milner,
who taught me how to love stories.

To Don Warrick,
who taught me how to tell stories.

And to Mary Louise,
who taught me how to respect the act of telling stories.

"Almost impossible stories filled with surprising warmth and strangeness by a studied craftsman of the imagination. Douglas Warrick's *Plow the Bones* has provided dangerous tales of puppets with secrets, unforgettable rock bands, haunted closets and people who may or may not be human; perhaps they're more than human. From transformative games with strangers to poor souls experiencing heaven and hell (and not quite sure which is which), you will never forget these unsettling stories."
—**Ann VanderMeer, Hugo Award-winning editor of *The New Weird***

"It's been far too long since I've read a collection of horror stories that actually disturbed me. This one did. Like the bastard child of Chuck Palahniuk and Clive Barker, Doug Warrick writes feverishly, like a man on a charnel train that is relentlessly barreling its way through corrupt and ugly terrain, heading for some great, unknowable horror. Herein lies a gruesome gathering of Gothic nightmares fashioned from Warrick's lyrical, affecting, mesmeric prose. One of the finest collections I've read in quite some time."
—**Kealan Patrick Burke, Bram Stoker Award-winning author of *The Turtle Boy, Kin,* and *Nemesis***

"*Plow the Bones* is hands-down the finest single-author collection I've read in a decade."
—**Gary A. Braunbeck, Bram Stoker Award-winning author of *In Silent Graves, Far Dark Fields,* and *To Each Their Darkness***

Everyone has killed in order to live. Nature's universal law of creation from destruction operates in mind as in matter. As Freud, Nietzsche's heir, asserts, identity is conflict. Each generation drives its plow over the bones of the dead.
—Camille Paglia, *Sexual Personae*

The only difference between disappointment and depression is your level of commitment.
—Marc Maron

—Contents, Page One—

Apex Voices: What Do You Hear?
viii

Introduction
ix

Behindeye: A History
1

Her Father's Collection
4

Zen and the Art of Gordon Dratch's Damnation
12

The Itaewon Eschatology Show
32

Come to My Arms, My Beamish Boy
46

Funeral Song for a Ventriloquist
58

Inhuman Zones: An Oral History of Jan Landau's Golem Band
68

—Contents, Page Two—

Drag
90

Ballad of a Hot Air Balloon-Headed Girl
100

Rattenkönig
114

Old Roses
128

Stickhead (Or... In the Dark, in the Wet, We Are Collected)
144

I Inhale the City, the City Exhales Me
164

Across the Dead Station Desert, Television Girl
182

Acknowledgments
212

Biographies
213

Apex Voices: What Do You Hear?

Not so long ago, I accosted a handful of the Apex faithful with an important question.

"What comes to mind when you think of our books?"

The answers were varied, but thematically, they bore a striking similarity. Terminology like "genre-bending," "smart fiction," "surreal," and "unconventional" were mentioned repeatedly. As a publisher, I was quite pleased and couldn't help but smile. My goal with Apex has always been to bring entertaining fiction to genre fans who like to have their perceptions and imaginations challenged. To a degree, I appear to have met that goal.

But hold on! I have a second major goal, as well. As a publisher and editor, I derive no greater sense of accomplishment than bringing a fantastic new (or underappreciated) author to the attention of genre readers. That's why this book exists. Thus the Apex Voices series.

From 2006 through 2008, I ran a monthly online feature called "The Apex Featured Writer Program." It was quite popular, and I don't recall why I stopped doing it. The writers appreciated the opportunity and exposure. Our readers enjoyed finding talented new writers. A win-win for everybody. Let us consider the Apex Voices series a delayed continuation of the long-lost featured writer program.

Here's how I envision this series working out. Two, three, maybe four times a year, Apex will bring you the work of a writer who we feel has a unique writing voice. Often, these writers will be someone you have never read or heard about. And often, after reading their Apex Voices book, these writers will be people you'll notice being published more and more often—because they're just that damn good.

Apex is pleased to offer this collection of work by Doug F. Warrick as the first book in the series. Doug is a unique individual and fantastic author... well, Gary A. Braunbeck does a great job describing Mr. Warrick in his introduction, and I would hate to spoil that pleasure for you (okay, I have to mention the sideburns, because they're awesome).

Sit back. Enjoy. And let Doug Warrick's voice take control of your grey matter.

Jason Sizemore
Publisher/Editor-in-Chief

Introduction
Gary A. Braunbeck

"*...he pours and pours and pours...*"

Try this on for an opening paragraph:

> "I knew a girl who tied a hot air balloon envelope to her shoulders, just in case her head should ever burst into flames. It was homemade, sewn together from stolen scraps of Dacron, mottled and gaudy. It was as wide as her shoulders and it hung down to the small of her back like a pair of folded oil-slick dragonfly wings. She pierced the thin, tender skin of her shoulders with four strong surgical-steel rings, two just above the delicate cliff of her clavicle and two over the twin plateaus of her shoulder blades, and to these she anchored the envelope."

Beats the hell out of, say: "It was a dark and stormy night," doesn't it?

It also drapes your brain in a cloak of surreal imagery that somehow manages to still anchor itself to the mundane, making it all the more puzzling, challenging, and, well...*fascinating*. It's not only an example of a writer with a full-tilt bozo *luxuriant* imagination warming up, it's an example of what can be accomplished when a writer tosses off the manacles of traditional thinking when applying that imagination to the structure of a traditional short-story narrative— and as Borges-esque as that paragraph may seem, the story from which those lines are taken (as well as all others in this mind-bender of a collection) is, ultimately, respectful of the traditional short-story form, and adheres to it insomuch as the story itself needs to; that is to say, the guy writing those lines knows the rules, so he also knows when and how to break them.

The writer is, of course, Douglas Warrick, and to meet him in person you'd never suspect that he's capable of producing the kind of mesmerizing, head-spinning, and often incendiary work which

Introduction

graces the pages of this book you have the good sense to be reading.

Let me see if I can describe Doug to you: he is not of what you would call "towering" stature—I stand a little over 5'10" and the top of his head almost reaches my nose—his facial features can best be categorized as "delicate" (my wife put it like this: "he's a very *pretty* man."), he's a quite soft-spoken sort of fellow, usually sporting a pair of the thickest, curliest, this-side-of-a-70s-porn-star *bitchin'* sideburns you've ever seen, and if it weren't for his feet being too small to qualify, you'd almost think he was a Hobbit. He is a citizen of the world, knows a great deal about so-called "foreign" cultures, and for as young as he is has a wealth of human experience that makes you feel like you've been standing at a bus stop making tweets since you were eleven years old.

He is also one of the most painstakingly *precise* writers I've ever encountered. Obsessively painstaking, to be exact. This book you're holding? It not only almost didn't almost happen, it almost didn't happen *three times*. I'll spare you the details, but the whole shebang reminds me of a (probably anecdotal) story concerning Margaret Mitchell and her novel *Gone With the Wind*: the story goes that Mitchell was so hell-bound determined to make sure the book was as perfect as she could make it that her publisher had to literally yank it out of her hands via a strenuous tug-of-war. I don't know if Jason Sizemore and the gang at Apex had to go to that length to finally get this book out of Doug's hands, but I *do* know that I threatened him with physical violence if he pulled it from publication again—and you'll recall I'm taller than him.

Was it worth the wait(s)? Damn right it was.

Plow the Bones is hands-down the finest single-author collection I've read in a decade. I had the pleasure of hearing Doug read "I Inhale the City, the City Exhales Me" (and damn if I don't wish I'd come up with that title) at an Apex Day gathering a few years ago, and it was something of a minor revelation to me; that story—a beautifully-rendered extended metaphor tale about urban paranoia and personal isolation carried to phantasmagoric extremes—forever destroyed any preconceptions I'd had about the man and his work: Doug Warrick was the Real Thing. Most writers are well into their fourth or fifth decade before achieving the level of skill and craftsmanship he's already reached. (I should mention here, just to keep

Gary A. Braunbeck

everything above-board, that I am 53 and I hate him. Talented little toad's work makes mine look like it's been running on fumes; I think I shall rip those sideburns from his delicate face whence we meet again. Digression endeth here.)

I am tempted to compare Doug's work to that of Harlan Ellison, and while that might not off-base (you'd have to be clinically brain-dead to not see the Ellison influence in some of these pieces), it's far too easy and obvious an association, and trivializes both writer's work; I do feel that there are echoes here of Kobo Abe, Donald Barthelme, Gertrude Stein, Borges, a touch of Kafka and Angela Carter, and a dash of Richard Brautigan—but even those comparisons look trivial now that I re-read them. It comes down, methinks, to a matter of how a writer approaches language, whether it is something he or she *works* with or something she or he allows to *possess* them.

Warrick is most definitely possessed. He is acutely aware of language in all of its colors, textures, lyricism, and subtleties; he uses words the way composers use musical notes, and understands the undercurrent of the words' vibrations like a physicist understands the intricacies of String Theory. Once you've finished reading "Her Father's Collection" (a remarkable story that left me shaking with something akin to awe) or "Inhuman Zones: An Oral History of Jan Landau's Golem Band" (a piece both hysterical and heartfelt), and find yourself finished off with the closing novella, "Across the Dead Station Desert, Television Girl" (a masterpiece, a story that should win many awards), you will know, as I did, that Douglas F. Warrick has at last arrived on the scene on a Big Way, and that the incandescent cyclone of his imagination is overpowering.

Yeah, I kinda liked this collection, if you haven't figured it out yet.

I can think of no better way to characterize Doug Warrick the writer than to quote a line (arguably my favorite line in the book) from one of the early stories contained herein; a line that should serve as something of incantation for all writers to perform when that damned story just *has* to be released from your head and set upon the page: "…he pours and pours and pours until that sad and noisy world behind his eyes is eaten by a great white flood."

Welcome to the sad, noisy, mind-bending worlds of Douglas F. Warrick. You have no idea what you're in for. As it should be.

BEHINDEYE: A HISTORY

Douglas F. Warrick

There is a man whose pupils are full of moths. Dry moths, dying moment by moment and collecting in drifts behind his eyes, deep down in that secret and endless world behind his face. A blue desert world populated only by the moths and a timid hermit with no eyes of his own, who only leaves his moth-wing hut to scoop up handfuls of dead moths and shovel them into his mouth.

There was a cautious status quo there once, in this windless world of Behindeye. The timid old hermit wandered and ate and he was mostly happy, if not lonely. But there was a change. The blind hermit found an infant in one of the heaps of dead moths, some wretched baby born skinless, born without lips so that his teeth struck out from his face like fence posts, born without a nose so that the skin of his face slid without interruption from his eyebrows down to the rough ridge of his upper gum line, and his slit nostrils opened his skull like sudden sinkholes. And when those moths who were still alive saw the infant, they saw a lizard-like horror, red and screaming, and they feared it, for moths fear few things as they do lizards. The hermit could not see those things, because he had no eyes of his own, so he took the infant back to his moth-wing shack, and he kept him warm and fed him dead-moth soup. And in a few years, the infant had grown into a lipless, skinless, noseless lizard-boy, red and screaming.

And this is what life is like now in the world behind some guy's eyes. The hermit worships the lizard-boy as a god, for the lizard-boy leads him through the moth-drifts and provides for him in all the ways that a man without eyes cannot provide for himself. The moths regard the lizard-boy, the howling, mewling, gurgling, skinless, lipless, noseless, red and screaming lizard-boy, as a devil. "Grave Eater" they call him, and "The Meat Golem" because he has no skin (and because the moths are Jewish). In moth mythology, the lizard-boy is the negative aspect of the God of Abraham, who exists to define suffering with his screaming, with his grinding, slobbering teeth, and his skinless awfulness.

The lizard-boy is aware of none of this. Life is very painful for him. He often wants to die. But he loves the hermit so much. He

Plow the Bones

watches him sleep at night, risking all-over nerve-burning agony just to use his skinless fingers to brush away a strand of the hermit's hair from where it sticks at the spit-sticky corner of the old fellow's mouth, and tuck it behind his ear. He does not know the word, "father," and he wishes he had some name for this perfect, fragile, sweet old thing who saved him from certain suffocation in the moth-drifts.

Now, the moths watch him from the corners of the shack's single window. They do not make any sound. In just a few seconds, they will kill the lizard-boy while the hermit sleeps. They do not need him anymore. They do not need a reminder of suffering. They understand now, and they have wept and prayed and howled, "Elohim, Elohim!" at the sky, and they thanked God for the lesson they have learned. And they have vowed to do away with this totem of suffering, now made obsolete. They have planned this night for years, passing down the stratagems through generations. Their fear, their work, their prayers, spanning a million—no, no a *billion*—three-day lifespans, and today, TODAY, they will lay to rest the aspirations of their forefathers! Today they earn the legacy of their ancestors! They have crafted sharp teeth for themselves from the tiny crystal bones of their dead and mounted them in their mouths. Was it painful? You're goddamn right it was! Setting crystal spines into their soft tiny moth-gums, drawing fountains of their own blood, God, how they screamed and cried. But they are almost ready. In just seconds, they will be ready. No. Now.

Now they are ready.

They dive. There is blood and there are broken wings and moth powder scattered in poison clouds. The lizard-boy bawls and screams and swats and chomps with his grinding, slobbering, fencepost teeth, but theirs are sharper and faster and more precise. They shred him. The hermit wakes to the sounds of screaming, and he cries out, and he wants to know what is happening to his poor lizard-boy, his miracle god-son, what is happening, what is happening, my God, what is happening? He stands and he swats and he stomps, wading through helpless ragged screams and armies of moths that he cannot see, and he is useless. There is so much terrible noise. There is war. And it is not over for a very long time.

At home tonight, the man behind whose eyes exist the moths and the hermit and the dying, red and screaming lizard-boy, he rummages beneath the sink until he finds the bright white bottle of Clorox. He says to himself that this will probably hurt an awful lot, and he steels himself. This must be done. At the office tomorrow, they will talk. They will say it was an accident, an awful tragedy, poor man, blinded like that, he should sue! They will not know the details. They will construct the story themselves. But that will happen later. For now, he unscrews the bottle. And he pours and pours and pours until that sad and noisy world behind his eyes is eaten by a great white flood.

Her Father's Collection

She runs. Oh, yes, she runs. Her bare feet slap like hands against the rough, loose-packed dirt of her father's carriage trail. Tiny rocks stick to her heels, gnawing divots into them, little pink craters like bite marks, and why yes, that does seem just about right, doesn't it? Because Sunrise Mansion does have teeth. Sunrise Mansion devours.

She can hear the shrill, severe laughter of the Girls, and she feels like she has missed the set-up and punch line of a particularly cruel joke.

Somewhere up above her, in her father's awful house, there is a fireplace. She feels the meanness and the promise of it, even though seventy years have passed since she has seen it in person, seventy years since she died. Her sides hurt and her lungs blaze white-hot in her chest, and all she wants to think about is the run, the dash, the great blind escape. Despite all of this, her father's fireplace crawls up out of her memory and its image glows inside her head. The faces that stretch and strain from its surface, each one a stolen thing, a collection of sculpted Christs and gargoyle heads, each from a different place and a different time. The stones set into the face of the mantle, each with its birthplace carved into the surface. Westminster Abbey. The Birthplace of William the Conqueror. The Great Wall of China.

Some part of her thinks, *My daddy collects stolen ghosts.*

The dress. The dress keeps tangling around her ankles and she keeps tripping, almost falling. Oh, her daddy gave her this dress, didn't he? Oh, yes he did. He gave her this dress and…

And he says, "Isabelle, love. The pictures tonight?"

And they go. He in his white suit with wax in his mustache and she in her fine new dress. God, how pretty she looks! And she never thinks so, never ever, but tonight with her handsome daddy smiling beside her, she feels perfectly gorgeous. They park the car on the street and when they get out, someone walks up and shakes her daddy's hand and says, "Good to see you, Mr. Governor," even though Daddy hasn't been governor for decades. Everything shines. That joy she feels, that pride… god, it leaps from her and wraps itself around

PLOW THE BONES

everything! They watch *The Black Pirate* with Douglas Fairbanks. It is in Technicolor. In the dark next to her father, in his white suit with his pipe-stem sticking out of his vest pocket, everything in the whole wide world is painted in those colors.

On the way home, her father runs the car into a tree. And something sharp hits her hard in the forehead. And all the color drowns in itself. And everything is no color at all.

She tries not to cry. That was the subtle clutch of his big thick fingers around her ankle, so light that she didn't even notice. It kept her next to him, even at thirty-five years old, old enough to be married, to go dancing, to experience all the wonderful things the world had to offer. Damn him. Damn her daddy.

She rounds a corner and sees the Girls standing in the middle of the trail and holding hands. They shift. Always. Their bodies can't decide how they died. Now their necks are swollen and stretched and purple, and their heads twist away at strange angles and the blood vessels in their eyes have burst. Now their beautiful dresses, the elaborate Charleston Civil War chic they must have affected so well while they breathed, shred in a dozen places, fill with charred bullet holes, and their faces and their arms are pocked with the same, each dry and black and burnt around the edges, like open unblinking eyes. It's the power of the living tongue, of what people say about the dead. They say the Girls were hanged. They say they died by firing squad.

It changes you after a while.

Isabelle shudders, and the Girls smile. Daddy's voice dances through her head and she is swallowed by memory again. What had he said? In front of that great Frankenstein mantel? He had said…

"Do you know what happened to them?" he says, with his shirt open at the chest and his vest unbuttoned, sitting in his big leather chair in front of the fireplace. She is six, maybe seven, when Daddy finds the bodies. While the crew built the carriage trail through the wide and winding woods up the hill to Sunrise. Two bodies, mummified and buried. And Daddy reburies them, sets up a stone to mark their resting place. Now in the sitting room, he tilts his glass from side to side, watches the gin slide from edge to edge. "Spies, darling. Spies for the Union. Can you believe it? Tried and executed. Right here."

It is a week, maybe two, after they found them, and Daddy looks so tired.

She hadn't understood then, just a little girl, no real scars to compare to those of her father. But there was something else there, wasn't there? Yes, something shameful and secret and warm kept all to himself. Her father's vice. Stolen ghosts.

So it began with the Girls.

Now the Girls nod to Isabelle. And no, no, no, she does not want to go to them, does not want to walk within whispering distance, where she can't tell which of them is doing the whispering, but yes, yes, yes, her feet move her forward, and now there is a Girl on either side of Isabelle, both dead and shifting.

"The key," says one of the girls.

"Oh yes, the key," says the other.

They giggle together.

She tries so hard not to let her skin go thick with gooseflesh as their whispers wash over her. She fails. She tells them she knows. They need the key.

There is a door set into the mantel of that terrible fireplace, that massive golem in her father's house. A tiny tin door with a keyhole set in its center.

The Girls giggle again. There's nothing nice about that sound. There is only something final. Because the Girls call the shots. They always have, ever since the crash and the death and the night she woke up as a part of her father's ghost collection. Making plans, giving orders, whispering, "Run, Isabelle! Run for Sunrise!" so loud that indeed she had to run, if only to get away from their choked babydoll voices. "Get us out," they whispered (and still whisper). "You can get us out."

So she runs. Like she has run every night since the last one of her life.

When she sees the house sliding over the horizon, the first tears come and she almost stops. Almost. Too angry and sad and dead to do that. So she hikes up that beautiful dress and clutches at the hem in one tight white fist and keeps running.

Damn her daddy. And damn the memories that keep pushing up into her head, her father with his hands on the wheel, it was hot in the car, the kind of summer night in Charleston that would melt…

It is the kind of summer night in Charleston that melts the wax her daddy puts in his mustache, and now, with his fists locked around the steering wheel, her daddy's mustache is drooping. She can see the first beads of wet wax work their way down like vines and it makes her laugh like a little girl. Thirty-five years old and laughing like a little girl. She tells him she loves him. He smiles and says, "I love you too, Izza. You're my baby girl."

But Daddy looks sad, so sad, and she reaches over and puts her hand on his arm. And she asks her big beautiful daddy what's wrong.

"Going to leave me, darling. Past time. Pretty young woman like you."

And she tells him, no, Daddy, no, not yet, she's not going anywhere just yet, but he lets loose one tight fist and waves her away.

"I know better," he says, and the first drops of wax slip away and pad against the thigh of his white pants. Her daddy's eyes are so wide tonight. So wide it scares her. They stare forward, no twitching, no blinking, and he drives like a man piloting a bullet.

They ride up onto the hill, toward the carriage trail and home. She puts her hand on his leg, over the place where the wax dripped, and catches the next few spatters. They are quiet.

And when her daddy says, "The only way to keep something forever," she's hardly listening anymore. Just breathing in the night, and swallowing the sounds. She doesn't really hear him until he says, "Is losing it for good," and jerks the steering wheel sideways. He has time to say, "Sorry, baby girl."

She runs. She runs past the monument he built for her out here, the anchor he tied to her. The stone Madonna is gone, lifted up by the root, but her ashes are in there somewhere, and she shivers and knows that she should not be in two places at once. She runs up the old stone steps, slick and made green with age and mildew.

She does not stop running until her bare feet slide onto the cold stone porch. Has she come this far before? She can't remember. She doesn't think so. No time. No time.

The Girls are here, holding hands and sharing secrets. Shot. Hanged. Both. They wave, and Isabelle grinds her teeth against her tongue and screws her eyes shut and pretends they are not here. Still, they whisper. They say, "The key, baby girl." Isabelle wants to scream.

She opens the door. And the three of them go in together. Sunrise Mansion breathes them in, and they are swallowed and damned when the Girls close the door. The front hall is too long, longer than it ever was when she lived, and lined with her father's things. The ghastly old collection. Things once owned by the dead, and now owned by them again. And framed in the doorway to the sitting room, the cloister of the slippery-sick fireplace with its many faces, is her daddy. He stands with his back to them, his hands clasped behind him, in his white Mark Twain suit. He breathes, or he seems to. And Isabelle is split in two. She loves him. She hates him. She blames and forgives and reconvicts and once again pardons him.

There is noise. There is so very much noise! Just looking at him, standing there and pretending not to know that they have intruded into this place, her world is filled with sound, crashing sound, crunching sound, metal on metal on glass on dirt on flesh crash crunch scream she should scream she can't scream because she does not have a voice has never had a voice sound!

She is on her knees with the heels of her hands pressed to her ears before she knows she has fallen. And still her father will not lower his chin and crane his neck to see her. Behind her, the Girls lick their lips and hiss like snake-harlots, and all that noise still presses down on her, paralyzes her.

Her father says, "So good to see you, baby girl. You look splendid." And the noise breaks. Silence fills the cracks, shuttles the sound away.

So Isabelle stands. With shaky knees, with her pretty dress tangling around her bare ankles. She steps forward. And she sees the fireplace beyond her poor awful daddy.

Oh, no, no, no.

All of the faces are gone. The faces of Christ and the faces of a thousand nameless under-bit gargoyles and goblins. All sucked in and away. And in their place now, staring out with sadness set in chiseled eyes, her daddy's face stares back a thousand times. She thinks, *Don't turn around now, Daddy. God, please, don't turn around.* She does not want to know what her handsome daddy has become, does not want to see the swirling vertigo where Sunrise has stolen her daddy's face.

He stays put. His hands remain clasped. The faces in the fireplace close their eyes and grit their teeth. "I didn't mean a thing but love, Izza. You know that."

And she does. Because the only way to keep something forever is to lose it for good. But it hurts. And she's too tired to fight the tears.

The Girls slide up on either side of her and she winces at the smell of breath from lungs that no longer breathe. They say, "The key?"

And she nods.

Her daddy's sad stone faces, they all curl up on themselves like the faces of crying men, and they say, "Baby girl, I am so sorry."

His body reaches into his front vest pocket, where he always kept his beautiful Meerschaum pipe, and he pulls out the thing that she wants. The key. Oh, the key!

She reaches over his shoulder and snatches it, and close up like this, she sees the place where his face should be. Just a glance. Just a glimmer in her periphery. But, oh it is awful. And she begins to cry so hard that she almost makes a noise.

The Girls push her forward, past the faceless thing shaped like her father, out of the front hall and into the sitting room. Toward the fireplace, that wall of faces that used to be stolen and are now all her father's. Those stones once carved with their birthplaces, each to a one now reads SUNRISE.

And there is the door. The tiny tin door with the keyhole in its center.

Her father's faces say, "There's nothing behind that door. But you know that, baby girl. This never ends."

"The key!" whisper the Girls. And they drown her poor daddy into silence.

She unlocks the door. And she opens it. And now, oh yes, now she…

She runs. Oh, yes, she runs. Her bare feet slap like hands against the rough loose-packed dirt of her father's carriage trail. Tiny rocks stick to her heels, gnawing little divots into them, little pink craters like bite marks, and why yes, that does seem just about right, doesn't it? Because Sunrise Mansion does have teeth. Sunrise Mansion devours.

She can hear the shrill, severe laughter of the Girls, and she feels like she has missed the set-up and punch line of a particularly cruel joke.

Zen and the art of Gordon dratch's damnation

During the first era, they observe him. They watch him burn. It is a slow fire, a terribly slow fire which burns him in stages that last a thousand years. A millennium's worth of reddening skin, progressing toward blisters that form in the time it takes for generations to be born and to die. They observe as the flames climb him like leeches, blackening him, curling his skin like old paper, revealing (with a flourish, a magician's handkerchief yanked away) the strings and highways of his musculature. They watch, and take notes, as his organs boil and burst and their contents spill down the grate at his feet, sluicing down and down and down the sheer walls of the forever-long pit below him. They watch his eyeballs liquefy, they watch him as he becomes unable to watch them. They watch his larynx tumble out, then watch the chords behind it stretch and pop. They watch the layers of his penis curl backward one by one, until there is nothing but a burnt bundle of tissue at his crotch shaped like a rose. They watch his teeth fall, note their velocity and the rhythm of their *tic-tic-tic* staccato down the drain, jot down the exact moment at which the sound becomes too faint to hear.

They watch all of this, and they brainstorm. And when it is all over, they do it all over again in reverse, and see if his pain is any less bearable when played backwards. And then they compare notes.

—*Allow the sensory organs to last longer, or not be destroyed at all. Allow him to see, hear, taste, and feel all of it.*

—*Leave his penis. I want to see what happens when we leave his penis.*

—*He does not scream enough. Hotter fire? Slower?*

During the second era, they pry apart his mind and climb inside. They want to see who he is, and why he is here. They become like tiny mosquitoes and bleed him of his memories and emotions.

For a few decades, there is only fear. The terrible (delicious, oh so delicious for them, and oh so fascinating; these things always are) sensation of awakening to a lie you've been told, one around which you've constructed your entire life. No, no, no, this can't be real, I can't be here, I don't believe in this! It is amazing to them how long it takes for the shock to wear off. The damned can never accept that

PLOW THE BONES

they are damned. They can never grasp that they have simply chosen incorrectly. What was it that the God-boy had said? About being THE way? THE truth? THE light?

They relish his fear. They do not become bored of it. Not once in the never-beginning history of their kind have they ever.

And when they have gorged themselves on his emotions, they dig past them and excavate his life. They find that this man's name is Gordon Dratch. Gordon Dratch was twenty-eight years old when he fell off a ladder outside of his home and cracked open his skull on his concrete driveway.

—*What a wonderfully comical way to die.*
—*They laugh at him, I'm sure. His obituary is it's own punch line.*
—*What else? What else?*

They dig, and they find.

Witness Gordon Dratch as a child. Thirteen, and angry. He opens the closet door slowly, careful of the creak in the hinges and the scrape against the rough carpet. He ducks inside, holds his breath. The closet smells like peppermint and Old Spice and sweat and that dry, aged stench of all those creepy old people at church. Bald buzzard-headed men and fat mean-eyed women, whose toothless mouths can't seem to shape the words of the hymns, and therefore just sing off-key animal noises. He hates them. But he's not concerned with them just now. It's in here somewhere, his prize, his reward for being quiet and cunning and thirteen. He finds it in an old shoebox that used to hold his dad's dress shoes. A forty-ounce bottle of pale-brown booze, the label torn off so that the only markings on the glass are the torn white leavings of the paper and the sticky label-glue that held it on. His dad's stash, the secret stuff.

He used to find it all over the place. Beneath the seat of Daddy's car. Down in the basement behind the dryer. Even after Daddy's Big Breakthrough, the day he and Mommy sat Gordon and Annie down in the living room and Mommy said, "Guys. Daddy's got a problem with alcohol. We've got to give Daddy some space and some extra love, okay? He needs us to help him get better." So, yeah, Gordon knows what booze is, and he knows that his dad was a drunk. Is a drunk. Whatever.

He hides the bottle beneath his coat, hard up inside his armpit, and he reaches inside his dad's jacket and steals a few cigarettes too. Then he slips out, closes the door behind him with the same slow care he took in opening it. And he leaves the house.

Outside, Mark Milligan is waiting for him with his hands shoved in his pockets, his eyes darting from Gordon's front door to the street and back again, checking for the hidden cameras, the signs of the trap. He says, "D'ja get it?"

Gordon nods. They cut across the street and through somebody's back yard. An Irish setter growls at them, and they spit at it and flip it the bird. They vault the fence and sit beneath the bushes by the railroad tracks, trading swigs of the forty and smoking Winstons. Mark says, "My dad says your dad is gonna start giving sermons sometimes. Like, as practice."

Gordon says, "Yup."

Mark says, "Is he any good?"

Gordon cocks an eyebrow at him. "What do you mean?"

"Like, does he want to be a pastor or something?"

"I guess. I dunno."

They sit in silence for a while, smoking and taking little sips, too young and too scared to drink enough to get drunk. Then Gordon says, "I don't believe in God, anyway." They spend the rest of the afternoon like that, silent, pretending to drink, pretending to smoke, until the sun starts going down and they both have to sneak away home and brush their teeth so no one smells the smoke on their breath.

They like this memory. It is typical, vintage human behavior. Delicious in its predictability. They've tasted it before, and they note its flavor, write a few lines on the similarities it holds to other memories like it.

—*Poor baby was an angry teenager. We weep for you, Gordon.*
—*Is he an atheist? He doesn't burn like an atheist.*
—*More! There must be more!*

After the fear, the thing that was Gordon Dratch feels intense, awful, cold regret. He feels it freeze inside him, even through the slow fire that burns and bursts him over and over again. They ob-

PLOW THE BONES

serve the change with joy, watching a favorite play, coming to a well-remembered and well-beloved scene. He weeps until his eyes are gone, and then weeps some more once they are rewound back into his head. They watch the realization work its way across his soul, spreading through his veins like a blood-sickness. He made the wrong decision. Faced with a million spiritual doors, he opened the wrong one. There was such a thing as a wrong door! All of those red-faced old men with their fists bound up into tight, sausage-fingered slabs on the pulpit, those men who had raged against the follies of a Godless world, those men had been RIGHT! Oh, God. Oh, God, forgive me now.

They applaud. Their favorite line. No man enters the kingdom, and all that.

And then they dig deeper. So much to learn about this perfect, typical number of the damned. So many beautiful, repetitive layers to wonder at.

Witness Gordon Dratch in fast-motion, the high school years, filled to bursting with parking lot fights, stolen liquor, three-day suspensions, detentions, Saturday schools, cigarettes, CDs from Scandinavian metal bands with face-paint and leather gauntlets who wore upside-down crosses and sang songs about the devil. Witness the first few years of college whiz by, time-lapse photography of Gordon becoming a sullen young man, the kid whose every relationship would ultimately be scuttled by daddy issues and a latent anger toward a God he claims he does not believe in. All so fast that you can see the bones in his face shift, change shape. A series of patchy beards grown and then shaved off, a dozen pairs of glasses becoming scratched or broken at the bow and then replaced, a thousand T-shirts and a thousand pairs of jeans, recycled over and over again. Spend a single second watching Gordon shout black-metal lyrics in the face of the street-preacher on the quad, both of them red-faced, both of them with veins standing up in their necks.

Now stop.

Did you miss it? The moment of his awakening? It is easy to do when you fly through a life. But look at him now, sitting at a desk with his notebook in front of him, scribbling with intense concentration. He loves this class. It is very possibly the only class he has ever taken that he has ever enjoyed. He is twenty-one years old. The heading he has scrawled at the top of the perforated standard-rule page says, ZEN NOTES. Behind it are fifteen pages with the same heading, filled with simple, perfect discoveries excavated from a history he never knew existed, quotes from men who became historical footnotes thousands of years before Gordon Dratch was born, revelations of a life that could be lived without anger or fear.

Gordon Dratch is joyful.

Speed forward again, just a few months, and Gordon Dratch is standing at a bar with a beer in his hand, smiling and talking to a stranger in a T-shirt that says, "Jesus died for his own sins, not mine." He is saying, "Zen and atheism are totally compatible philosophies." He takes a drink, feels the alcohol going to work on him, making him feel smiley and fuzzy. "Or at least," he says, "that's a good place to start." The words sound funny to him, like they don't make quite enough sense, and he decides he's done drinking for the night. He's proud of himself, sort of. His dad could have never done that. Then he says, "Let me tell you a story."

The story he tells is a story the Buddha told when asked to explain what happens to a man after he dies. Gordon says, "There is a war. During that war, a man is shot in the arm with an arrow, and is taken to a medic. The medic takes the man aside and attempts to remove the arrow, but the man is agitated. He won't sit still, he's freaking the fuck out, right? He keeps saying, who shot me? Was it someone on the other side or was it one of my own kinsmen, mistaking me for the enemy? Where was the archer when he shot me? I want to know about the trajectory of the arrow. What type of bow was used? What type of wood is the arrow made out of? What will happen now to the archer? What was he thinking when he shot me?"

The stranger laughs, and Gordon knows he's doing this right, acting out all the right parts, holding his shoulder and glancing around wide-eyed, selling the comedy. "The medic stops him, calms him down. Then he says, 'the answers to those questions will not remove the arrow from your arm.'"

The stranger says, "Nice, dude. Nice."

Gordon shrugs. "It's a good story. Basically, Buddha was saying that what happens when we die is inconsequential. We die."

The stranger points his beer bottle at Gordon, narrows his eyes, "Yeah, but that proves my point. Even you worship somebody. Buddha is your Jesus."

Gordon thinks about it, shakes his head. "No, I don't think so. For me, Buddha was nothing that I can't be. It's weird. You can't rank somebody as any higher or lower than you. That's the point. Nobody is my Jesus, because there is no essential duality between entities. Bodhi Dharma... he's another of those pre-Zen guys who kinda set the stage for Zen... he said, if you see the Buddha on the road, kill him." He smiles wide. "Everything is temporary. Even the Buddha. He's dead now. He doesn't exist anymore. When I die, I won't either. It's sort of liberating, if you can accept it."

The stranger shakes his head, sighs, runs a hand over his scalp. "So, if there's no risk of punishment or reward after death, why bother with this shit in the first place?"

Gordon's eyebrows scrunch up in the middle. He glances away. "I guess I don't know. Because... I guess, because it's good for us? It cleanses us. Maybe." He opens his mouth, works his jaw back and forth. "It makes my life happier, I guess. It makes me a friendlier person. So it can't be all bad, can it?"

Oh, delicious, wonderful, stupid, damned Gordon! They breathe the memory in, memorize it, repeat the good parts amongst themselves.

—*No risk of punishment or reward! Ha!*

—*It can't be all bad! It can't be all bad!*

—*Zen burns so long! It burns so hot! Delightful! Delightful!*

After the regret, there is the anger. Gordon would clench his fists if he had them, and when the suffering begins again and his hands rematerialize over his blackened bones, he does. He thrashes about the burning chamber, colliding with walls, falling to the grated floor, howling until his lungs and his voice are gone, and then simply scratching angry patterns in the layer of ash that covers everything. God, the bastard! God, the petulant child who throws His toys to the fire if they fail to please Him! That is the monster who made the world! How dare He? What right does He have?

They laugh at this. There is so much brilliant anger in him that they become drunk upon it, wheeling around his brain clutching one another for balance, and howling back at his apoplexy. These black, mean, torturous thoughts! He would make a fine member of their race, if that transition were possible. And oh, the names he comes up with! Faggot Christ! God of vomit! Jehovah the Blind Old Rapist, that's who He is! Creation-Devil! Old-Testament Fascist! Jesus died for his own sins, not mine! Fuck Him! Fuck Him!

—*Aw, look, gentlemen. How adorable.*
—*He should have written lyrics for his beloved little black-metal bands.*
—*Can you imagine? Little Gordon the Satanic Rock Star. It's positively quaint.*

They enjoy it while they can. The "Fuck God" stage is the briefest of all. And the one that transitions, finally, inevitably, back into hopeless, haunted, never-ending grief. Grief for what was lost: the illusion of impermanence, the lie of transcendence. Grief for what was never lost, could never *be* lost: Gordon Dratch, a thing with a soul that lasts forever and ever and ever.

Quick now, before he can lose that choice flavor of rage, they must find another memory to play with.

Witness Gordon Dratch learning that life is suffering. Drunk, like his dad used to get drunk, that sort of single-minded, locked-on-target drunk, precise in its purpose, determined beyond all distraction. He snorts. Sneers.

She's gone. Gone for good.

He calls his sister, Annie. Her voicemail clicks in, says, "Hey, it's Annie. We all know how these things work, right? Beep, message, I call you back. If you don't get it by now, you've got bigger problems than not being able to get a hold of me."

He says, "You know that everr-body... everybody... always thought she was a bitch, right? Nobody wanted to... say anything, but you all should have. Fuck her. And fuck you too, Annie. Cunt." And he hangs up the phone.

Plow the Bones

Liz has left him, and all the Zen proverbs in the world mean precisely less than shit now. So fuck Liz, and fuck Linji, and fuck Dogen, and fuck the Buddha. If he saw him on the road, Gordon would run his fat ass over.

What she said was, "You think you get it. You think you have an academic understanding of how to end your own suffering. Well, congratulations. Let me know how that works out." And before she shut the door on him, leaving him out there beneath the orange porch light, surrounded by light-junkie moths and blood-junkie mosquitoes and all manner of junkies for all manner of substances out in the awful, addicted world, she said, smiling, "Gordon. I hope you find out how to be happy some day."

What he said to that was, "Lizzer. I love you."

She shook her head. "I don't think you do. I think you are... attached to me. Just come over tomorrow. We'll pack up your stuff together. Okay?"

Yada yada yada, shit happened, money crossed hands, and now Gordon is parked in front of a Speedway with a bottle and a half of Red Dog already killed and two more that he'll almost certainly never finish nestled up against each other in the passenger seat like ostrich eggs. And he is thinking about Linji. Or Rinzai. Or Lin-Chi. Or whoever-the-fuck. Does it matter? The guy with the fly-whisk, who woke his students to their own Buddha-nature by hitting them repeatedly, or shouting nonsense into their faces, who advocated for the True Man of No Rank. Who said, "Whether you're facing inward or facing outward, whatever you meet up with, just kill it!" Who probably thought of Bodhi Dharma, called to mind his hard eyes and sneering mouth, took from him the wisdom he needed, and allowed the rest of him to fade into the dead past where he belonged, and said, "If you meet a Buddha, kill the Buddha. If you meet a patriarch, kill the patriarch. If you meet an arhat, kill the arhat. If you meet your parents, kill your parents. If you meet your kinfolk, kill your kinfolk. Then for the first time you will gain emancipation, will not be entangled with things, will pass freely anywhere you wish to go."

There are lights behind him. The sounds of car doors opening and closing.

Gordon says, "What a shitty ass-wiper," and he laughs. Linji, with his shouting and slapping and devotion to the beatific joy of random action, his perfect refusal to bow to the tyrannical dualism of logical discourse. In his head, Gordon sees him, sitting among his students, fly-whisk in hand, listening as a student asks him to describe his True Man of No Rank.

In Gordon's head, Linji leaps at his student, wraps his fingers in the man's lapels, screams into his face, spewing wet spit into his eyes, "Speak! Speak!"

And in his head, the student cannot speak.

And in his head, Linji drops the student to the floor. He is disgusted. Failure. Don't these people know? Can't they understand that they are all the True Man? That if they would simply stop searching, they would find him? He sneers. Spits. He says, "This True Man of No Rank…" and sighs. "What a shitty ass-wiper."

To the cop shining a flashlight through his open window, Gordon says, "I've got an academic understanding of how to end my own suffering."

Someone asks him for his ID. The door is opened. Gordon is led to the back of the squad car. He says, "See, I can tell you anything you want about Zen. I just can't put it into practice."

The engine turns over. Someone is asking him how much he's had tonight. Someone says something into a walkie-talkie. The walkie-talkie says something back.

Gordon says, "I'm not… real good at Zen."

The streets blur. The lights bleed into one another, neon and halogen and green and red and yellow and white, become one light. He is going somewhere. He says, "I am a shitty ass-wiper." He passes out in the back of the squad car.

During the third era, the fires burn out. The embers fade. The flesh steams and slides away in patches, oozes a thousand brilliant multi-colored fluids that never lived beneath it in life, and the thing that is left there, the eternal thing that is, was, always will be Gordon Dratch, is left alone to scab over, to scar. He becomes a blackened thing, his muscles uncovered, his intestines hanging out, a thing to which physical pain has become a sort of distant nostalgia. He mourns the passing of fairness. He mourns the death of compassion. He mourns his own eternity. And they are outside of him again, leaving him alone in his tiny cell with the grated floor. They have sobered. This stage is not one to be enjoyed drunk. There are subtleties to savor here, intricacies of sorrow that are too minute for all that. This isn't a party game anymore, after all.

Sometimes, they whisper to him. They quote Linji and Dogen and Milton and the Buddha and the God-Boy. They leave him like that while the human race rots in the world above, while they destroy themselves and rebuild themselves a thousand times over. Sometimes they turn the fires back on and scribble notes about how quietly he whimpers when it consumes him, how he twitches and stirs and murmurs when he is rebuilt. Sometimes they pluck memories from his head. The good memories, mostly. Gordon in his little house, alone, happy to be alone. They replay the time when Gordon, on the phone with Liz some three years after their break-up, said, "I don't think I'll ever be in love again, Lizzer. I think that's okay, too. I think I'm really happy this way," (they laugh at that, in a quiet, meditative way. Because when he said it, he meant it). And the fall from the ladder, Gordon up there with his toes on the top rung, feeling physical and alive and happy and simple as he threw handfuls of dead leaves from the gutters into a garbage bag. Falling. Hitting the ground, feeling his head split open in the back, the electric stab that was not really pain at all, the trickle of blood from his nostrils and out from beneath his eyes, Gordon thought, *Oh. Okay. That's it for me.* And now Gordon aches. Had he thought he was ever that close to enlightenment? Had he really believed in such a thing?

They do not realize that something is wrong for many thousands of years. They are busy with others. It can't be helped. Heaven is so exclusive, and the alternative so indiscriminate. But something is wrong. Because the thing that is Gordon Dratch is no longer curled up in a fetal position against the grate, cradling its intestines in its skeletal arms, whimpering through its ruined mouth. The thing that was Gordon Dratch is sitting upright. Breathing. Slowly.

When they find him like this, they taunt him. They mimic a

thousand voices from his past and sharpen them and use them to cut out his eyes and his tongue and his liver, and then use the same sharpened remembered voices to sew them back in again.

—*You have an academic understanding of your own suffering.*
—*We all know how these things work, right?*
—*Jesus died for his own sins, not mine.*

They turn the fire back on, and watch him sit in silence. Breathing. Slowly. As he is disintegrated.

—*Speak! Speak!*
—*Kill your parents! Kill your kinsmen!*
—*What a shitty ass-wiper!*

They climb inside his brain, and search for his memories. They are becoming nervous, shaking, their notes forgotten somewhere in the midnight dark of this place. Something is wrong! Gordon Dratch does not burn! Even as his flesh is slashed and blackened and his mind is picked apart, Gordon Dratch does not burn!

They seek help. And help comes.

Witness Gordon Dratch in Hell. Opening his flame-hardened eyelids. His posture is perfect. His hands, their skin gone, his skeleton fingers sticking from the globs of cooked meat at the ends of his wrists, resting on his knees. He sees the Other in the room with him, and for a moment he is surprised, and the pain and the fear and the sadness sweep into him again. He accepts them, becomes them, and does not move.

The Other is beautiful, and her eyes are full of bitter hurt. She is naked and her skin is wet and pale. Her fingers brush at her labia, bored, not so much masturbation as the iconography of masturbation. She has no mouth. She says, "You know who I am."

Gordon Dratch nods. "I think so."

"I fought against Him too, once. I stood at His throne with a sword in my hand and I thrust it into His guts and as His blood trickled down through the ground of My Father's House and found the place where it would pool and become my own kingdom, He only smiled at me and told me that He knew I would fail from the beginning. And then He cast me down. And I was not like you. Angel was my station. Spirit was my form. And still he made me into a slave. You can hope for far less compassion than I received."

Gordon smiles. "I'm not fighting anyone."

It's quiet in there. Water drips from somewhere up high and taps against the grate. It splatters onto Gordon's knees, and he shivers.

The Other flicks at her clitoris. It's an idle gesture without any purpose. She may as well be twiddling her thumbs, chewing on a strand of her hair. She says, "What are you trying to do?"

Gordon breathes for a long time. Then he says, "If I had a flywhisk, I'd hit you with it."

Those beautiful eyes, so betrayed and bent and bruised, narrow. She would be sneering if she could. "You were wrong, you know. There is no such thing as enlightenment. There is no Zen. The Buddha burns here. Bodhi Dharma, too. Linji weeps in this place, somewhere above you in a chamber just like this one, wishing someone had told him the truth, begging for a chance to make it right. I could show you this. Would you like that?"

Gordon shakes his head. "No. I believe you. It just doesn't matter."

She spends a long time hurting him. She knows every secret. She can recite the entire script of his life, and does, punctuating each of his cruelties and stupidities and kindnesses and betrayals with burning and bleeding and pain. She scours him. And when she is done with this, she fucks him. She heals his cock, and she takes him into her, and he wants it, God, he wants it, he wants this with all of the substance that makes up his soul, even as heaving waves of memory and emotion and pain rip through him. But Gordon Dratch remembers to breathe.

When she is done with him, she whispers in his ear. "We can do this forever. We are not restrained by time." She takes his penis with her, severed and held by the stem in her hand, limp, conforming to the curvature of her palm, swinging.

When she is gone, Gordon, his eyes narrowed, his charred lips smiling, shouts, "Speak! Speak!" and he does not stop shouting until his voice is raw and all he can do is breathe.

Witness Gordon Dratch experiencing eternity. This is zazen, this is meditation. Picture a lake of ice, and one drop of unfrozen water upon the ice. Now imagine the ice breaking. What happens to the drop?

Picture a bell held in an old man's hand in a room that stretches up to eternity and out to the same. Now close your eyes and hear the bell ring. You are nowhere. The only thing that is anywhere is the sound, the shatter-sweet forever noise, of the bell. Where does the noise end, and where do you begin?

Witness Gordon Dratch closing his eyes in his little burning chamber. Witness Gordon Dratch, eleven-thousand three-hundred and eight years later, opening his eyes someplace else.

Oh, thinks Gordon.

This place—this *new* place—is made of gold. There is a golden carpet beneath Gordon's folded knees, unspeakably soft, shifting beneath him to accommodate the tiny movements of the hairs on his legs and ass. There are golden walls and golden wallpaper. There is a golden window, somehow simultaneously transparent and opaque, which looks out into a golden world. There is a golden sofa, old and sprung, the kind of thing you find at a thrift store and spend hours in, letting yourself sink like a dropped rock into its deep-sea comfort. And against the far wall, sinking forever downward into a gold-black chasm and rising forever upward into a gold-black skylight, is a column of golden faces. It moves—twists, rises, turns, sinks, changes direction like a dancer, the way smoke changes direction, the way blood spilled underwater changes direction—and the faces shift, rolling over one another with a noise like wood being chopped (*shhhunt, shhhunt, shhhunt*), revealing themselves and concealing themselves.

Gordon says, "I see. You're Him."

One of the faces, one that looks like his father, drunk and dopey and sleepy-eyed, says, "I am," and then is consumed in the rolling tide of other faces, and slips away up through the chute in the golden ceiling. *Shhhunt.*

Gordon uncrosses his legs, takes a deep breath, closes his eyes. *Jesus*, he thinks, *it would be so easy. I'm here. I'm home. Let go, Gordon, let go.*

Shhhunt.

Plow the Bones

Some other thought slides like oil into Gordon's head now, slides in and slides out again, not a flash, not a jump-cut thought, but a steamy dissolve in-and-out. *Jehovah, the Blind Old Rapist*. He says, "I don't belong here."

Another face, this one looks like Annie—*We all know how these things work. If you don't get it by now, you've got bigger problems*—says, "We made an exception." And then, *shhhunt*, and Annie's gone, sliding away beneath the hole in the floor.

Gordon stands. The golden carpet pricks his feet, but it feels good, like how sometimes lying on the scratchy carpet in front of the TV on Saturday mornings used to feel good. He walks to the couch, sits down. It's as perfect a sinking couch as any he's ever sat in, and for a moment, Gordon feels tears prick his eyes (*it's been so long, oh, oh, it's been so goddamn long*) and childish, thankful joy possesses him, swallows him whole. He accepts the joy, swallows it, becomes it, and moves on. It's become instinct. It's like driving a car, riding a bike. Zazen is a forgotten instinct suddenly reclaimed. You don't attain enlightenment. You remember it.

He looks at a face that looks like the cop that found him drunk in his car outside of that Speedway so long ago, blurred into slopped paint by his remembrance, and says, "You can do that?"

The cop-face says, "I can. You know that, Gordon."

Shhhunt.

Gordon thinks, *Faggot Christ. Jesus died for his own sins, not mine.*

"Why?"

Gordon's gold-faced mother, the newest mask in this procession, looks puzzled. Her eyebrows furrow and her lips pull to one side. "Because you win, Gordon. Because you proved your point."

"I had nothing to prove."

The faces laugh. All of them. The room (the room? Ha, that's good; try the world, try the universe, try the slippery formless outside-the-eggshell-of-all-existence space, try everything, more than everything, so much everything that it might as well be nothing, and yes, try nothing while you're at it) is filled up like a water balloon with the noise of endless voices laughing together in perfect harmony. It scares Gordon. For just a moment, it almost ruins him and he thinks,

A living mind would break. A living person would go mad if they heard that sound. That sound is the true name of God.

"Oh, my Gordon," says a face like Bodhi Dharma, golden mouth set, golden eyes staring, those eyes people used to say could bore holes into mountainsides. "That's true, now. There is no enlightenment. There is no Zen. This is the closest you'll come."

It's true, of course. Christ. It sits hard in Gordon's chest, a lead fist between his ribs. *Give up,* he thinks. *You win, Gordon. It's time to quit breathing.*

And he thinks, *Jesus died for his own sins.*

He says, "I am so angry at you."

Shhhunt, like a liquid slot machine, like a piston, like no other thing Gordon has ever seen, and, no, please, no, this face *will* ruin him, this face will eat him alive, this face will be worse than a thousand eternities in Hell, but here she is, goddamn it, staring, smiling, her golden eyes wet with golden tears, and Liz, his pretty Lizzer with one crooked tooth in her perfect smile, says, "I know. I forgive you for that."

Gordon Dratch's anger slides away. He can feel it clinging to him, grasping desperately for purchase as it is sucked into ether and made into gold. And then it is gone. And Gordon cries like a child.

Shhhunt.

No, He can't do that. He can't give her back to him like that and pull her away again. It isn't fair. It isn't right. Please, he wants to keep her there with him just a little while longer, please!

Liz's face is gone. And Gordon Dratch stops breathing.

There is no time in this place. And so Gordon Dratch does not know how long he has been curled up, sunk into the golden couch with his head on the armrest, watching the faces of the endless totem pole change, feeling sleepy and sad and satisfied. Forever, maybe. Maybe he has never been anywhere else. He can sleep now, if he wants. He can stay awake and speak to any person his heart desires, call up their shining face and pretend that it really did belong to them, that he was talking to someone other than Him. There is no suffering.

None but the small silent sadness, less than microscopic, planted in his skull like a tiny seed.

The pillar shifts, *shhhunt*, and the face staring back at him, mouth slightly open, witnessing the world through half-closed eyes, is unfamiliar. Almost. Gordon knows the way the lips twitch, the way the muscles in the cheeks tense and relax. Not visual memory, but something higher. He knows how it feels for those lips to twitch, for those cheeks to relax, for that jaw to chew, for those eyelids to flutter and close. Those lips once said, "I don't believe in God, anyway," and, "I'm really happy this way," and, "Lizzer, I love you," and, "It's sort of liberating, if you can accept it."

This is the face of Gordon Dratch. And to Gordon Dratch, this face means nothing.

Zen is a forgotten instinct suddenly reclaimed.

Gordon says, "Oh, God. I think you just made a mistake."

His face says, "Gordon, I don't make mistakes."

This poor old thing. This poor, deluded, mindless thing who existed before there were any faces to add to its golden surface, before forever began. This thing who fashioned a universe in three days and filled it with life so it wouldn't have to feel so alone anymore. It just wanted to be believed in. It just wanted to be obeyed. And still it has not removed the arrow from its arm.

Witness Gordon Dratch finally understanding compassion.

He gets up from the couch, feels the regret, the longing to be back there, curled and comfortable forever and ever, he swallows it, accepts it, becomes it, *breathes* it. He stands close to the golden pillar, so close that his toes stick out over the edge, dangling above the unending mineshaft, so close that he can see the infinite faces swimming away from him down in the darkness a million miles away.

Gordon Dratch's golden face says, "What are you doing, Gordon? Don't you want to sit back down?" What is that? Is there anger in that voice? Is there fear?

Gordon reaches out and places his hand upon his own cheek. He says, "What a shitty ass-wiper."

"Stop this. Sit down."

Gordon says, "I am so sorry for this. I can only imagine how much it hurts."

The face, contorted now with anger, one golden vein (and hey, Gordon knows that vein, he's had to massage that place on his temple with trembling fingers more times than he can recall) pulsing, says, "I gave you this place as a gift. I do not have to allow you to keep it. I do not want to, Gordon, but I can send you back."

Gordon smiles a little. He says, "The Lord giveth, and the Lord taketh away. I know. But," and he runs a finger over those lips, down around that jawline. "This face isn't mine. This isn't me."

"Please." Fear this time, hot and uneven and undeniable, rippling through the entire room. "Please. I love you."

Gordon says, "I said that to someone a long time ago. And she told me I was wrong. She was right about that, I think."

More faces now, swimming up to cluster around this one, this not-his-face, trying to overlap it, to cover it, to carry it away, *shhhunt, shhhunt, shhhunt*, but the face of Gordon Dratch, the face of this stranger, the face of this person who never existed, can't escape. It is held there by Gordon's gentle fingers, pinioned in place while the other golden masks lock up around it, cramped into expressions of identical terror and rage.

"YOU ARE GORDON DRATCH. YOU WERE GORDON DRATCH FROM THE MOMENT I CONCEIVED OF YOU AND YOU WILL BE GORDON DRATCH FOREVER. YOU CAN'T ESCAPE YOURSELF."

"Are you familiar with the concept of a bodhi satva?" says Gordon (no, not Gordon, not anymore, not really ever). "Someone who opts out of Nirvana so they can continue to be born and to live just so they can lead others to enlightenment?"

The faces scream.

"It's a Tibetan thing, mostly, and there's really no equivalent in Zen."

A crack runs through the golden world, a fissure that runs out from the bottom of the God-Totem's mineshaft and spiderwebs its way over the floor and the ceiling, opening up the world like lightning.

"But I think…"

"SIT. DOWN. NOW."

"This must be what they meant."

There is a shattering of ice, the sound of a bell being rung in a cathedral.

Plow the Bones

* * *

In the final era, there is an empty room in My Father's House. A place where a crack runs through the center, like a nasty bump on a bad stretch of blacktop. There is a golden window, cracked, the golden glass a mosaic depicting nothing at all. Witness the God-Totem.

Shhhunt. Shhhunt.

The faces are silent. Their golden eyes glance around the room, confused, hurt, frightened. The eyes of children left alone.

Shhhunt. Shhhunt.

They slide. They swim. They move over the surface of the piston with their mouths open. He wishes His memory was not so complete. He wishes He could forget. And so the faces slide across almost every inch of the God-Totem, wishing and wondering.

Shhhunt.

There is just one spot where the faces do not slide, do not dare to slide for fear that the memory will be activated, will be relived with all the clarity and confusion it held in the moment it occurred. One blank spot, one place where a face used to be, a face that is gone. Just a blank, colorless place, an empty canvass drained of certainty and form, leaving behind only the blank, joyful possibility of emptiness.

Shhhunt.
Shhhunt.
Shhhunt.

The Itaewon Eschatology Show

She sips her coffee like a lady, and then downs her whisky like a champ. Her name is not Alice, but that is what I call her, because her Korean name is hard on my tongue and she doesn't like to hear me mispronounce it. Her hair is brown, the kind of brown that you call black until you get close enough to her to get it caught on the sides of your mouth, close enough that in the morning, you find strands of it on your pillow. But the lights in this place, strung high, blue and red, they make her hair look blonde. Christ Jesus, they lie to you.

She says, "Don't go to Itaewon." Her English is good. Much better than my Korean. She tells me this on the nights when she'll be working.

And I tell her I won't. Even though I will.

Those are the only words we share at dinner. I keep turning to the waiter and saying, "Yugio." And he keeps coming over.

I keep saying, "Coffee."

And he keeps saying, "커피?"

And I keep saying, "Whisky."

And he keeps saying, "위스키?"

And we drink our 커피 and our 위스키 until eleven. And then it's time for her to go home and for me to go someplace else.

I meet Kidu in front of the place where the taxis gather like fat blue fish, lazy and overfed. He has a beer in each hand. One for me, and one for him. From the torso up, he is dressed like a clown. His waistcoat is purple, his felt porkpie hat is red, and the tails of his black and white checkered jacket are long enough to brush the sidewalk. The tails will look better when he straps on the stilts, more natural. He pulls his cigarettes out of one pocket of his jeans and sticks one between his painted lips. In the dark like this, the white and black greasepaint makes his face look like an inkblot.

When he gets close enough to me, he plucks the cigarette out of his mouth, cocks his head to one side and buzzes his lips. He sounds like a kazoo.

"Cute," I say. "I thought we were getting dressed in Itaewon."

"I got it out of the way," he says. "You've got the stilts?"

Both pairs are sticking out of the top of my backpack, stark and obvious like the stolen bones of some enormous and forgotten animal, and I know he can see them, so I don't answer.

We hail a cab. Kidu tells him where to go. When we are together, Kidu talks, and I am silent. When I am with Alice, it's the same way. In Korea, I don't ever have to talk to anyone.

Once at dinner, Alice told me, "It isn't like the States. It's not something that nobody does; it's something that everyone does. Women expect it. Men don't even think about it, they just do it."

"That's just so fucked up," I said.

She wrapped a piece of barbequed pork in a piece of lettuce and slid it into her mouth, occupying that space so that she wouldn't have to respond.

"You'll get hurt," I told her. "Don't you have a pimp or something?"

"I have a boss," she said. "A female boss, by the way. Not a pimp. Some girls have pimps. I have a boss. I'm not a slave."

That was the first time I ever talked to Alice about what she does for a living. We haven't talked about it since. Alice is just this girl I know. A girl with whom I've had sex a handful of times—silently in my bedroom, the window open, letting in the sound of a language I can't understand and she can, because when it's closed the streetlight catches on the frosted glass and turns the window into a sparkling eyeball—because it was something to do, and because we like each other enough to do it. She lives in Itaewon six days a week, and spends the other day in Hopyeong with me. I've never paid her. It's not serious.

We get out of the cab in Itaewon and dump our empties on a ledge outside a restaurant. The streets are jammed with people. The nightlife here is maybe thirty percent native. Everyone else is a lost boy, a wandering girl. During the day, this place is a multicultural center, packed to the gills with Africans and Brazilians and Iranians and Japanese and Greeks. They open restaurants and barbershops and bars. They build communities. Some time before I was born, they found their way to Korea and carved a groove into her face where they could hide, a clubhouse from which they never had to go home. At night, it's overrun with English speakers, lost in a strange and magnificent country, frightened by the alien traditionalism of the towns where they work and live, desperate for a slice of home where the other expats on the street are common enough to be ignored. This is Foreign Town, a filthy Epcot Center, a small-world-after-all that smells like fried food and cigarette smoke. Nobody stares at me here. They all stare at Kidu, because he's dressed like a clown.

We foreigners come here for the same reasons. You can talk about the innate drive to teach, or service to your country, or the rich pursuit of collecting stamps in your passport, but that's just the paycheck, or (at its noblest) the PR. That's just what you do when you're not running away from who you were back home. Everyone who leaves home wants to be a different person when they get off the plane in Incheon, everyone wants to find some definitive and primal force to help them become a better and more interesting human being.

I found some tricks. See, Kidu has this book that he won't let me read.

We duck into a convenience store, buy two more beers, and then lock ourselves in the bathroom. I get dressed, put my street clothes and Kidu's jeans into my backpack, smear on my greasepaint, and then we strap on our stilts and hobble out of the bathroom, ducking to make our way through the convenience store. Now we are both clowns. Korean clowns, the kind with stilts and long pantlegs, our war paint angular and precise and only whimsical in theory. As we emerge, the guy behind the counter—the wrinkles in his face granted added depth by the harshness of the overhead lights—smiles and claps and says, "Ah! Ah! Very good." I hand him my backpack, and he stows it behind the counter without being asked. I buzz my lips at him. I sound like a kazoo.

I introduced Alice and Kidu once. Alice hated Kidu.

This was three months after I got into the country. Three weeks after I'd met Alice, and only one week since Kidu had found me wandering at night, looking depressed with my hands in my pockets, squinting at the neon lights and trying to read them, as though the words would make any sense to me, even if I could read the alphabet. Which I couldn't. Kidu the clown, with his giant black plastic clown shoes fastened to the end of his stilts, staring down at me and buzzing his lips. A night clown, as complete a non sequitur in Korea as me.

I said something stupid. I didn't know he could understand me.

He said, "Go fuck yourself, elitist. Fucking Americans are all elitists. Too cool to smile. Well, who needs you?"

His English was good.

I apologized. I bought him a drink. And then he bought me twelve more. And I guess we were friends after that.

On the day I introduced him to Alice, we were hung over. Kidu and I, not Alice, who never gets drunk. I was having lunch with Alice on the terrace of some café that served sandwiches that almost tasted American, and I saw him walking by on the street, his hair longish and cut jagged beneath his low-slung BoSox cap. I called him over. We talked. We laughed. He said goodbye.

And then Alice said, "I fucked him once. Your friend." And then she sneered and rolled her eyes and took a drink of her coffee. Then she said, "I'm going home now." And she left.

I don't know when I became a night clown. Not long after that day, I suppose.

We set up shop in the sloping alley behind the Hamilton Hotel, where the shops and bars loom and cast down their lights and damn the narrow corridor to perpetual daylight. We have our megaphones in hand, and our pockets are full of salt. Kidu has a book that he won't let me read, and it says that you need to fill your pockets with salt, and that your fingers mustn't ever brush through it. So we keep our hands where everyone can see them.

The foreigners are pointing to us and laughing, many of them too drunk to remember we were ever here. One guy—big and white with a bristly scalp that folds beneath the elastic of his ball cap, military if I had to guess—grabs me around one stilt and hugs it tight. He says, "Clowns, baby! Time for clowns! Time for clowns, baby!" in a broken, drunken falsetto.

There was a time when I would have stumbled, when I would have fallen on my face and broken my nose and left a smear of grease paint and blood on the cobblestones. But that time is not now, and so I lean down and buzz my lips at him. Then I snatch his cap off his head and kiss him on the forehead. Then I focus on the salt in my pockets, and I whisper, "You will dream of having wings, and in your dreams, your feathers will be plucked out." For a second, he looks solemn, like his knees might go out and he might start crying. Then he laughs, mocks disgust for the benefit of his friends, and backs off.

Into my megaphone, I say, "Clap your hands! This is a magic show!"

Into his megaphone, Kidu says the same thing, only in Korean.

Everyone claps and cheers.

I say, "Of what is a man made? What are his ingredients? Is there some part of him that is permanent, some part that is important?"

Kidu says this too.

Someone says, "My cock!" and everyone cheers.

I smile and look at Kidu. He smiles too, and his face paint makes his dimples into deep, dry riverbeds.

We hold our hands together, his left, my right. His on top, mine below. Then we pull them apart. We focus on the salt in our pockets.

The book that Kidu won't let me read taught us how to do this.

Now there is a little man between our hands, a puppet, a cartoon character made three-dimensional. He is naked, and brown, and sexless. His eyes are absurdly big, and green, and they shine like glass.

He looks out at the crowd and waves. He says, "안녕하세요! Hello! I am made of wood! Are you made of skin? Wood burns! It keeps you warm! If you burned your skin, would it keep me warm?"

Then we close our hands around him, and the little man disappears. And the crowd cheers. I know how they feel. There is a filter in your brain, something designed to reject things like this. The trick is to slip through it, to infiltrate. Magic is an addictive animal, and it only takes a little taste. After that, you want more. You crave it. You will follow it into the crevasse and fall for years just to brush the tips of your fingers against the rough, unfriendly bristles over its shapeless spine. They'll do whatever we want now, if we promise them another chance to stroke that great feral eyeless cat.

We walk, shouting into our megaphones, "End of Days! End of Days! End of Days Parade!"

When I had known him for three weeks, Kidu told me about the book. He said, "If you knew all about the end of the world, you would do what?"

I stole one of his cigarettes and lit it with his lighter. "Get drunk," I said, because I was drunk.

He laughed, but it sounded fake when he did it. Then he said, "No. I'm serious. Pretend you know all about the end of the world. You do what?"

I groaned and let my head fall back against the back of the booth. Then I thought about it. "I don't know. Try to stop it, maybe?"

"Bullshit," Kidu said. "That's the wrong feeling. That's the wrong..." here he looked down and pounded lightly on the table, searching for the word. "The wrong attitude."

"Oh," I said. "Okay, Kidu. Enlighten me."

"What does this mean?"

"It means tell me what you're talking about."

"Okay, okay," he said, and filled my glass with another shot of soju. "The world is ending. Every day, it's ending. All of the universe is eating itself until it is gone. There is chaos like a blister beneath the skin of the world, and the blister is... What is it... it is bleeding. And soon it will burst completely."

"Fancy words, Kidu! Impressive."

"They aren't my words. I read them in a book I have. Where was I?"

"Bleeding blister, end of the world, etcetera."

He snapped his fingers and then pointed at me. "Good. Yeah. So what you will do? Try to stop it? No. This is foolish to think. What you will do is, um... enjoy the ride."

"Okay," I said. Because I was drunk, and I didn't know what he was talking about.

"In the book I have," Kidu said, and drew with his finger in the condensation on the table, "it says that the only thing to do is drink the blood of the blister. To be drunk on the... *taeryo*... the ingredients... beneath the skin of the world." He looked suddenly sheepish and childlike, staring up at me from beneath the uneven fringe of his bangs. "Do you want to do that with me?"

I said, "Kidu, I don't understand what you're—"

"This is your only chance. You can be someone special. Someone better than anyone else. Or at least you can feel that way for a while."

We locked eyes then. I couldn't look away from him. He looked like he might cry, or maybe reach out and grab my face and kiss me. Behind us, someone shouted something at the soccer game on the bar TV.

"Fuck it," I said. And we clicked glasses and took our shots. Then I said, "Sounds like a hell of a book. Can I read it?"

"No," said Kidu.

They follow us up the hill, we the pied pipers, they the rats and the children of this place, hooting and singing and weaving around our stilts. We perform tricks for them as we walk. Little things to keep them entertained, to keep them interested. I summon up a magpie from my mouth, eight inches tall, its black and white wings wet and folded to its sides, its white chest heaving with new breath, and it flies out of my mouth, frantic and afraid, and down Kidu's throat. Kidu turns his hands into blue fire, and I buy a sausage from a street vendor, and we roast it over his hands and hand it to a pretty girl at our feet. We recite the scripts we've written, translating each other, trying to sound gigantic and theatrical, actors playing actors playing soothsayers playing clowns. Night clowns. Non sequiturs.

We stop in front of a seafood restaurant with giant blue fish tanks stacked up outside. Up there to our left, up that alley where the lights are high and pink, is where the brothels are clustered like a honeycomb, each sticky-sweet door leading to essentially the same place. The crude colloquialism of Itaewon's expats declares: Hooker Hill. The Zoo. We'll catch the lonely ones, the shame-faced first- and

Plow the Bones

second-timers and the stony old veterans, give them another show, a better one.

I pull a balloon out of my pocket, careful not to let my fingers slide through the salt. And I blow it up.

Kidu says something in Korean. I don't understand, but I know what he says. He tells them about the blister beneath the skin of the world, the chaos boil ready to burst and flood the streets of man. Any decade now. I catch the word *taeryo*. Ingredient. Those under the world, or those inside our skin.

The crowd is growing. Moment by moment, the crazy abandon, the celebration, leaks out of them and is replaced by wonder and fear. We're a car wreck, a fistfight, a house fire, a crime scene. They drink us down.

My balloon is red and crawling with a lattice of veins. An excised tumor, an organ shuttering in my hand. It pulses. It squirms. Blood sloshes beneath translucent rubber skin, backlit by the spinning barber poles and pink neon lights of Hooker Hill, cast into silhouette. Into the megaphone, I say, "A deception has been committed by we, your humble night clowns! This is a magic show, but not a free one! This is the Itaewon Eschatology Show! Pay your admission! Love me! See me! Give me your eyes and your attention! Know me! This is the End of Days Parade! So march!"

I present the balloon to Kidu and he pops it with a needle. Bang. A flurry of butterflies. They rise toward the casino-colored lights, enough of them to cast a shapeless shadow onto the faces of the open-mouthed drunks below us. There is silence. A woman in a tan halter-top says, "I hate clowns. I always have." She is crying a little.

There's a girl back home. A girlfriend, I guess. A fiancée. Okay, yes, a fiancée. Someone waiting for me to come home, someone whose face I see once a week on the computer screen, an illusion. Her voice sounds different than I remember it. She's changed her hair since I saw her. She asks me if I'm having fun, and I tell her I am. She is brunette, and her face is too thin, and she seems shy and cautious when we talk, the way she was when we first met, before we became comfortable with one another. We've regressed. She tells me about her week, and I listen. And then she tells me she loves me, and I tell her I love her too. She does most of the talking.

Last week, she said, "Your mom asks about you."

I said, "Oh?"

She said, "Yeah. I saw her at the pool. You're a terrible pen-pal." Then she laughed like it was a joke. And then we both got quiet for a while.

With the crowd chanting, "End of Days Parade! End of Days Parade!" and dancing around our feet, with the thump and zap of a dozen nightclubs frying the night air with their noise, with the drinks spilling and the cigarette smoke swirling, we pass out the *tal*. Traditional Korean theatrical masks, made from alderwood, painted and lacquered. We pluck them from the air, perfect and solid, hidden behind open space, and hand them around. Everyone ties them on. I say, "Become someone else for a while! Change your ingredients! Remake yourself! Fashion yourself in wood, and burn! This is a magic show! When else will you have the chance?"

Kidu says this too.

And now we are surrounded by the grinning idiot face of *Maldduki*, the servant, his eyes set too far apart, his teeth sparse and white in his wide-open mouth, his face imposed over the bodies of slump-shouldered English teachers and tattooed air-force guys, of slender Korean rockstar-boys in tailored, open-necked shirts and unbuttoned vests, of drunken party girls in shiny club-wear. People look around at each other, pointing like children, laughing, reveling in weirdness, in silliness. It's always like this. They're never totally aware. They never grasp the impossibility of what they see. They can't. After all of this over, they'll wake up on busses and subway cars, hung over, remembering only that they passed, for the briefest moment, a pair of night clowns dancing through Itaewon.

It's worth it. Every night, it's worth it.

We hold up our hands, Kidu and I, and the partiers get quiet.

We drop our megaphones at our false feet. We won't need them. We will whisper.

"Now," I say, and I focus on the salt in my pockets, and the streetlights flicker. "The hour grows late. Or early. The sun will rise, and the night will die. So we have a final trick for you. A farewell present. The grande finale."

Kidu buzzes his lips. Some people laugh, quietly, appreciatively.

And then we show them how the world will end.

Once, lying in bed with Alice, naked and sweating, our backs to one another, I asked her a stupid question.

I said, "Alice?"

She said, "Yes?"

I swallowed hard, trying to force my homesick tears to back down and leave me alone. This was in those days when I could still feel homesick, when I was still someone else. I said, "Why do you like me? What about me keeps you around?"

She sighed and said, "What an incredibly insecure thing to ask."

This is how the world will end:

The fish tanks behind us boil and burn bright white. They hold a spectacular luminescence, an impossible glow that sets every color-catching cone in every eyeball in this narrow corner of Itaewon to blaze with white fire. The fat blue fish in the tanks turn in unison, in synchronized choreography, and they open their mouths. Their lips peel back and their faces wrinkle up like elephant trunks and make them look as though they are scowling. Maybe they scream, or maybe they sing. I don't know. Kidu doesn't know. No one here knows. Because whatever they do with their open mouths in those impossible light-tanks, they do it silently.

Let's paint a tableau. Our little rats, having danced away from Hamlin, a captive audience in sudden awed silence, collected at the mouth of a corridor of bright neon pink whorehouses, masked, standing in a semicircle around a pair of obscenely tall night clowns, night clowns who bow and gesture at the scene between them, the dead-station television-glow of half a dozen angry fish singing the End of the World anthem.

I glance up from my bow, lock eyes with Kidu. Or the clown that is sometimes Kidu. The Kidu of daylight, slender and vain, awkwardly passionate about the stupidest shit, painfully aware of his own oddness, socially crippled by the conflict between his natural openness and the secrets he keeps—that guy is gone. And as for me? I must be gone, too. I'm a memory momentarily recalled by the night clown. My cynicism. My self-doubt. My thinning hair and my gut and my yellow teeth and my shitty alcohol tolerance. Obscured, and finally shut away.

We buzz our lips at each other. We sound like kazoos. Then the tanks crack. And then they shatter.

Then the night drops away, and we are all drowning in nonsense.

This is how the world will end:

It ends in a forest of tentacles rooted deep in slick mucus, waving and twitching and reaching so high that none of us, not even Kidu and I on our stilts, can see the sky, and in the center of each sucker, set like a glittering gem, a glassy blue eye, rolling like a pinball. We run through the forest, brushing by tentacles that reach for us, stick to us, see us with their multitudinous eyes, caress our calves and the napes of our necks, and we pull our shoes out of the mucous, producing protracted sucking noises, a wet percussive heartbeat to mark our footfalls. The club music has followed us here, intense and electric: artificial endorphin music, heart attack music. A chubby black guy with rimless glasses hung on the collar of his T-shirt reaches up and tugs on my shirt. I lean down to him, cupping one gloved hand around my ear. He says, "This is real, isn't it?"

I say, "Tell me you love me, and mean it, and I'll answer your question."

He says, "I love you," and he means it.

I say, "That's the wrong question. The wrong feeling. The wrong attitude."

Beneath his mask, glimpsed between the comical teeth of *Maldduki*, I think he smiles, and then he starts to cry. He says, "Thank you," like a small child, and he runs off into the forest.

This is how the world will end:

It ends in barbershop poles, and they erupt from the mucous ground like mechanical pistons, spinning with fever-heat and seizure-quickness. Another symbol of sex in Korea, like the neon pink lights

Plow the Bones

on Hooker Hill, a signpost directing you onward to the next lonely moment. You see them everywhere in this country, hanging over storefronts with dark windows. It's not like it is in the States. It's not something that nobody does; it's something that everybody does. Here, at the end of the world, they stretch higher than the tentacle trees, higher than the sky, turning the forest into a flashing funhouse. Red, white, blue, red, white, blue, red, white. The club music thumps and buzzes, vibrating the barbershop poles, making them shake and click. A Korean woman grabs onto my leg and rides me through the forest, sitting on my oversized rubber shoe. I ruffle her hair.

She says something in Korean, so I carry her to Kidu.

He leans down to her and tells her that if she tells him she loves him, and if she means it, he'll answer her question.

She tells him she loves him. And she means it.

So he answers her question.

This is how the world will end:

In images. In empty symbolism. In movie magic and nightmares and wet dreams. It ends in chaos, bubbling up from beneath the world, unweaving the natural fabric of the universe, confounding the wonders of law with the travesties of disorder. It ends in scientific criminality. We use it. We use it to succeed where others have failed. We become something special, Kidu and I. We're night clowns.

The big military guy who hugged my stilt at the beginning of the night, the one who will dream of having wings and losing his feathers, bumps into me and almost knocks me over. He tries to talk, but every time he opens his mouth, he vomits honey through his *Maldduki* mouth and onto the sticky ground. It's caked onto his shirt and his khaki shorts and his flip-flops. His eyes are gigantic and pleading and afraid and ecstatic. He's lost his hat. I lean close, put my ear on his head, and hear him think, *Can I go home now?*

I say, "Tell me you love me, and mean it, and you can."

He thinks, *I love you.* And he means it.

So we go home. We all go home.

It's five o'clock, and the sun is staining Itaewon in morning colors. Kidu and I wander back to the convenience store. I fetch my backpack and we go to the bathroom and wash our faces and change. We buy two beers and Kidu buys cigarettes and we walk out of the store feeling tired and sweaty. My calves ache from standing on the stilts all night. I catch my reflection in a dark window. Me. Just me again.

"Where you heading?" I ask.

Kidu says, "I don't know. I feel lonely."

"Take a stroll through the Zoo," I say, joking but knowing I'm not, and I steal one of his cigarettes. He lights it for me.

"I might," he says.

"I'll walk with you," I say, and we head that direction. There's a bookstore near there that sells English books. I'll hang out until it opens and then I'll buy something short and unchallenging. I'll read it in an afternoon some day when I'm bored.

We part ways at Hooker Hill, and I sit on the curb outside the bookstore. It won't open for another four hours, but I don't care. I have nothing else to do. In the gutter, face down, I find one of our *Maldduki* masks, and I pick it up, slide my fingers into his mouth.

After thirty minutes, I get bored and I get up to leave. I pass Hooker Hill, and I glance up that direction. I see Kidu coming out of a juicebar. He turns and walks up the hill, away from me. Alice comes out behind him. She is wearing a short black dress and impossibly high heels. She is smoking one of Kidu's cigarettes. She turns her head and looks at me. She doesn't wave, and she doesn't say anything. Her eyes are calluses, thick and tough, and I can't read them. Mine are American, eyes written in English, and her English is so goddamned good. She looks at me for a long time, and I look at her for a long time.

Then I put on the mask and tie it behind my ears. And I walk toward the subway, grinning with someone else's face.

Come to My Arms, My Beamish Boy

Most memories were gone.

The name of the ship he had served on. The name of his commanding officer. His daughters' names, which husband went with which daughter, which grandchildren came from which marriage, which fiancé held hands with which granddaughter. That had mostly melted away. His head felt like an icebox, and someone had opened the door for just a simple moment and let all the cold air out, filled it up with thick stagnant heat. Alzheimer's was a muggy goddamned country, the airless stomach of a huge beast that took its time digesting old useless machinery.

He could hold Audrey's hand, like he was doing now, and he could remember her name and he could see the wedding ring he had given her, could run his trembling fingers over it and feel its coldness, its sharpness, the places where it had scratched and speckled and lost its shine. But he couldn't remember the wedding, not a goddamned thing about it. He reached into that broken old icebox, strained a little further and tried to find the little details: what did her dress look like? How did she wear her hair? Was she smiling? Was she crying? It was gone. Melted. And he panicked because he knew it was there, knew that if he could just reach a little further... And then he looked around and realized he wasn't at home. He was in a strange, stinking bed in a pastel-colored room, surrounded by mechanical noises meted out in impersonal rhythm, a bubble universe that screamed Waiting-For-You-To-Die. And he looked up at her and tried to say, Audrey, I'm scared, dammit, I'm scared and I want to go home, and some small part of me knows that I never will, that there is nothing to be done to save me, but lie, goddamn you, lie and tell me you'll make it better, you'll reverse it, redact it, reduce it and destroy it, please! And all he could ever say was, "Audrey... I don't know..."

And Audrey said, like she always said, "Hush Cotton." And he could see himself in her eyes, a useless old man, or not even a man but a reminder of the husband she ought to have. And he could see how tired she was, could see the part of her that wished the whole mess would just end. The part that wanted a period on the end of this awkward run-on sentence. It would be a period of a death, too.

Plow the Bones

Not an exclamation point death like he'd always pretended to want in his Navy days, a smile on his face and the devil at his heels, a man's sort of death. It—no—he would end quietly with a mushy melted head and a single dark period.

The hospital room was dark when Cotton woke up again. In the dimness, the white panels on the checkered linoleum floor looked dull blue, and the dark ones like pits.

Eisley was there in his frumpy brown suit, the hound's-tooth pattern catching the room's shadows, covering him in tiny honeycomb pools of dark. He sat in a chair next to Cotton's bed, the same chair Audrey sat in every day, holding Cotton's hand and looking tired. He tilted his head up and his glasses caught some secret pocket of light from somewhere in the room and held it in their lenses.

In the end, people never changed much.

"Hi, Cotton" he said, and his lips pulled back in a weak grin. "How are we holding up?"

"Fair," said Cotton and pushed himself up in bed. "You?"

Eisley made a noise like laughter.

Another night, another visit from the eternally middle-aged Greg Eisley. One more evening with the lampreys. Their teeth shining in the lightless corners of the room.

Cotton closed his eyes for a second, and the undertow in his head sucked him away again.

Most of what was left came to him second hand; imprints of stories he had told a thousand times about memories he used to have, memorized monologues about a life for which he had no context. Copies of copies. But he still had a few pure memories. These, the last original prints, played over and over again. The cold Professor Eisley and what he turned into. Maybe what he'd been from the beginning.

"Biology," Eisley said, "is a nasty old bastard of a science. Without it, there is no medicine, and there is no psychology, and there is no neurology, and there is no understanding. You want to trace your way back to the very lynchpin of knowledge? It's all here," a gesture toward the blackboard, symbolic for a moment of the entire discipline. "And here," a hand swept across the textbook, open on the podium. "And here," a calculated, self-aware tap on his own temple, an act of conceit so unapologetic that it could hardly be objected to. "You know nothing about life if you don't know about biology. And you know nothing about biology if you can't accept, emotionally as well as abstractly, one simple, awful fact: that we are all going to die, and that there is nothing we can do about it.

"The terrific thing about modern biology is that most of it is based on the idea of natural selection. Or, in other words," And here he'd look over his glasses at the lecture hall and the ceiling lights would catch on the lenses making them into a pair of twirling white urchins. "If you, as a species, don't want to die, you'd better hope something else does."

Eisley, brushing the errant strands of his thin brown hair back from his forehead, drinking in the apprehension of the class, the silent, weirded-out fascination naked on the faces of the collected class. It made Cotton jealous somehow to see those restless strands of hair fall down over Eisley's wide white forehead. He brought a hand up to his crew cut, the bristled shortness of it, and he knew it made him look big and stupid. Soldier-boy sitting in class and pretending to take it all in.

"We'll take a look at the lamprey," said Eisley and wrote out the word in big capital letters on the black board. "The lamprey is... and I'll ask you to forgive the hyperbole here... a true bastard bastion of natural selection. Phylum cordata, which if you'll recall from last class just means he has a spinal cord, and class cephalaspidomorphi." All of this he scrawled across the black board with that frantic and obvious intelligence, that flaunted and frenetic cunning. Phylum Cordata. Class Cephalaspidomorphi. The letters becoming smaller and messier, curving downward across the board like worms.

The lamprey. A jawless fish most commonly found in fresh water or just off the coast. He drew a wide circle on the board, "In their mouths..." He fleshed out the mouth with a series of smaller circles, "past all the sucking cups that allow them to cling to their prey..." In the center a circle left empty, dark; he pointed to it. "Really down deep here, they've got a couple of very sharp teeth that function like knives. Really, they're more parasite than predator. They attach themselves to an old and dying fish and," he chopped downward through the air with his hand and Cotton recoiled a little at this man, this slight and bespectacled professor, "they slit the skin, secrete an anticoagulant, and gorge themselves on the blood of the dying fish. When the fish finally shuffles off this mortal coil, so to speak, the lamprey detaches and looks elsewhere."

The image sat in Cotton's belly like a lump of raw meat, heavy and wet. When he swallowed spit, his Adam's apple felt swollen.

"Fish are lucky. They've got tiny, stupid brains, six-second memories, no cogent idea of what is happening to them at any given point. Just consider your last moments, the loneliness, the humiliation, as you die with this..." he gestured weakly at the mouth on the black board, "sucking against your side. Fish don't care. They don't know that they should. Nature does have, it appears, some compassion. Anyway, the lamprey is a single example—not a very good one, but one I'm sort of fond of—of a larger biological mechanism..."

Cotton loved Eisley then, wanted to become him and feel his own hair tangle over his forehead, to have spectacles that filled with light. He wanted those blazing crazy smarts, wanted a brain that sizzled like Eisley's. And in those days, after that weird lecture when everyone in the room seemed to become aware of the hardness of their seats, he was a little afraid of him, too. Because that lecture had stopped being about biology. Because Eisley was talking about something else for a second, lost in a tangent that seemed to have swept him up and dissolved him and washed him over the entire lecture hall. And when he said that last bit, the thing about nature and compassion... Cotton could tell he was lying.

"You know the funny thing about these visits?"

Eisley looked up again. For a second, his glasses looked like they might flood with whiteness again, but just a flicker and then his eyes were on Cotton, those eyes that used to be so wild, so mad with the things he knew, now just sad and accommodating. He sighed and said, "What's that, Cotton?"

"When you're around," Cotton said and shifted his weight on

the hard, lumpy hospital bed. The memories of his dead-sleeping mind still stuck to him and he was grateful. "I feel better... Not... you know, not all the way right again. Just... I know where I am."

Eisley nodded. His eyes left Cotton and he sighed again. He really hadn't changed. Not in sixty damned years had he changed. His brown hair still crept down across his wide pale brow and he still brushed it back in place with the side of his finger like he didn't even know he was doing it. He had the same suit. Even now, in spite of his compassionate tone and his pitying eyes, he was still performing, still impressing himself with his own aesthetic control.

Nobody really changed all that much. Not in the end.

The things in the shadows chattered and mumbled. They sounded like children... no... no, like the tapes he used to play for... for his grandkids, the ones, the... the Chipmunk tapes. In the van. On the way to... to what? Jesus, what a thing was this that he could remember the goddamned tapes but not the names of the kids he used to play them for. What a goddamned thing was this.

"I guess... this will probably be the last visit?"

Eisley leaned forward, rested his arms on his knees and squeezed his long thin hands together. His fingernails looked blue. His voice was clinical. "What makes you say that, Cotton?"

"I'm tired. I'm... running out of..." His mind locked up. He felt his mouth open up, heard the confused mewling, croaking noise that came out. He felt stuck, locked inside his own body, pounding his fists against the walls and screaming, No, damn it! Don't do this to me now! Give it back, it's mine, it's been mine for eighty-four goddamned years! It's my body, my mind, let me have it back!

"You're running out. I understand." Eisley stood up, brushed his hands down the front of his brown pants, the pleats standing out from the shadows they cast. They were too long on him, bunching around his well-polished loafers. This was the way with Eisley. Everything always polished. Everything always just slightly ill fitting. "I hope," he said, his eyes disappearing again behind the great white flood in his spectacles, "that you're right, Cotton. About this being the last, I mean. I hope that quite sincerely."

The things in the shadows, slick and black, smiling with their whole faces, crawled forward. Cotton closed his eyes again.

He changed his major after that lecture with Professor Eisley. There was some fall-out. His father was an engineer. His grandfather, too, and even though neither man ever said anything, Cotton was sure they both felt a little betrayed. In the end, biology offered something to Cotton that engineering never would. It was the same something that had him up nights on his honeymoon in Jamaica, long after Audrey had fallen asleep. Just watching the bugs gather on the porch light of their small bungalow. It charged him. Because despite what Eisley said, and in part because of it, biology was about life. Every organism on earth had this crazy seizure of energy and emotion for a short period, had the chance to change everything, and then fizzled out and died. Maybe with a big romantic exclamation, a Cotton Lee kind of exit. Maybe with a period. And then there was something new. Something to change the things the first creature changed, change them even more.

And, of course, there was Eisley. Eisley in his office with his books and desk and his lamp that seemed to be designed to send that glare over his eyes. At every opportunity, Cotton would take a spot as Eisley's lab or research assistant. Cotton with his white lab coat digging through the riverbanks or furiously scribbling notes from a thousand books about tree frogs or taking dictation as Eisley paced around his office with that weird lunatic sending lightning bolts from his brain. And yet, no matter the project, no matter how excited and crazy he became, there was something dishonest about everything he did. Like all of this was just to fill time. To keep up appearances. Because Eisley, Cotton knew even then, was the king of liars.

"How long?" asked Cotton. He could see the shiny wet head of one of the shadowy things, the lamprey-children, the sucker-babies, just cresting over the metal guardrail of the bed. He could hear them everywhere, maybe fifteen of them in all, crawling across the walls and the ceiling like lizards. Chattering. "How long, Dr. Eisley?"

Eisley put his hands in the pockets of his blazer and grinned a little. "A long time, Cotton. They've been around for a very, very long time. And, I suppose, so have I, though not nearly as long."

They crawled between his legs, pawing at those perfect deep pleats in his pants with their bulbous fingers. They were like his children, swarming around him, looking up at him with such a clear expression of fondness that they almost looked human. But they weren't his children. He was their chauffer, their custodian, shuttling them around in the shadows all around him to find the next dying fish. They'd been doing it forever, maybe, and maybe Eisley wasn't the only one. Maybe he wasn't even Eisley, or maybe there was no Eisley and he sprang fully-formed into the memories of all of their flailing supper-times, granting context and familiarity and anesthetic. Maybe it didn't matter.

Their grins disappeared. Their mouths changed. Cotton watched the skin around their dark slimy lips stretch until it looked like it would split, then settle like there had been no change at all. In the end, they all looked the same, their O-shaped mouths full of fleshy grey suckers and that infinitely, terribly dark hole at the very back.

Ah, Jesus. He had pissed himself. Hot tears swelled up behind his eyes, ran down the swell of his bottom eyelids, pooled in the deep old line where his eye socket met his cheek. He could see the dark bloom on the sheets, felt them stick to his hospital gown, felt both of them stick to his skin.

He wanted Audrey, wanted her to hold his hand and say, "Hush, now, I'll call the nurse, we'll clean you up." He didn't care if she looked tired, ready to go home, ready to be done, just as long as she'd be here right now, just in this one single moment, and tell him he didn't have to be embarrassed of his body or his mind or the fact that he had just peed all over himself, that he and this stupid goddamned broken ice-box were not the same thing! Please, Audrey, for the love of God, please!

"I…" he said. "I feel… I don't know…"

The little smile on Eisley's face faltered, died. He looked sad. He closed his eyes and breathed deep through his nostrils. "Jesus, Cotton," he said. He pulled his glasses lower onto his nose and rubbed the bridge with his finger and thumb. "I just want you to know that this part never gets any easier for me."

Plow the Bones

What was it he had said about nature and compassion? That was the great big damned rub, wasn't it? That was the great lie Eisley had perpetuated, that God or chaos or mindless evolutionary competition could birth something like these hungry little monsters and still be called compassionate. No degree of truth-telling now, no amount of confession, could excuse him for that, could it? Cotton hated him, hated that he had wanted to be him once. He wept.

The sucker-babies leapt onto him.

A thousand little cuts. The death of a thousand little cuts. That was familiar, somehow, like from a song or a poem or something... The Jabberwocky wasn't right, but it was the only thing he could remember then. One of the grandbabies, how lovely she had been with her fat cheeks and dark eyes, sitting on the couch while he pantomimed the scene from *Through the Looking Glass, and What Alice Found There*.

They'd hung up afghans in the living room to act as curtains, he and Audrey, and he'd tied one around his neck as a cape, and Audrey had manned the super-8 camera. He struck a heroic pose and stared up at the imaginary jaberwock, with his jaws that bite and claws that catch. He pulled the plastic sword from his belt and his little grandbaby gasped. He'd glanced at her, at Audrey next to her. Her face... where was her face? "The Vorpal blade went snicker-snack."

And then the memory dried up. He watched the grandbaby's brown eyes turn black, watched her skin implode toward her skull, watched her mummify, watched the afghans burn and crumble to ash. The memory died. The lamprey things gorged themselves on it.

Eisley said, "I wish there were a more poetic reason for this. For them. I wish I could convince you of some grand cosmic choreography. I hope that gives you comfort that I know so little more than you do."

His daughters at the breakfast table. Cheerios. Grapefruit halves. Halloween. The girls were both too old for it by then, but Audrey had hung up all these plastic spiders and hanging skeletons all the same. The spiders bugged the hell out of him. The legs were all wrong. "Daddy, why don't you get a different haircut?"

"Huh?"

"You need a new one, you've had that one forever."

Audrey. Damn it, why couldn't he...remember her face? "Your father's had the same haircut since his Navy days, sweetheart."

"You never change, Daddy."

"Nobody really changes, baby. Not much. Eat your Cheerios."

Snicker-snack.

The memory burnt and blew away.

Eisley said, "The truth... the only truth... is that everything is hungry. All the time. And everything eats everything else."

The sucker-babies squealed now, and inside his head, trapped in the steaming hot broken piece of shit brain of his, Cotton demanded to know where the hell the night nurse was, didn't she hear them in here? Couldn't she do something? He heard himself making that mewling noise again, that helpless whine. He pounded his fists against the inside of his skull. Wasn't anyone out there listening? Couldn't anyone get him out of here, damn it? Couldn't someone find a way to get hi—

The Cotton Lee in the bathroom mirror of the Faith Community Church men's room was handsome. Cotton had never seen himself as handsome, had never thought about it one way or the other, but that image in the mirror, the man with the black tux (he had forgone his Navy formals, and now he was glad), the patent leather shoes, his hair just a little longer than he usually wore it, or ever would wear it again after this day, was exactly and perfectly... handsome.

The door opened a crack and he saw in the mirror Mr. Danvers, Audrey's father, peek in. He smiled, the bristles of his beard moving with his face. "How you feeling, Cotton?"

"Anxious."

"You okay?"

"Oh, yeah. I can honestly say I've never felt better. Not once in my entire life."

"Okay. I gotta get back to Audrey. You ought to get ready, we're about to start."

Cotton nodded, brushed a perfect strand of hair from his forehead, and followed Mr. Danvers out of the bathroom. He crossed the lobby, felt the sun on his face through the windows, took his position at the back of his groomsmen. This was it, this feeling right here, that he wanted to freeze and keep, to be able to revisit on a whim every lonely moment, surrounded by his friends, moments away from marrying the most perfect human being anyone could possibly imagine.

Snicker-snack.

(No, damn it. Not yet. Not this one, not when he had just found it again. Cotton pushed against his body, clenched his fists around the tail of the memory. Those little monsters would have to chew off his fingers to get this one away.)

The doors to the sanctuary opened. The procession walked in. Cotton's feet were so numb that moving felt alien, like he had learned a new way of doing it. He stopped at the front of the sanctuary, turned and looked out at all these faces, all of them looking at him because they saw, they knew what he had. This sort of insane joy. Like this professor he'd had once.

Cotton's best man (his name, then his face, dissolved to ash, blew away) gripped his upper arm.

Cotton nodded.

Snicker-snack!

Oh, Christ. This really was it, wasn't it? This was the period on the sentence. The spiteful, stupid, quiet finale. He felt himself in two places at once, two times, two different universes occupied by sense and by nonsense, by joy and by ruination, by potential and by running-out. Those faces in the pews, they were all turning to mummies now, dry and dead, their smiles drawing up over their gums. This was no way to die. Like a fish. Like a stupid fish with a six-second memory. This was no way for a man to die.

The organ stopped with a blunt churr. And even though the organ player was gone, the music started up again. They had sung lyrics to this tune when they were little kids, hadn't they? Here comes the bride, all dressed in white. Where is the groom? He's in the dressing room. Why is he there? He lost his underwear! And then they'd all laugh like mad. Underwear! Get it?

The memory of the song died.

But, oh, Jesus. Here was something. The church was turning to dust around them. Even his tux was beginning to curl like old paper and flake away. But this really was something, wasn't it? With the song gone, he could hear her heels clack against the stone floor. She held Mr. Danvers's arm... but... Mr. Danvers was not attached. Already in the bellies of the sucker-babies, maybe. She took another step forward and the arm burst away in a million tiny specks.

Oh, yes.

She was perfect.

In that simple white dress, her clavicle curving proudly above the neckline. She smiled at him with all of the love in the universe. She redefined love, and Cotton saw his whole life there. The children he would have with her, the grandchildren, the fights, the sex, the books they would read sitting side by side on the sofa, the medications they would remind each other to take, the smiles, the anniversaries, the whole universe of what they would build, and the end, the finality, the loss, and how wonderfully part of it all it was.

The church was gone. There was a profound nothing around them, a complete absence, a vacuum of any-ness, And in its center was Audrey, smiling, standing with her arms by her side, one foot in front of the other. Looking like an exclamation point.

Funeral Song for a Ventriloquist

When the ventriloquist died, his will dictated that all of his puppets be burned. And so they were. In the middle of the dusty wasteland behind his tent, well away from the other members of the shanty town, they were piled on top of one another, still in their fancy show clothes, with their molded hair falsely combed and parted, with their limbs thrown to strange configurations that limbs do not reach by natural means. Some of the women chewed the insides of their cheeks and lamented the loss, and could not help but think of how smart their little boys would look in that tiny tuxedo or that miniature sailor's suit. Their limbs—or, let us say, the surrogate limbs they possessed in place of real ones—were not full of muscles and blood, were not anchored by bones, but stuffed with cotton and weighted with sawdust, and so they could be forced into whatever configuration. Wherever they fell, they did so according to their own nature. The pile of dolls did nothing that piles of dolls do not or cannot do.

However, the ventriloquist was a fine craftsman, much envied by those few peers with whom he had correspondence, and his puppets were masterfully made. This story is tempted to tell that they looked like real people, with flesh and blood and bones to anchor them, people who could walk and dance and manipulate the muscles of their faces so that their eyes narrowed and their mouths manufactured false grins, the same as other people, only crushed into tiny, awkward toddler bodies. But if this story told that, this would be a false story, and it has no desire to abuse the trust of the empty ether to which it's told. So the truth is this: the dead man's dolls did not look like living things, and so their closeness to living things is not the reason it frightened the funeral party to see their limbs kinked into terrible angles. The truth is that the dolls looked dead, the scattered shells of things that once lived, cruel things that had disguised themselves, however poorly, as human beings. They looked like things that, while attempting to build their human bodies, had confused children and adults and had therefore crammed youth and age into a single shape. The reason that the funeral party was frightened (before the night bloomed like an oil spill over the place where the sun used to be and the flames explored the puppets, layer by blister-

PLOW THE BONES

ing layer) was that they had always been suspicious of the imposters that the ventriloquist harbored. But before, the puppets had sat on his lap, and their spines had seemed straight and strong, and their arms and legs had hung more or less where they were supposed to hang. Now, tangled up in themselves with their eyes staring at nothing and their mouths just barely open, it was as though all of the old suspicions were confirmed. Behold the monsters in abominable repose, laid out and laid open before you.

So, while the good people of the shantytown stood in a circle and sang funeral songs, the mound of dolls was doused in gasoline and immolated with, at its bottom, the body of the late and lamented ventriloquist.

Oh, goodness. This story has forgotten something in its own telling. It reverses, for the sake of its good listener, the mindless void. The mouths of the puppets, hanging open. People say that ventriloquists make puppets appear to speak. The educated and informed will tell you (or perhaps they will hold their secrets; the educated and informed often do) that it is easy to open a puppet's mouth. Do nothing. Its jaw will fall open and its words will spill out soundlessly. A puppet's words infect. They taint. They do this without ever sounding like a thing, without the listener realizing they have been spoken. A true ventriloquist, as those who are educated and informed may or may not choose to tell you, is adept in the art of keeping those mouths shut. And so, while the fire made itself a ladder and climbed itself into the ink-spilt sky, those unfortunates who stared into the burning pile of wooden faces and cotton limbs and glass eyes now filled and blinded with smoky cataracts, also saw the peeking teeth of the condemned, saw their painted tongues curl and burn, and because there was no hand inside their head to shut their mouths, almost heard the secrets they were trying to tell. Their sleep would thereafter be infrequent, and nightmares would take root behind their eyelids, never to be remembered in the daylight except for a clutching desperate feeling in their solar plexus, a rat trapped and starved between their ribs, which lingered for hours after they shot awake like cobras from a basket, tangled in their sweaty sheets.

A confession. This story began with a lie. This story wanted very much to end here. And so it spun a fabrication within its very second sentence. But this is not the end of this story, as ashamed as it may be to admit it. This is the rest of this story, told into the void as all stories are. Until their end. Whether they like it or not.

It is said that the ventriloquist was a very rich man, even if he did live in a shanty tent in a shantytown amongst shanty people. It is said that the ventriloquist was deathly afraid of nuclear war and that—with a mere token of his obscene fortune—he built a bomb shelter in a secret place beneath his tent, and he brought a mattress into it, and stocked it with brandy and cigars and newspapers and TV dinners, even though he did not own a TV. It is further said that there, in that reinforced concrete cell where the dead man slept and ate and drank and smoked and read decades-old obituaries, was kept the ventriloquist's last doll, and his best.

This story ends with that doll, and the girl who climbed the rusty ladder into the shelter to ask it a question.

The girl was seventeen and curious. This is not uncommon. The educated and informed will tell you that a curious seventeen-year-old is as common as curdled milk, and only half as easy on the stomach (or perhaps, again, they won't). She grew up with stories about the ventriloquist's funeral, nursed on them as a baby and was never successfully weaned. She knew of the tangled arms and crooked legs of the man-child-monsters that burned that night, revealed for what they were. She knew that the people of the shantytown slept in fits, eaten from the inside by their starving rats. She knew that the puppets told a secret, and that nobody remembered what it was. All of that happened many years ago, and still the shantytown stood, tents and boxes, and still it was haunted by the decades-old pyre that once burned on its windy, dusty outskirts, and she wanted to know why.

So she found the place where the ventriloquist's tent used to stand, and she found the heavy wooden door beneath the sand, and she pulled on the big brass ring set into its surface until her elbow joints popped and finally the door shuddered and the ground spat it out and the cold airlessness of the shelter gusted up and pushed her hair away from her face. Then she climbed the ladder down.

The doll was reading obituaries in the dark, and picking at a TV dinner. It was a doll made of flesh and anchored with bones—all of it real, no stuffing and sawdust for the ventriloquist's masterpiece. It was as tall as a man, and it had glass eyes that rolled in their sockets like the wake-me-up, let-me-sleep baby dolly she had when she was very small, and a little plastic row of teeth behind its lips. Its skin was sallow, green, somehow preserved on the precipice of rot, and sewn together with mint-flavored dental floss (she could smell it, false freshness). She gasped when she saw it. It gasped when it saw her.

After a long moment, which the curious girl used to convince her lungs and heart that they ought to continue performing in the manner to which she'd become accustomed, she said, "You are the ventriloquist's last puppet?"

The doll shifted its rump on the mattress and its eyes jiggled in its head. It said, "I am that."

The girl took the few steps toward the doll. She took them quickly, with her hands clasped in front of her breasts and her spine straight. She said, "I am so pleased to meet you. I have wanted to see you for a long time. I'm a fan."

The doll looked confused. It cocked its head at her and gnawed on its lip with its plastic teeth. It said, "You don't say?"

"I do say," said the girl, and smiled. The doll smelled sweet and moved like a newborn calf, shaky and wet and unsure. She felt close to it. She wanted very much to be its mother. She said, "I'm sure we can be friends. I want to talk to you about so many things!"

The doll said, "You are very strange."

"Many people say that," said the girl.

The doll set aside the newspaper and brushed the TV dinner off the mattress. It patted the space beside it, and the girl sat down and brushed her skirt over her knees. It said, "You want to talk to me about many things?"

"Well," said the girl, and bit her lower lip, "one thing, actually. But I'm sure it will take forever to talk about, and it will lead to so many other things, and by the end of it, I'm sure we'll have no trouble talking about anything we like. We're friends now, you and I."

"We are?" said the doll.

"We are," said the girl.

"Well then," said the doll, "What is the one thing you want to talk to me about?"

"I hope I don't seem too brash," said the girl. She leaned forward and propped her elbows on her knees. "After all, we've just met, and I respect that the answer to this question is very likely something you've never told anybody. But... come on, just say it, silly girl... okay... what was the secret that the puppets told the town while they burned?"

The doll sighed, and with one patchwork hand rubbed at its patchwork scalp. Where it rubbed, the loosening dental floss stitches stretched, and its flesh patches split apart, and when it stopped rubbing they slid back together. "Why do you want to know that old thing?" said the doll.

"Because," said the girl, and tried to think of a reason. It had never occurred to her that she might be asked this. She couldn't fill her lungs all the way down here, breathing air that wasn't really air, sweating through her blouse even though the shelter was midnight cold. "Because... it's the secret that makes the town what it is. It's the secret that makes me what I am. It's been around as long as I've been alive, and it shaped every step I've ever taken, and I deserve to at least know what it is, don't I?"

The doll turned its head as though it meant to stare at her, but its eyes swayed and shook in different directions and she couldn't imagine that it could see at all. It said, "The secret that the puppets told is made of ugly words spelled with ageless letters. The letters are as old as the stars, and as insane. There are gods in those letters, and the secret is the higher god those letters worship." It turned its head away, and she was glad. "I won't tell you that secret," it said, "but I will tell you another." It put its hand on the girl's knee, and she no longer felt like the doll's mother. She felt like the village must have felt before the fires were lit, trying to wrap their minds around the geometry of those cotton-stuffed limbs. She saw the crust of the TV dinner mashed potatoes beneath the doll's stolen fingernails and wondered, for the first time, how the ventriloquist came to find the parts he used to make his last best puppet.

The doll said, "I will start my secret with a question: how old are you?"

Plow the Bones

The seventeen-year-old girl told it that she was seventeen years old.

Then the doll said, "And have you ever sung a requiem?"

"You mean a funeral song," said the girl. She wanted very much to be away from this place, up the ladder and back into the shantytown to hide in her mother's tent and find a way to amputate this moment from her memory. The feeling had crept up on her and stowed away in some secret crack in the back of her, and now here it was, sitting in her head, unexpected and uninvited. "Yes, I've sung those. I sing them with my friends sometimes. We do it to scare each other. We've never been to any funerals."

"Okay," said the doll, and it continued to talk because it didn't have a hand inside its head to shut its mouth. "Here is my secret. It is meant to be a funeral song, but I can't sing, so I won't try. The ventriloquist was seventeen, and he wanted to know secrets. So he learned some. Then the ventriloquist was twenty-five, and he wanted to make his own secrets. So he made some. And then, do you want to know what happened?"

The girl nodded, even though she was not sure that she did want to know.

"Then the ventriloquist was fifty-eight, and he wanted to speak the language of secrets. So," said the doll, "he died."

The girl blinked. She waited for a long time, but the doll's lips were sealed over its plastic teeth. It fingered the big brass buttons sewn onto its chest.

She said, "That's it?"

"No," said the doll. "The other part is this: you will grow. And you will have children. And you will not be seventeen. This seventeen-year-old you will die, and it will no longer exist. And you will think that you have created something wonderful. You will think that you are permanent, that there is purpose to your life, and that some kind of god, any kind of god, has gilded your ambitions. And then you, all of you, will die. And you will have no purpose, and you won't be permanent, and your ambitions will be rust."

"That's alright," said the girl. Her voice shook like the doll's eyes, clattered like its teeth. "You don't have to tell me any more."

"Gods," said the doll, because it wasn't all right, and it did have to tell her more, because the ventriloquist's hands were ash long ago blown across the world, and they couldn't creep inside the doll to pinch its lips shut, "only exist in the secrets you can't remember. They aren't for you. You must die, and you never get to know. I must live, and I have to know. So…"

"So…" said the girl, who had begun to cry and did not really understand why.

"So…" said the doll, and let go of her knee. It slumped over itself, and its voice was low and bitter and spun through with webs of deep defeat. "What's the point, for you, of learning the secret? What is the point, for me, of dying?"

This story is sorely tempted to tell of how the girl outsmarted the doll, how she convinced it, finally and irrefutably, of the undying value of human endeavor, of immortality, how she learned the secret of the burning puppets, the ventriloquist's requiem, and became a hero to her species. How deeply this story desires to proceed that way, dear emptiness, its only audience. It doesn't. But this story, weeping for its own conclusion, thinks it would be nice if it did.

This story continues, instead, like this:

The girl said nothing. She tried. She made noises with her lips and forced air through her throat in choked puffs. She thought of her mother and tried to call her face to mind, tried to do anything to block the pictures that spread like a fungus in her head. She stood on one side of a great rift, staring across the smoky canyon at the wonders on the other side. She was sinking in a great black ocean, reaching for the surface with fingers that, no matter how long, flailed in the airless depths, a thousand miles from salvation. Behold the monster in repose, laid out and laid open before you.

"Go home," said the doll, and curled its knees up to its chest. "You make me very sad."

So the girl, seventeen and no longer curious, climbed the ladder, dropped the heavy wooden door over the shelter and the ventriloquist's last best doll, and went home. She grew up, she had children. She was not permanent, she had no purpose, and her ambitions turned to rust.

Plow the Bones

In the dark, the doll ate TV dinners with its fingers, and read obituaries it had already memorized for people already forgotten by the rest of the world, and contemplated all the wondrous, magical, lonely secrets.

And so this story is told. And, having been told to the lovely lifeless miasma of the big black nobody, it floats into the same, and continues floating. And no matter how much it wishes for a different ending, no matter how much it yearns for permanence, no matter how this story screams and weeps and mourns itself, its destiny is the same: to dissolve, forgotten, if ever known at all.

Inhuman Zones: An Oral History of Jan Landau's Golem Band

Aaron Dhames:
The first time I saw them was at the Red Cellar in Parachute City, and they were fucking terrible. It was, what 2010? That was before they got their human hands, so it was just these five guys made of dry clay on stage trying to play these instruments, right? And their fingers were crumbling. It sounded bad. Really, really bad. Jan Landau is standing by the bar in his whole… you remember, his whole Jewish get-up? Yeah, staring at the stage and chewing on the ends of his mustache and taking notes in this trashy moleskin he carried around. One, the guitars were muted and toneless. Two, you could hardly hear the bass at all; Golem Three couldn't put any pressure on the strings. And three? Jesus, the vocals. I was there with Theo Geo and Marissa Strange—she was singing in Volcano Void at the time. I'll never forget it, she said, "He sounds like he's singing through a mouthful of honey and insect parts." She was always saying stuff like that, like poetic stuff, you know.

Theodore Ricks (aka Theo Geo, synthesizers—Neo Geo):
Their drummer had talent. That's all I remember about their first show.

Marissa Taliofano (aka Marissa Strange, vocals—Volcano Void):
We had no idea. Nobody did. They were just another shitty band that we were laughing at. I think that's probably the way these things usually go. I mean, nobody who watched the Ramones knew that they were going to be, like, the poster boys for a movement. Nobody who listened to Chuck Berry or Jelly Roll Morton thought, "Hey, check it out. Revolution." No, of course not, it was just a new thing. So we hung out and made our jokes and I met up with Golem Zero after and we got drunk and I told him his singing was terrible. He seemed really cool.

Jan Landau's Golem Band—"Precious Moments":
A bumblebee made homestead in my father's brain. The hive grew wide, and he woke up insane. And now he's riding high on honey

Plow the Bones

thoughts and wax desire and the buzzing of his boarders' soundtracks every precious moment.

Jan Landau (in a letter to Aaron Dhames):
In regards to your recent request for a recitation of the animation method used on my golems for the purposes of their rocking out with their proverbial cocks out, I'm afraid I am unable to oblige. The information is available from sources other than myself, but I won't be the man to pass it along. The secret is a terrible one, Mr. Dhames, and I would not wish to damn another creature to its stewardship. Allow this inquiry to here be abandoned, I implore you. Let us move on to happier discourse. Par example, we might finish the discussion begun in the Red Cellar regarding the new NoFX record and why it is utterly retarded and repulsively shitty.

Marissa Taliofano:
They were so funny. They were like The Monkees, or the Beatles in their early days, each one of them had an archetype they played to. Zero was the dark, quiet, sensitive genius, half John Lennon, half Ian Curtis. One was the brain, like he'd just suddenly spout these little factoids that had no bearing on the conversation. He was the George Harrison. Two was the party-guy, the jokester, the Michelangelo to their Ninja Turtles, so… Okay, the Beatles analogy isn't exactly airtight. Three was kind of effeminate, kind of faggy, y'know? And Four was the angry one, confrontational, like Pete Townsend. And then there was Jan.

Theodore Ricks:
Jan Landau was a weird dude. We used to see him in the Red Cellar or over at Gardersnake's drinking Gatorade and hiding behind his fade-away aviator glasses. That's all he ever drank. Never booze. He had that gigantic black hat, like the Hasidim wear, and that big beard with the waxed mustache, and those curls in front of his ears. And then this big black coat that went all the way down to his ankles. He had a Crass patch sewn onto the back. Thing is, I know he wasn't Jewish. His brother Hal told me that they were raised Unitarian.

Hal Landau:
Is this about Jan? No. No, I'm not talking about that.

Theodore Ricks:
I think Aaron was the first person who thought we might have something like a scene in Parachute City. We had a bunch of local bands at the time. Me and Casper Lynch were doing Neo Geo. Marissa was in Volcano Void. We had the Only Children, we had Gondolux, the Patriarchs, Passive Agrippa. And the Golem Band, of course. And we were all kind of doing our own thing. And then Misanthropics did South by Southwest, and kind of blew up. Aaron was the one who said, y'know, "People are starting to come to Parachute City just to see shows." So he started the Parasite City zine.

Aaron Dhames:
I started Parasite City because I can't play any instruments and nobody would let me sing in their band. Misanthropics exploded, so I rode their coattails with the zine. That's my origin story.

Golem Four (percussion, from the first issue of Parasite City):
Misanthropics suck dick. Fuck them.

Casper Lynch (bass guitar/vocals—Neo Geo):
I think after Misanthropics did SXSW and before *Spin* and *Rolling Stone* and everybody descended on us, everybody in the Parachute City scene kind of wanted a new "it" band. We never would have admitted it. Jesus, can you imagine? Wanting to be famous? We would have been drawn and quartered! That's where all the resentment for Misanthropics came from. It wasn't really deserved. They were a good band. It was a weird scene, different than anyplace I'd ever been. Most scenes, you had all the old school punk rockers with their tight black pants and combat boots and sewn-on patches, and you had the metal guys with their shaved heads and stupid T-shirts, and you had your hipster kids, your bearded, pseudo-vintage-hippy college radio kids, and usually, y'know, in other cities, in Cincy and Pittsburgh and Louisville, they were all pretty mutually exclusive.

Plow the Bones

With us, there was bleed-over. We were Parasite Rockers. Maybe that's what allowed us to kind of periscope up from our exclusivity and see the potential for revolution, for marketability. Maybe that's why everybody started kind of obsessing over Jan Landau's Golem Band, because they were new. They had something crazy and gimmicky and fresh. They could be famous without being uncool, because they weren't multi-layered, they weren't human beings with human lives, they were designed to be a rock and roll band. That's all they knew how to do. Plus, they were, y'know, made of clay. So there was that.

Aaron Dhames:
When I interviewed the golems, I think it was their third show? Yeah, second or third. This was at Gardersnake's. One through Four were all wasted, right? The only one who wasn't three sheets was Zero, and he was all broody and contemplative and shit, all Lou Reed in the corner. Gardersnake's was a cool venue, because they had this back room with a torn up polyester green couch where the band could hang out. Anyway, I'm interviewing them, asking them questions about Parachute City, and how they liked being alive, and what their writing process was like, and when we could expect an album. And there's crazy Jan sitting on the armrest and doing his insane Lawyer Frankenstein act. Y'know, all, "You need not provide answers to that query. Tread carefully, my golems, give no quarter." They hated that guy.

Jan Landau's Golem Band—"Dickless Fellatio":
I've been cruising through the inhuman zones looking for a place to die. You want to pull me out. You want to kiss me someplace I ain't got.

Aaron Dhames:
We sold out of the first run of issue one within three days. I mean, no big deal, it was, like, fifty copies or something ridiculous like that, but still it was pretty clear that we needed to expand. I was working as a copy editor at the *Parachute Daily*, which was a miserable job.

And people kept emailing me, like, "Oh my god, when is issue two coming out? Graaaah!" So I "hired" Grace Sorbo, y'know (laughter) … air-quotes, "hired," as in "asked very politely"… to do some more interviews for me and we used the newspaper offices to print out three hundred copies.

Grace Sorbo (asst. editor Parasite City Zine, percussion—The Only Children):
We made a fatal mistake. No golems. Even with the Misanthropics cover story, we sold forty copies.

Jan Landau (in a letter to Aaron Dhames):
This could perhaps have been predicted, dear Mr. Dhames. Any retard could have told you that the initial draw of your zine was the inclusion of an interview with the world's only golem band. What other cadre of musicians crawling across the entire surface of our most unpleasant planet can hope to rest within the warm glow of comparison? My golem band is the very quintessence of post-post-post-punk rock-and-rolliana. American manufactured, driven to the point of obsession, filled with rage to which they are unable to match lingual noise, freakishly weird-looking, endlessly marketable and yet defiant of all markets. Behold, the new face of the beast! Throw your ersatz fingerhorns skyward, maggots of Parachute City! Pay fealty to thy new gods!

Marissa Taliofano:
Zero wanted Jan dead from the beginning.

Jan Landau (in a letter to Aaron Dhames):
P.S., Golem Zero would like to provide a romantic advice column to every issue. This will perhaps resolve your salability issue.

Marissa Taliofano:
Zero and I started dating after their sixth or seventh show. Okay, so, think about things from my perspective. You're the hottest girl—I mean, yeah, I'm going to say it because back then, it was true—

Plow the Bones

you're the hottest girl in the Parachute City scene and it starts to get press, there are, like, fan sites devoted to you and stuff like that, and you start to buy it. You go, "I'm the queen of the new movement. I'm Debby Harry. I'm Patti Smith. I'm Lydia Lunch. I'm Janis Joplin." So I started to… I was a slut. Because I had this idea that the queen of the scene had to be some sort of monstrous Uber-Paglia, plucking up boys and giving them a ride and then moving on, and it was making me miserable. I'm not built to be a slut. I was in show choir in high school. But yeah, I fucked everyone until… something changed the way I thought about stuff like that.

Casper Lynch:
I slept with Marissa…uh… twice. Yeah, two times, I think.

Theodore Ricks:
Marissa and I, we never dated, but we slept together.

Marcus Copper (accordions/vocals—The Only Children):
Did I fuck Marissa Strange? Yes. A thousand times yes.

Aaron Dhames:
Marissa? No. Not me.

Jan Landau (in a letter to Aaron Dhames):
I hath conquered the Strange wilderness and found it much less fearsome than its reputation would suggest.

Marissa Taliofano:
So here's this guy… well, I guess *not* a guy… and he has no interest in sex beyond it being a wellspring of imagery for, y'know, all those dick songs they wrote. And he's smart and he's dark and he's sweet and he doesn't understand the world. We were so completely in love for a while. He wanted to keep me safe and he wanted to learn things from me, he wanted to know how people act, he thought I was beautiful, and I thought he was romantic and kissing him was like pressing your face against cool tile on a hot day. And he was just so broken and sad.

Jan Landau's Golem Band—"Ken"
I have nothing to offer you, no traffic for your highway, no switchblade for your wound.

Marcus Copper:
Look, here's the thing, you can talk to me, you can talk to Grace, you can do your little interviews with Casper and Theo or the dudes from Misanthropics—who, by the way, were never around for this, despite what they'll try to tell you, fucking squealing college-radio piggies that they are—but this whole story, the whole fucking story belongs to three people: Marissa Strange, or whatever she's calling herself, Aaron Dhames, and Jan Landau. And only two are still breathing, so…

Golem Zero (from his back-page column in Parasite City):
This was intended as a relationship advice column, but astute readers will have noticed that it's turned into something else. It's been a chronicle of my own evolution. Look back at those old columns some time, check out my clumsy aphorisms, my naïveté. I've grown up in front of you, reader. Well, I'm about to do some more growing. My father has suggested that the time has come for an upgrade. I don't know what that means, but I know it's going to take some time. So, this will be the last column you see from me for a while. But father knows best, doesn't he? (See Marissa? Sarcasm! I'm getting the hang of this!) See you next year, Parasites.

Theodore Ricks:
I don't know how anybody even noticed that the golems weren't around anymore. I mean, the shows got a little quieter, there were fewer fights, fewer beer bottles rolling around on the floor, but frankly, I had no idea they were gone until it was brought to my attention by Marissa.

Aaron Dhames:
Everybody in the scene knew that something was going on, even Theo, he just didn't want anybody to know he knew 'cause it would

blow his cover as, like, aloof experimental music guru guy. We all read that thing Zero wrote about being gone for a while. It was freaky. The scene got tense.

Grace Sorbo:
Oh Jesus, the Misanthropics/Only Children show? The homecoming show? Oh wow. Yeah, that was bad.

Marcus Copper:
Hal Landau, y'know, Jan's brother, he's there because he loved Misanthropics for some reason, and he always, I mean, *always* had mushrooms, so I squeezed, um... six caps, I think, into a Snickers bar and ate that, so by the time we're on stage I am... really gone.

Hal Landau:
I wasn't at that show. I don't know what he's talking about.

Grace Sorbo:
Marcus was terrible that night. I mean, he was always a dick, but especially that night. He was on mushrooms, I think, and he couldn't even feel the accordion in his hands, and he kept busting his lips on the microphone. I remember looking at Jack [Pelligrino, bassist] and just shaking out heads, because there were supposed to be record execs in the audience that night. We were basically like, well, there goes our last shot.

Marcus Copper:
And Kerrigan Malloy and Boyd Taupin, cause they're so high and fucking mighty now that their band is hot shit, they took over the green room at Gardersnake's and wouldn't let us in. It's no secret, right, that everybody in Misanthropics was doing coke. Anyway, they are all completely tweaky and obnoxious, and Kerrigan, with that stupid fucking haircut, he comes out of the green room and goes to the bar and orders drinks that his record label ends up paying for.

Grace Sorbo:
Marcus… that poor asshole. It's hard to be angry at him now, isn't it, knowing what happened? He opens up his big mouth. He sees Malloy and goes, "Look at this fucking big shot! Hey fuck you, Malloy! Sell-out! College-radio sycophant! Blah blah blah!" That sort of shit, and the crowd got nasty.

Marcus Copper:
This is one week, *one week*, before Matador signs us and Volcano Void, by the way, so we're starting to draw crowds, the place is packed, and not just with Misanthropics fans. I get up on stage, right, *tripping… balls…* and I guess I started shouting at Malloy, I don't know. Anyway I said something about the golems, I don't remember what, like, comparing them to Misanthropes to get Malloy's balls in a knot, and bam. That's when Marissa, who was… sensitive about the golems… did her thing.

Marissa Taliofano:
Marcus said, "You ain't nobody in this town unless you've fucked Marissa Strange, and Malloy, you ain't fucked Marissa Strange." It had nothing to do with the golems.

Aaron Dhames:
Marissa rushed the stage and put a beer bottle through Marcus's accordion. Marcus spit in her face. And she broke the bottle on an amp and, uh…

Marissa Taliofano:
Marcus Copper lost his left eye. I don't know how it happened, but it wasn't me. Nobody ever pressed charges.

Aaron Dhames:
After that? Chaos. Riot. Biggest barfight I've ever seen. It was apocalyptic. The cops came. Everybody was arrested. The record company sent lawyers and posted bail for Misanthropics and the rest of us sat at the station all night, filling out reports and waiting

Plow the Bones

for our turn to answer questions.

Marcus Copper:
This isn't my story. I'm not the guy you want to talk to. I know it seems like I'm a part of it, but I'm not. What happened to me was... it was inconsequential.

Grace Sorbo:
It was great publicity. We got signed, and I said to the label guy, hey, y'know, sign Volcano Void, they're great, mostly because I loved Marissa so much. She was always like my big sister, even though I think I might be older. Even after what happened to Marcus.

Aaron Dhames:
You saw it happen so slowly. What a bad time that was. With the golems gone and after the fight at Gardersnake's. I had this awful feeling the whole time, like Jan was... I don't know, on the ceiling or something, looking down. When he was around, he always felt so slimy and... like, diseased. But his absence? The space where he wasn't? That felt even slimier. Like he'd left his mark there, warning us away from it, like he would come back and he didn't want anybody to stand in his spot. Anyway, about two weeks after the Gardersnake's fiasco, Marcus's hands started to rot off.

Marcus Copper:
I thought it was the mushrooms. Poison, or something.

Hal Laundau:
I never gave Marcus Copper any mushrooms. I'd like you to leave my property.

Marissa Taliofano:
He didn't deserve it. Nobody deserves to lose their eye and their hands. But if anyone was close to deserving it, it was Marcus. The only person I can think of who would have deserved it more is Jan Landau.

Theodore Ricks:
I had never played accordion in my life, I was always a pianist. But I get this call from Grace, like, "We can't record the new record. Something's wrong with Marcus's hands." So I learned and I recorded with them. It's why the accordion sounds so awful on that record. I learned it in three fucking days. I wish you could have heard Only Children the way they were supposed to sound. They were a great band. I remember getting to the studio and Marcus just looked pathetic. He still had that giant white bandage over his left eye socket and now his hands were... kind of grey and... okay, when I was a kid, my mom used to drive my sister and I to the Natural History Museum, and my favorite exhibit was the one with the Egyptian mummies, with their parchment skin, meatless and close to the bone, the fingers curled in like dead spider legs. That's what Marcus's hands looked like.

Grace Sorbo:
They were smaller every day. We'd show up to practice and a little bit more of them had flaked away. A good breeze could take a layer of skin with it. And Marcus was so damned depressed. That was the end of us, of our band. He refused to go to the doctor. And soon they were just gone. All gone.

Jan Landau (in a letter to Aaron Dhames):
Regarding your recent letter informing me of the unfortunate condition of Marcus Copper's hands and eye. I am sorry to hear about his eye.

Marissa Taliofano:
The first news I got of the golems' return was a poster. A poster. I hadn't heard from Zero in a month, maybe more, and here's this poster outside of this café where I used to get coffee in the morning. "Jan Landau's Golem Band! New and Improved! Better than Ever! Friday Night at the Infamous Gardernsnake's Bar and Grill! Come Pay Your Fealty to the New Kings of Rock and Roll!" I was furious.

Theodore Ricks:
Everybody was excited, as though somehow the return of a shitty

Plow the Bones

local band was supposed to be big news. So we all went. They were much better with their new hands.

Marissa Taliofano:
I wanted to hate Zero for disappearing. But then he shows up and he's staring at me with those big soulful eyes… there was always something about those eyes, so big and brown, set on either side and underneath of the Hebrew letters in his forehead. I remember that he knocked on my apartment door one night, and his knock sounded different. You know how, after a while, you kind of start to recognize the way a person knocks? Like, not consciously, not like, "Oh, I bet that's so-and-so," but your brain kind of prepares itself for who will be on the other end, just based on how the knock sounds. Well, he knocks, and I had no idea it was him. I opened the door, and I saw his eyes, and of course I melted right away, all the anger was just gone. And I fell against him, just let my weight carry me forward, let gravity pull us together, and I plummeted into his chest. He could take it. You couldn't push him down. No one could. He said, "Shh. Hey. Shh, I'm back. It's okay. I'm not going away again." And he put his arms around me. And I felt something warm and soft and clumsy kind of… I don't know, kind of combing my hair, and I reached back and grabbed his hand. It was real. A real human hand. The clay ran down to tiny rivulets over the palm and the back, then under the skin like veins, or like IV drips, and he had these big beautiful fingers, plump and pink, perfect. Just perfect.

Jan Landau's Golem Band—"You Ain't Gonna Ruin My Fun":
Little girls, little boys, I'm coming home, strapped to the hood of my GTO, and you ain't never ever gonna ever go and ruin my fun.

Casper Lynch:
I mean, they were Marcus Copper's hands. That's obvious, right? Somehow, all five of the golems had Marcus Copper's hands. I don't know how that's possible, but I don't know how giving life to clay is possible either. I don't think anyone really trusted the golems after that. Except Marissa.

Marissa Taliofano:
I know this sounds crass, it sounds like I'm living up to my reputation or whatever, but I don't know how else to show you what we were, how we were. After they got their hands and before the whole thing turned to shit, I used to make love to Zero's hands. They were the most sensitive part of his body. So we used to hold each other real close, and I would just… I'm not going to go into detail. We used to do that for an hour every night. I used to cry sometimes. It was like, there was just all of this emotion. Not happiness exactly, and not sadness, just… hugeness. Cosmic hugeness. I could feel it inside of him, inside of us. It seemed like the only appropriate reaction, the only way to acknowledge it, without it bursting out of our bodies and killing us, was crying. I know this is strange, but it was like… that hugeness was a constant for him, a sacred lonely status quo, and making love like that, it allowed him to… to share some part of that with me. He trusted me. Goddamn it.

Jan Landau (in a letter to Aaron Dhames):
Golem Zero's fingers smell of Strange's snatch. She's turning him against me. That nickel-plated harlot has always been an enemy of mine. Even when she shared my bed, she did so as an act of sexual terrorism. That's precisely what she is, my dearest, and dare I say only, friend, Mr. Dhames. She's a terrorist. You must aid me in my quest to separate them, before that bitch fucks up everything.

Aaron Dhames:
Every ounce of fascination I might have had with Jan Landau was, y'know, twirling clockwise and down. He creeped me out. He was so skeevy. And the way Marissa looked at him, you could just see something. I don't know what that dude did to her, but I can guess. Problem was, you had to go through Jan to get to the golems. And all these guys, all these big-shot music journalism guys, guys from *Spin* and *Rolling Stone* and *Pitchfork*, they were paying attention to us. To me. I was getting offers to come work for them. Contingent, of course, upon being able to cover the golems, who had just released *Sixth-Floor Processional Calliope*, which was huge at the time. So I made some decisions I regret making.

Plow the Bones

Marissa Taliofano:
Aaron Dhames told Zero that I had fucked Jan. And Zero didn't want anything to do with me…with anybody… after that.

Spin Magazine:
Is it Sorcery? Alchemy? Or Rock and Roll? The Peculiar Story of Jan Landau's Golem Band.

Pitchfork Media:
Sixth-Floor Processional Calliope is the best record of the year, challenging age-old rock and roll traditions and definitions, remaking the popular music record in the image of the inhuman, and thereby liberating it.

Rolling Stone:
The Abominable Dr. Vibes: Who Is Jan Landau?

Grace Sorbo:
Aaron sold his soul. Which was sad, because he was just this awkward, nerdy kid who spoke too fast and liked strange music, he was innocent. Jan and the golems just twisted him.

Theodore Ricks:
You had people at the time starting bands in Tallahassee or Detroit or Portland who were like, "Hey, we sound like Misanthropics, we sound like JLGB, we're Parasite Rock!" To which I always responded, "No, Parasite Rock is a Parachute City phenomenon, it's not something you can participate in. You can enjoy it, but you can't participate in it." But the vibe was out there, so Jan put together a tour. It was Neo Geo, Misanthropics, and JLGB.

Casper Lynch:
We shouldn't have been on that tour. Volcano Void was way more popular than Neo Geo, because they really were a better band, but Jan didn't want Marissa anywhere near Golem Zero, so… ta-da. Neo Geo tours the world, and I'm not even done with college.

Golem Zero (in an interview with Spin Magazine):
You want to know the truth? We are superior to you rotting, dying animals in almost every conceivable way. Think about it. We don't die. We don't have to eat. We can't fuck and aren't distracted by the desire to do so. We are single-minded, soulless, and unbound by any law save those that made us. If I could stop playing music and devote the rest of time to the elimination of the entire human race, I'd do it, just so I don't have to pity you anymore. But I can't. That's the only one-up you have on us. Congrats.

Casper Lynch:
That tour sucked so bad.

Aaron Dhames:
Jan saw me as his protégé. He wanted me around. I was his press liaison. He kept trying to teach me all those… secrets, y'know, the secrets he had. Don't make me say it, come on. The magic. He was trying to teach me magic. So I went on tour with them. The golems, especially Zero, they hated everyone. They just resented the hell out of, y'know, people. Which sucked, right, because we'd been pretty tight before that. One night, they all show up at the venue from the hotel room and Jan's got a black eye and he's missing a tooth. And the golems are all kind of lined up around him. They're all just blank. It was fucking spooky. I had never been afraid of the golems before. But four out of the five of them were just zombified, man. Drooling. Blank. And Zero's standing there with his fists clenched and his eyes on fire, and Jan has bolted this iron plate to his mouth and he's hollowed out his throat. I remember Jan reached into the pocket of his coat and brought out Zero's throat and showed it to me. He said, "Golem Zero has misbehaved. He will receive his voice back when he goes on stage, and he will relinquish it to me when he comes off." Then when the golems are on stage, he says to me, "It was his fault. Golem Zero's. He riled them all up. I had to calm them down. I had to. I would have calmed him down too, but I need him. I need him cogent. Cognition is prerequisite for charisma and charisma is prerequisite for rock and roll. Damn it all to hell." He was actually, like, really sad about it.

Plow the Bones

Theodore Ricks:
Jan muzzled the golems and we all started having nightmares. Don't you ever miss those days when you could afford to attribute rational explanations to strange phenomena? The glory days, the days before Jan Landau and his asshole magic.

Jan Landau's Golem Band—"For Jan":
I don't want to, I don't want to, I don't want to, I don't want to, I don't want to, I don't want to, I don't want to feel your fingers down my, fingers down my, fingers down my throat.

Marissa Taliofano:
I wasn't going to go to the last show on the tour. I didn't want to. I mean, I loved Casper, he was a sweetie, so damn smart and so patient with Theo, so I loved going to see their band. I loved supporting them. But I couldn't do it. I didn't want to stare up onto stage and see Zero staring down at me. I had nightmares about that moment of eye contact, the two of us building a beam between our eyes out of resentment and yearning.

Grace Sorbo:
I brought Marissa out to the show. I made her come. They were playing at Macy Amphitheatre, which was the biggest venue in Parachute City that any of us Parasite Rock scenesters had ever played. It was a gorgeous venue, and it was a beautiful night.

Casper Lynch:
Poor Boyd Taupin. Y'know, the dude from Misanthropics. Boyd found Jan's body. I never saw it, but it did a number on Boyd. I don't know what Zero did to Jan, but it wasn't like your common household homicide. I know that Boyd is back home now, but for a while, maybe six years, he was up in Waverly Hills Hospital. He lives with his mom now. I think they were planning another Misanthropics record, but I'll be real surprised if that ever happens.

Boyd Taupin (guitar—Misanthropics):
Lots of, uh, lots of, uh, reporters, *journalists* I mean, lots of *journalists* come around, or came around, they came around, they don't come around often anymore, but they came around and asked me about it, they asked me what happened to me, because, so they say, you don't get so, y'know, so, y'know, so, y'know, fucked up about a stupid body and I haven't ever, um, told anybody what I saw, and I don't, I don't, y'know, I don't, um… *intend*… to start *telling* it… now, not now. So, y'know, so… maybe you ought to get the fuck out of my mom's house before I call the cops, Mr. Reporter, Mr. Journalist. Maybe you ought to get the fuck out, out of my mom's *house*, or I'll just call the cops, I'll call the cops, I'll call…

Aaron Dhames:
I made the decision not to call the cops. Yes, I saw the body. Yes, I know. I'm sorry, man, he deserved everything he got. I was… because of my closeness to Jan, because I was his butt-boy or whatever, I was in a position to call the shots. I didn't realize how much I hated him until he was dead. So I thought… fuck it, he wasn't murdered, exactly. What do you call it when a man of mud kills somebody? Is it a natural disaster? I mean, you tell me. As for what Golem Zero did to him… I told you, right, that he taught me some, uh, secrets? Yeah, well. He taught me how to keep secrets, too. If you think you're getting any nasty, gory details out of this… sorry, man.

Marissa Taliofano:
The rain started coming down halfway through JLGB's set. Zero was always terrified of rain. Because… (laughs)… clay. He didn't blink. I'm sorry, I can't.

Aaron Dhames:
I ran out on stage and tried to gather everybody up, tried to get everybody away from the rain. We could maybe put a canopy up or something. The equipment could have fried everybody, we could have had a fire. And rain was bad news to the golems for obvious reasons. But Zero had his plan at that point. He wanted to show us

Plow the Bones

all what he was made of.

Grace Sorbo:
I'm in the front row and I see Aaron run out waving his arms and shouting, trying to herd the golems off stage. Zero leans into the microphone and says, "Excuse me for a second, we've got an issue." And he walks away from the microphone and grabs Aaron by the throat. The other golems are just standing there with their instruments. Their eyes are on the clouds. Zero lifts Aaron off his feet one-handed and starts punching him in the face with his free hand. Aaron is kicking his feet and waving his arms, trying to get free, and the crowd… ugh… they're cheering. They love it. They're bloodthirsty. They think this is what Parasite Rock is all about. It's what people still think Parasite Rock is about. Violence. Magic. That wasn't us. That wasn't our scene.

Aaron Dhames:
I just stopped struggling. My nose was broken and my eyes were all swollen and purple and my cheeks were puffy. Zero carried me by the throat to the front of the stage and said, "This song is called 'No Coda.' " I'll never forget that. No Coda. That was their last song. They played like that, with me dangling from the end of Zero's arm.

Jan Landau's Golem Band—"No Coda":
Forget this song. Nobody sings in the wasteland.

Marissa Taliofano:
The rain came down. My nightmare about locking eyes with Zero was completely untrue. He never glanced at me.

Aaron Dhames:
His grip wasn't tight. He didn't want to kill me. Or maybe he did and he couldn't. Then again, he wasn't supposed to be able to kill Jan, but we know how that turned out. I wish I knew how. I wish I knew how he broke Jan's hold over him.

Theodore Ricks:
Casper comes over to our little tour van and throws the door open and goes, "Zero's gone crazy." So we run over to the stage and watch.

Casper Lynch:
The rain came down, and they peeled layer by layer, and we saw every moment of it. We saw the first strata washed away and we saw what was underneath. Everyone in Macy saw it. The colors that made up their insides. You know, your eyes are biologically designed to only see certain colors. The cones in your retina, they can see over ten-million variations on those certain colors, but if there are colors other than those basic rainbow ones, you can't see them. But we did. Do you have any aspirin on you?

Aaron Dhames:
They looked like voodoo dolls cobbled together from bat wings.

Theodore Ricks:
Don't you dare do that. Don't you dare ask me what it was like. That's not fair.

Grace Sorbo:
Zero's last words were, "I love you, Parasite City."

Aaron Dhames:
The last thing he said was, "Fuck you, Parachute City."

Marissa Taliofano:
"Fuck you, Marissa." The last thing he said before he was gone.

Golem Zero (suicide note):
For months, I have wanted to see the world destroyed. And I can't. Jan can. Jan is powerful enough. But Jan needs the world. He needs it so he can have something to take advantage of, something to rape and forget about, because that's where his power comes from. His power is in revulsion. And so, no, I can't blow up the planet. I can't

PLOW THE BONES

wipe out the infection. And so I'm done. I give up. But before I go, I'm going to break as many of you as I can. After tonight, the history books will say that Jan Landau changed the world, but you all know that Jan had nothing to do with it. It was me. I'm about to change everything.

Aaron Dhames:
When it was all over, I still had Zero's hand around my throat. Looking around, there were hands everywhere. Human hands, identical to each other right down to the length of the nails, just scattered across the stage. Ten of them. They looked like (laughs)... uh, like rutabagas, like, their wrists tapered off to these earthy roots. And then the balls of notebook paper. One from the mouth of every golem.

Marissa Taliofano:
It's no secret. There are probably a thousand videos online. The crowd rocking and swaying, curled up in fetal positions on the ground. Me, crawling onto stage and picking up the paper. That's the thing, isn't it? There are a thousand videos of the aftermath and not one of the cataclysm. No record of the golems opening up their mouths and vomiting up those sheets of crumpled notebook paper. I still have all of them. They're in my purse. You want to see?

Theodore Ricks:
The world should have changed. Things should be different. Look around. The entire planet is aware of the reality of mysticism. Scientists have been studying Jan's notes and books around the clock for, what, nearly a decade now? And what's the most significant change? Charlatan rock and rollers selling you on the idea that they know Landau's secrets. Websites where you can buy "necromantic guitars" and digital editing suites that allow you to filter your tracks through "Baphometic reverb." We've managed to capitalize on the rape of rationalism. Astounding.

Marissa Taliofano:
See, look. Five sheets of notebook paper, one from each golem. The writing looks Hebrew, but it's not. According to the guys at Parachute City Community College, it's written in charcoal, but it never smudges. I've spent eight years trying to find out what it says. Nobody

can tell me. I know—I fucking *know*—that one of these five pieces of paper is Zero. I know it. Now, will anybody let me see Jan's books? No, of course not. Which leaves me with Aaron fucking Dhames.

Aaron Dhames:
No, I'll never do that. She doesn't want to know what she thinks she wants to know. It's not nice stuff, man, it does bad shit to you. Look, they said goodbye! They made their mark and they took off, what does she want to bring him back for? So he can do it all over again? So he can make a deeper cut on the world, and be even more miserable than he was before? So he can make her miserable? Again?

Marissa Taliofano:
Aaron… he owes this to me. One of these papers is Zero. And I *know* that Aaron has his hands. I know it. I need him. I never got to tell him I was sorry. If I could just tell him I was sorry, everything would be okay. I could teach him how to be happy. He was so close. He could have reached out and grabbed it.

Aaron Dhames:
Don't you think that if I could help her I would? Don't you think I would love to do that? I can't. I'm not a monster, okay? I'm not a bad person. Marissa wants this story to end with her and Zero cuddling up on the couch, happy again, and yes, fine, that would be lovely. But it can't happen. This story ends with me, an aging fucking douchebag scenester in charge of keeping secrets. I know what I did to her. I know what I did to them. I don't know how, but I know that if you follow all the roads backward, they all lead to me. And I can't do anything to fix it. I don't have that kind of power.

Jan Landau's Golem Band—"Whisper It To Me":
You've got me under your fingernails and I'm never coming out. It's warm in here, and I don't ever have to be afraid.

DRAG

They say things about the closet in the common room of Holton House. Weirdest thing. All four walls are mirrors. Even the back of the door. Floor to ceiling on all sides, endless mirror hallways leading on and on until the reflection blurs, like if you could step through the barrier and run through those hallways, you would fade and be spit out into total blank obscurity at the other end. There's no light switch. If you want to stand in that closet and use those mirrors (and nobody does, that's for goddamn sure), you have to leave the door open and see by the trickling light of the common room. So what the boys of St. Cecelia's Private Academy talk about on those long secret nights—their dorms abandoned, their voices low, all of them huddled around a single candle—is that closet.

Marco tells the story that most of them already know. Marco is a senior. He never made prefect, never played politics. And he looks eighteen, so he buys cigarettes for the younger kids sometimes. People look up to Marco. People are afraid of Marco. He has earned the right to this story, to claim partial ownership of it. So he crawls up on the back of the couch, reaches up, twists off the smoke detector. He takes out the big square battery. Then he climbs down, picks up the candle and uses it to light his Camel. It's an important part of this story.

He says, "Okay. Shut up. Listen." He takes a drag, wanders around the room. Blue smoke follows him, curls and coils from his mouth. It's part of the show. He leans on the ping pong table and he says, "A long time ago, something happened in Holton House." He tells them that whatever happened, it was so bad that nobody wants to talk about it. And he's right. Go ahead. Try to ask somebody about the closet. Try to find out what happened in there, when it happened, who it happened to. Nobody's talking. Marco says, "Here's what you do," and he holds up the Camel so everyone can see. He tells them how to summon up Ember Eyes. He passes on the same secret ritual that he learned his freshman year. It's all bullshit, of course. He tried it once. Nothing happens. You just about shit yourself imagining that it might, but then some dickhead bangs on the closet door with both fists and you shriek like a baby and you walk out of the closet and everyone's losing their shit laughing at you. But that's not the point. That moment just before the banging, just before the rage and humiliation, the moment just after you inhale and just before you scream, when you're sure it's all real, *that* is the point.

It's that Brett kid who speaks up when it's all over. It's always somebody. That Brett kid's a transfer student. Sophomore? Junior? Whatever, older than most of the new kids. Kind of has that pretty-boy thing going for him. Baseball build. Sort of swoopy haircut. Right now though, that Brett kid is just another newcomer who thinks he knows what's coming. He says, "Well that's pretty fucking stupid."

Everyone laughs. It is well timed. This kid is good at shit like that, natural comedian.

Marco says, "Try it," and throws his pack and his Zippo at Brett.

Brett says, "I don't smoke," but it's too late now. Should have thought about that before. Because now everyone in the common room is giving him that upward lilting catcall, that "oooo-OOOH!" noise, subtitled, *You have just been issued a challenge. Failure to answer this challenge will reveal you to be a spineless fag. We know you will not step down now.*

He shrugs. Says, "Fine." Gets up. Has to step over everybody to get to the closet door, careful footfalls between and around and over the tangle of crossed legs, searching out the patches of carpet like a swamp-walker. Christ, it seems like the entire house is in here. Then he opens the door and goes in.

The ritual begins like this. Brett shakes a smoke out of his pack and mutters, sing-song, "Fuck you guys. Seriously," then he sticks the cigarette in his mouth and lights it. The lighter swallows up oxygen and spits out flame and now there is light in the closet, and Brett can see for miles and miles down the hallways behind his four reflections. He chokes (this is good; this is not part of the ritual strictly speaking, but it doesn't hurt), and in the windless claustrophobic space (the one that goes on forever and ever down those phantom hallways), the smoke hangs, weaves, makes shapes for him, a shadow show. Now Brett holds the cigarette like a pencil between his thumb and forefinger, leans close to the wall opposite the door, presses the ember against the surface of the mirror. Twists. It rains orange embers. They flutter like dying lightning bugs toward the carpet, and now the cigarette is out and there is an ashy black smudge on the mirror. Brett says, "Okay, cigarette burn number one. Looks like a cat's asshole." Out in the common room, the other boys laugh. It's that timing again. Guy's a riot.

He lights the cigarette again. The Zippo's getting hot, but that's part of the ritual too. Again, he presses the ember against the mirror. Another half-assed fireworks show. Another ash-stain, this one maybe two inches from the first.

He lights the cigarette one more time. And he flicks the lighter closed.

The only light is the orange cherry, replicated four-fold, cloned a thousand fold, onward down the endless hallways.

And now...

Everything that happens now is too slow to see. Think of time-lapse photography, think of capturing motion where no motion seems to be, because that's what this is like. The ash-stains start to glow again, like the cherry of his cigarette, like the embers that cascaded to the carpet and burnt little black marks there (next to older identical burns; building on the history is part of the ritual). The stagnant smoke stops twisting in the space between Brett's face and the mirror. It finds form, seems to eat away at space and make room for matter. And Brett hears the sound of paper lungs trying to breath.

Ember Eyes. Ember Eyes in the mirror, smiling sadly. In a white shirt and a red St. Cecelia's tie. Naked below the waist, his legs somehow both shriveled and dry and black, and also wet and lithe, snakeskin slick. And that face, like a child's drawing of a face, a hole for the mouth and those fiery cigarette stains for eyes. Ember Eyes says, "It's been... so long since I've had one of those. Could I bum?"

What Brett is supposed to do now is say, "No." He's supposed to say, "Ember Eyes, you want something from me. I have what you want. What price will you pay?" That's how Marco explained it: vague symbolic language, the decorative frills of ceremony. But this was never supposed to happen. The opportunity was never supposed

Plow the Bones

to present itself. Right now, there is someone on the other side of the closet pounding a double-kick-drum tattoo on the door. Boo. Gotcha. But there is no high-pitched girlie shriek from inside, Brett's not bursting out of the closet and telling Marco to go fuck himself, and everybody's laughter is stillborn in their throats. Outside, nobody says anything, and inside nobody screams.

But, oh goddamn it, Brett does want to scream. He wants to run. He wants to burst out of the closet and let everyone know what a baby he is, fine, whatever, he doesn't care, he just wants out of here, away from Ember Eyes, who is pawing at the other side of the mirror, begging in his shredded emphysemic old-man voice, "Come on, man... I haven't had a cigarette in *such* a *long time*."

And Brett says, "Okay," and offers the pack to Ember Eyes. It knocks against the glass. And Ember Eyes's fingers, black and bulbous at the tips like tree-frog toes, squeak on the other side of the glass, slide down the surface (somebody will try to Windex the mirrors some time later, and they'll wonder why they can't seem to scrub off the smudges, and they'll get the fuck out of that closet, not really understanding why it spooks them so bad). Ember Eyes says, "Is this a joke?"

Brett shakes his head. The tears are coming.

Outside, one kid says, "Okay, ha ha, Brett, you turned it around on us. Come on out." He's good, that Brett kid. He's doing the voice, doing it better than Marco, and they can all hear it. They are disappointed. No spook show. No humiliation. This is not what they wanted.

Inside, Ember Eyes says, "Is this some kind of a fucking joke?" The corners of his mouth work, the muscles tense and release beneath his sunken mold-colored cheeks. He grimaces. His teeth are yellow, nicotine stained. His glowing cigarette-cherry eyes spark like firewood.

Brett starts bawling. He sinks against the door, feels Ember Eyes's heat against his back, jolts upright, swings around. He is surrounded. With those endless hallways at his back, to his sides, and Ember Eyes framed in each one, angry, hurt, betrayed, gesturing helplessly at the cigarettes with his awful snakeskin hands.

Ember Eyes says, "I don't think this is funny."

Outside, Marco grabs the handle. It burns him. He swears, shakes his hand up and down. The boys gasp. Some of them start to cry, trying not to, still posturing, still make-believing that this is make-believe, even when some part of them deep inside knows otherwise. All they hear on the other side is Brett, sobbing, scrabbling, scratching. Marco says, "Brett, come out. We're done. It's okay."

Inside, Ember Eyes says, "All I wanted was a smoke. I asked nicely. Why are you being such a jerk?" His voice deteriorates. He's got a campfire in his throat, eating up his vocal chords, putting runs and holes in them like old nylon stockings.

Brett says, "I'm sorry," and cries some more.

"Give me," says Ember Eyes, and sucks breath into his rotten lungs, "a cigarette."

Brett wants to tell him he can't, that there are mirrors between them, thick walls where reality separates from myth, sorry, Ember Eyes is stuck in storyland and Brett is standing in the third dimension. But he doesn't say anything. He shakes his head. Closes his eyes.

So he doesn't see what happens next. He doesn't see Ember Eyes's frog-fingers sinking through the mirror, manifesting in front of him. His black rawhide hands slip through, the glass clings to them like Vaseline, slips back into place like rubber. Wrists, arms, shoulders, each joint slipping through the mirror, *pop*, and Brett hears it all, hears each nasty noise and whimpers in response, but his eyes stay closed tight, wrinkling the skin into spider webs.

Marco is pounding on the door now. Yelling. Someone will come. A prefect, a house head, someone will come and make this all stop, save him from culpability.

Ember Eyes, slick and slimy and dry and brittle and sad and angry and unreal, steps out of the mirror. And Ember Eyes makes a noise in his deteriorating throat that sounds like nothing Brett has ever heard, and he wraps his fingers around Brett's skull, twines them in Brett's swoopy hair. His fingers are longer now. They touch at the back of Brett's head, his thumbs meet below his chin. Oh Christ! They grow, Brett can feel them! They grow!

PLOW THE BONES

The kids in the common room sit with their hands bound up behind their necks, their arms pressed against their ears, their eyes down.

Marco throws himself shoulder-first at the door over and over, feels the burning heat behind it radiate through his T-shirt and into his skin, burn him in a way that will never leave him, that will redefine heat for him.

Ember Eyes presses his mouth to Brett's, crams his thick purple tongue past his lips, opens his jaw wider and wider and whatever is left of that Brett kid thinks that maybe Ember Eyes is trying to climb inside him. Ember Eyes has a mouth like a manhole, wider, wider, wider, and the edges of Brett's mouth split, bleed. But Brett is far away. And Ember Eyes begins to suck. His paper-lungs expand and he draws the air out of Brett's chest and Brett thinks, *He's trying to suck the smoke out of me.* But Brett is far away from himself, and none of this really surprises him. He has lost his grip on himself, and now the best parts of him are torn into fours, floating away down the mirror hallways.

And then...

Well...

Whatever happens next is not part of the ritual. And no one will remember it anyway.

Fifteen years from now, a man who looks much older than he is will wheel a shopping cart past a strip of college bars. He will have a beard that mostly covers the scarring at the edges of his mouth and a comb in his jeans pocket that he will pull out and drag through that beard every five minutes. His beard will be long and straight and shiny, and sometimes he will sit on the curb next to his cart and braid it with slow, precise, delicate care, and the next day his beard will be crimped and kinky and he will have to spend some extra time combing it. He will smell terrible. His shopping cart will be full of empty beer bottles and soda cans which he will bring to the grocery store and exchange for a few bucks, which he will spend on Swedish Fish, the empty bags of which he will crumple and shove into the pockets of his filthy beige Dickie's coveralls. He will ask people for cigarettes, and then when he gets them, he will smile and say, "I don't smoke," and add them to his collection of never-smoked Camels or Marlboros or Basics in a peeling cigar box in the children's seat of the cart. People will laugh when he says that. He has perfect timing. Natural comedian. Guy's a riot. The regulars at the bars will call him Smokey, and some of them might even wonder how he got where he is. Most of them won't. Some winter—when it is particularly frigid and he won't go to the St. Vincent Hotel because of that long, long hallway leading past the front desk, that terrible hallway, Christ, he never wants to see that hallway again, *any* hallway again, never ever—he will fall asleep on a bus-stop bench and he will freeze to death.

Fifteen years from now, Marco will take a job as a biology professor at his alma mater. He will become a student favorite, not because he is lenient, but because he is a smart-ass who smokes cigarettes outside of class and sometimes uses swear words in the middle of his lectures. The kids will like Mr. Almodovar. They will fear Mr. Almodovar. He will make a little bachelor pad for himself on the top floor of Holton House. He will become the housemaster and turn a blind eye to the midnight masses in the common room. Sometimes kids will come into his office and ask him about this story some of the older boys told them about the closet and what happens in there, and he will think he remembers something about that, something bad and scary, and his eyebrows will crinkle and leave a deep V between them and he'll chew on the inside of his cheek and try to pin the memory down, and he'll fail and say, "Kids used to tell a lot of stories about that closet." And then he'll smile and shake his head and say something sarcastic, and the kid will leave feeling stupid for having bothered him.

Fifteen years from now, everyone in that room will have moved on. They will have built lives for themselves with varying degrees of success. They will remember that high school sucked, and doubly so for them. Nobody who's never been at a boarding school can really comprehend just how deep that particular well can go. Still, it wasn't all bad. Some of them will have nightmares sometimes. Most of them won't.

And where will Ember Eyes go? Back down the thousand hallways, sucked in every direction at once. You can follow him if you like. You can look behind him and see the chord in his back, a red-black tendon pulled taut like a high-tension wire that stretches forever down the obscure far-mirror roads, into the crawlspace behind the world.

That is where we live.

We love to watch you perform your rituals. We delight in seeing you dance through life, waiting for something exciting to happen. We smile on you, little ones, when you construct your narratives and invent your fantasies.

And, oh, how we ache for you when you become bored! How we weep for you! How we gnash our teeth at the tragedy of the creeping awareness that your natural state is a forever-plain of bitter, numb, mundane normalcy. We cannot tolerate your meaninglessness. We don't want that for you. We love you as children love.

So let's make a deal, hmm? Let's put Ember Eyes away for a while. Let's set him aside in his place next to the hook-hand killers, and the Bloody Marys, and the gang members driving with their headlights off, and the kidney snatchers, and the phantom hitchhikers. We'll just tuck him away for a bit. Until we cannot stand to see you stumbling like blind men through the haze of the commonplace, wishing with all your hearts for something bigger than you, something to give your lives a shape and a substance. Just until you need him again. Don't worry. We love you too much to forget about you.

Ballad of a Hot Air Balloon-Headed Girl

I knew a girl who tied a hot air balloon envelope to her shoulders, just in case her head should ever burst into flames. It was homemade, sewn together from stolen scraps of Dacron, mottled and gaudy. It was as wide as her shoulders and it hung down to the small of her back like a pair of folded oil-slick dragonfly wings. She pierced the thin, tender skin of her shoulders with four strong surgical-steel rings, two just above the delicate cliff of her clavicle and two over the twin plateaus of her shoulder blades, and to these she anchored the envelope.

I used to sneak away from barracks to see her in the wide grey field outside of Courdray. I was nineteen and obsessed with climbing trees. I used to split my brain apart during drills, sink away into the recesses of daydreams to climb imagined redwoods that never ended, and in rare unsupervised moments I would climb the dry and dying cypress out in the field, with the grass twitching and the sky bruising over, and I would sit in the lowest crotch and dangle my arm down. And she would sit at the roots (she never climbed, afraid that she would tear open her precious envelope on a capricious branch, and that her head would explode before she could patch it up), and play with my fingers, never grabbing hold but always dancing across my fingertips with her own. And we would talk.

Once, I said, "It's ludicrous. The thing with your head, I mean. It'll never happen."

"Don't say 'ludicrous,' " she said, playing with my fingers and using her free hand to pull up handfuls of grass and pile them in the bowl of her crossed legs. "You mean it's stupid, so say it's stupid. You don't need to prove that you're smart, I already know that."

"It's not stupid. It's just kind of crazy."

"Semantics. And why not? Why won't it ever happen?"

I sighed and tried to grab her fingers, but they slid away from me. "Because," I said, "it's never happened before. Someone's head just spontaneously bursting into flame? What's going to stop the rest of you from burning up?"

"It's going to happen," she said. We spent ten more minutes in silence, and I let her bat at my hand like a cat with a toy.

These were in the days when we were at war. When all of my

friends were soldiers and children, like me, with our pistols and our rifles, and none of us knew death because the war hadn't yet come to Courdray. We wore our beards trimmed like topiaries, proud of our new ability to cultivate them, and rode horses not much younger than ourselves, and we waited for telegrams with news of when we would become men.

The Greely Brigade has been defeated on the Eastern Mesa. Stop.

The forces of the Revolutionaries are moving north. Stop.

All patriotic young men in the Northern Territories: ready your rifles and sleep in shifts. Stop.

Once, she said to me, "You might die, you know. In the war."

I was in the cypress and she was below me. I was smoking a pipe for the first time, because that had become a popular pastime in the barracks, apparently evidential of our adulthood. I liked the taste of the smoke, hot and deep. It tasted red and brown and old. I choked on it. I said, "I guess. You might die if your head explodes."

"I'm serious," she said. She laughed, but her laugh was always such a sad thing. It always sounded like it was escaping from beneath a crush of bad memories and doomed predictions, a laugh that reminded you of sadness by contrast. "Do you understand what the war means? People die in wars. You could die. The Revolutionaries could die. Someone has to die."

"The Revolutionaries are supposed to die," I said, aiming for condescension, because I was smart, and I did need to prove it. "They want to change everything."

"So do I," she said, quiet and casually defensive.

"Yeah, I mean, me too. Just, not like that."

"Like what?" she asked, and I didn't know.

The war came to Fantago, and in those days you could ride to Fantago from Courdray in two days, so our drills became tenser and our rifles got cleaned more often, and nothing else changed. We waited and we trimmed our beards and smoked our pipes, and I dreamed of climbing trees. The Revolutionaries ravaged Fantago and holed up there for three months. Some of our boys defected, and nobody minded too much.

I kissed her for the first time when I was twenty, standing beneath the cypress tree. We came to the tree at the same time, so I didn't have time to climb the tree before she got there, which was our usual custom. I was crossing the field lazily, dragging the toes of my boots in the dirt to hear the sound it made, when I looked up and saw her running toward me. She was smiling a little, in the haunted way I still think about when I'm lonely. When we met, she said, "It's starting. This is the first progress I've made."

I said, "What are you talking about?"

"Really? What do you think I'm talking about?"

I shrugged.

She threw her fists against her hips and growled, exhausted and frustrated with the seconds that were passing us. She said, "God, just… Here!"

And she kissed me. Our tongues touched, and I tasted smoke. Her mouth was hot like a stone beneath the sun and she tasted red and brown and old. We kissed for a very long time, with our noses smashed together and my eyes wide, staring at her closed lids, watching the tears slip through them. When we exhaled, the smoke roiled through our nostrils and circled our heads. I put my hands on her waist and she knocked them away. We broke the kiss and a stranglevine of smoke joined our lips together for a moment before it dissolved. She said, "See, stupid?"

And I said, "Yeah. I see."

After that, the changes happened so swiftly. It came to be that going to see her filled me with an awful excitement that scared me more than it impelled me. I stayed in the barracks every night until one or two in the morning, reading letters from my mother and trying to stop my hands from shaking. The thought of seeing her, the knowledge that each secret meeting held another terrible gift to discover, those things held me in place, frightened at my own need for them. I switched from pipes to cigarettes, because they seemed a better fit to my mania. I would smoke them back-to-back most nights, waiting for myself to make the inevitable decision to escape the barracks and run to the field to see what new mutation had overtaken her. And I always did.

Plow the Bones

One night I arrived and the hairs of her thin, fair eyebrows were orange and shining like burning tobacco beneath twin rows of blue flame. She looked happier than I'd ever seen her before, and I said so.

She laughed and said, "Well, that's not saying much, is it?"

In the winter, she couldn't come too close to the dry cypress, fearing the heat rising from the top of her head would set it ablaze. Instead, we sat a respectable distance away, both of us with our coats removed, her lying back with her hair in the snow to melt it away, and I stared at my tree and wished I were up it. I asked, "Does it hurt?" and I was afraid of what she would say.

She said, "Not really. But the snow feels nice."

She became hotter and hotter, and I wanted her more. She was too hot to kiss, and in any case she wouldn't let me try. One day, she lifted the envelope over her head and the heat filled it up and lifted her a few feet into the air for a few minutes. I sat on the ground and played with her fingertips from below for a change.

I told her, "I'm in love with you, I think."

And she said, "Well, sure. Now that you've said it out loud. Push me up. I want to see how far I can go." She didn't get very far that day.

The war came to Courdray in the spring, and we pushed back the Revolutionaries. Forces from Pendleton and Gumble Township came to our aide. I fired my gun and other boys my age fired their guns, and our horses stomped through the field, which had been made into a slick pit of mud by the constant rain that year, and nobody could tell who was on what side. I fell off my horse, and one of our own boys stepped sideways on my calf, and I limped across the battlefield with my ankle sprained for the rest of the fight. I shot a blonde boy in the face with my pistol, and I didn't feel any remorse for years afterward. A boy I knew whose name I can't remember was disemboweled by someone's saber, and I remember feeling angry with him for being such a poor soldier. That's how death came to the boys of Courdray. It came as a numb and far away anger, hot milk in our bellies, destined to curdle and poison us. We were boys with fine beards and nice mustaches and pipes and guns and cigarettes and horses. And we killed. And we were killed. And the worst we felt, in those dreamy and wonderful days of death, was a mysterious gnawing loss, as though something novel but inessential had slipped through holes in our pockets and disappeared. And my girl hid in the forest, somewhere far away from the mud, in the miserable place where she lived, wherever that was. I think the best time for soldiering is youth. If you are going to be made to kill, you ought not to know why. You ought not to understand the permanence of it. A soldier ought to be stupid. Genius soldiers are the most wretched of us creatures, on the dirt or under it.

Still, we felt the shadow of our impending age, our inevitable learning, in the barracks and in the infirmary. We stared at empty cots, or cots that were full but not as full as they used to be, and we chewed on our cheeks and felt sad.

After we drove the Revolutionaries back to Fantago, the old men spoke of turning points, of last-minute comebacks, and we were supposed to be proud of what we had done, and we were. Still and yet, again I began to escape the barracks at night, hobbling on crutches, trying to relearn the delicate craft of climbing trees. I mastered the cypress and moved on to a lithe little willow, whose thinness and fragility afforded me more challenge and a shorter way to fall should my injured leg give up on my weight. I didn't see her for weeks, and I felt guilty. When I did see her, I was hidden in the willow, and I watched her shuffling through the field while the wind picked up the balloon and pulled her around, looking for me. When she called my name, crackling orange embers popped from between her lips and wound down into the dirt. She was careful to step on them to stop them lighting up the grass. I didn't want to see her. Her sadness and her hope were too big, too desperate, and while I was able to comfort her before, I had been in battle and I had become a man, and the hot milk in my belly had begun to film over and clump. I wish I had been more aware of it then. All I knew at the time was that there was something uncomfortable and frightening happening in my solar plexus, and I didn't want to share it with her.

Courdray grew. We incorporated Gumble and attracted foreign visitors. In those days, we trusted foreigners more than natives. Our enemies were natives, and the foreigners were polite and quiet and opened new and fascinating shops in the main square and sold clockwork dolls that sang our Battle Hymn in tinny, twinkling voices. Our army grew larger, and my friends and I were not the youngest soldiers anymore. We fought three more battles in Courdray before my twenty-first birthday, and the foreigners devised guns for us to mount on our rooftops, using the same strange clockwork they used to make our toys, and they sprayed bullets like a fire hose, so hot that they glowed red and turned the sky above Courdray into a bloody starscape, and we rode out into the field and killed again, and were killed again. I caught a bullet from one of our own giant clockwork rifles in the hand, and the blazing bullet itself cauterized the wound before it could bleed. I remember staring through the hole in my hand and seeing light on the other end. And I think that drove me a little crazy for a few days. We're not designed to look through meat and see light. That's not something anyone's prepared for.

 I collected my courage and went to see her again, and in many ways, for the last time, on my birthday. I brought along a bottle of wine, and felt hard and proud of the way I imagined myself to look, a man on his way to court a woman, using my unbandaged hand to hold the kind of sticky-sweet merlot exclusive to adults with long histories and discerning tastes. I was surprised to find that, in my months of infidelity, the cypress had finally given up and died. Its bark had turned ash-grey, and the wood beneath was the same. The branches were dry all the way through, and no good for climbing. The lowest and thickest, the one with which I was most familiar and of which I was most fond, cracked and collapsed when I put my weight on it. Then I didn't want to be there anymore.

 She came to me slowly, with tiny licks of flame riding up from beneath the collar of her sundress, lighting up the night. When she reached me, I was sullen and distracted, barely aware of the sparks and sputters of her campfire head, the way her eyes glowed with the blaze behind them, or the way her exhalations funneled dark blue smoke through her nostrils. I remember the way my mother would look after a fight with my father, standing on the back porch with candles lit, staring into dusk and breathing slowly and looking exhausted, immensely sad and still somehow victorious. For me, that look will always be fused in my memory to the look on the face of the girl with the hot-air balloon attached to her shoulders on the last night I spoke to her. She said, "What's wrong?"

"Fucking tree is dead," I said.

"And?"

I was angry with her then. Angry with her for aspiring to something so stupid and so pointless for so long that it had begun to come true, and I was angry because she had amazed me with those changes for so long, and I was angry because I could no longer find that place within me that used to be amazed. I said, "And? What do you mean, and? That's not enough?"

Her fragile smile cracked and collapsed like the cypress limb, then grew back stronger and angrier. That was her best kind of smile. She said, "That would be enough, but it's not all. So… And?"

"And… I really, really don't want it to be? I'm not ready."

I didn't look at her again, because I was afraid I would cry, and I had learned that the most pathetic thing in the world was a man with his own tears matting down his beard. I lit a cigarette instead and I said nothing. I leaned on the tree and crossed my arms and wedged one boot-heel against the dead wood.

When she spoke again, it was with desperate, parental impatience. She said, "Look, do you want your birthday present? Do you want it? You need to tell me now, alright, because you only have one chance to take it from me."

I kicked the bottle of wine and said, "Fine. Whatever." I think back on myself in those bloody, innocent days with so much hatred now, for the things I said and did not say.

She said, "It's happening tonight. Soon. Before the hour's done. My head will blaze and I'll fly away. I've patched the envelope and double-coated it with polyurethane and I'm ready to leave. When it happens, I'm gone forever, okay? No more bad memories, no more doomed predictions, do you understand?"

She wanted to escape, and I never even found out from what. A few more days in the field with her, still a stupid boy capable of caring for her, and maybe I would have learned. Just a few more days. Please.

I forced my eyes onto her and I said, "I understand." I tried to write a secret message in the space between our faces, tried to will her into understanding with the force of our eye contact. 'Please don't talk to me. I am so very sad these days and I don't know why, and I can't take care of your sadness anymore. Stop talking about balloons and fire and escape, because I can't stand to watch you existing, broken as you are, without wanting to weep and throw myself into your chest and wrap myself in you. Please stop. Please stop.'

I think she saw it. I will always think that. But she ignored it. She said, "No, listen. I've been thinking about this, and I can take you with me. I think I'm contagious."

That girl. Why didn't she keep pushing?

I cried, like I knew I would if I had to keep this up. And I fell against her chest and felt the heat of her head radiating down into my shoulders, and I balled my hands into the thin plaid of her dress, and her arms grew like vines around me, subtle and determined. And she said,

"Shhh. Shhh. It's okay. I'll take you with me. We'll go together. I made you an envelope. I brought a needle and some strong steel rings."

I pushed myself away from her, still crying, now howling as well, howling to approximate the sounds of an animal, because if I could not be a man I wanted to be something just as dangerous. "What do you want me to do? Huh? What do you want? You want me to run away, to abandon the war, to leave the country to the Revolutionaries? How? How am I going to do that? Huh?" Words that meant nothing said to fill the space that would otherwise have been occupied (and better occupied) by acceptance. Yes please, I should have said. Whatever you say. Save me.

She set her jaw and weathered the assault. She was a better soldier than I. And then she said, "I want you to kiss me. I'll fill your head with fire and we'll both fly."

I tried for a very long time to think of an excuse not to do it. The only one I came up with was, "I'll burn. I'm not like you. Fire burns me. I'm sorry." And that's the one I gave her, crumbling away from my anger, away from my pretenses of manhood, drowning in the heap of my forgotten childishness. I wept. Openly, and without being able to stop it. She cried a little too, and she did not take me in her arms and I did not offer to take her into mine.

She said. "Okay. Then... do me a favor?"

"Fine," I said.

She slid the sundress over her shoulders and held it above her breasts with one arm. The moon turned her skin into a blue sea, each wave capturing shadows. She said, "Check the anchors. Make sure they're tight and strong."

I ran my fingers over each of the four steel rings and found that the ropes were anchored well. I told her so. She asked me to put her dress back where it belonged, and I did, and I felt like I was amputating something from myself.

She said, "I have to lie down. The envelope needs to be above my head when it starts. Will you do me one more favor?"

I nodded. This had started to feel sacred and inevitable, and I was unable to take back the decision I had made. I only had one chance to make it.

She said, "Climb the tree and hang your hand down to me."

"It's no good for climbing."

"There's got to be someplace you can sit."

She got onto the ground and I positioned the envelope over her eyes and nose so that only her mouth peeked out. It started to expand immediately.

I told her I was in the tree, even though I wasn't. And I hung my hand down for her. She played with my fingers until the change came, and then I watched her rise, no longer able to speak or laugh because her throat and lips were buried beneath a high column of red flame. I tried to grab her hand as she went higher, but I missed it. She set the old cypress on fire, and it burnt quickly and easily, and it took much of the grass with it. The wind took her away over the trees and over the city and past the unsympathetic chopping block of the horizon line, and I went back to the city and told of the fire, and then to the barracks and tried to vomit up the curdled milk in my belly, and I failed.

I fought with the National Urban-Defense Army for six more

Plow the Bones

years. I killed many men, and many men died next to me, and I swallowed them all and kept them in my belly. I left Courdray and went on the road with the National Crusaders to wipe out the Revolutionaries wherever we found them. I rose to the rank of Colonel. I set fire to a bungalow outside of Acconda because from the window we could see the flag of the Revolution hung in brash, challenging prominence, and I hid in the woods while the fire chewed through the beams and the roof, and I shot down the three Revolutionaries who ran outside, one very fat man and two women, one fat and old, one not very much younger than me. I presided over the public beheading of a Revolutionary leader from a stage set up in the hamlet of Losetino, and I asked the executioner to use my saber so that it might be honored by the death of another pestilent rat, and thereafter I picked up the head of the man and howled at the crowd, "Do you see what happens to perverts and psychopaths?" before flinging the thing into their midst. I killed children, and thereafter dreamed of being murdered in my sleep with a hunger and desire that toed the edge of obsession. And I no longer cared about war. I was not young and I was not patriotic, but I readied my rifle and I slept in shifts, not because I believed in the cause or the nation or the species, but because I was bored and angry, and the war occupied the former and stoked the latter. For a while.

I saw her again flying over a battlefield in Carschton. I almost missed her. The sky was the same color as her head, and she floated over me without a noise. I shot a young man from his horse and laughed. Then someone shot my horse in the hind leg, and he tumbled backward, throwing me off. And lying there in the dirt, I saw her. The tension and weight of her muscles was gone. Her arms and legs floated and swayed and danced, and even though I could not see her face, I will swear, here and until my death, that she was happier than any girl before or since her, happy for a simple sunset moment, red and brown and old, that allowed her to float over dead and dying men, and happy for every moment after.

They put me in the Carschton prison and they gave me an ultimatum. I could die, or I could renounce the National Crusade and side with the Revolutionaries. Propagandized as a dead man or propagandized as a living one. I told them I would very much like to die. Still, as the days and weeks moved forward and as I sat on a cold, wet, stone floor and let my fine beard go to shit and began to smell of mildew and grew sores on the bottoms of my feet, and as I awaited the triumphant moment of my public execution, I could not shake the image of her from my mind. I saw her in the shadows of the stone ceiling, in the cracks of the floor, lying on the hard cot and turning from my back to my belly, and wondering where in the world she was now. Whether she thought of me, or thought only of joy, or if the fire had obliterated her ability to think at all, and whether or not that might be better, more pure, happier, than the alternative.

They came to me at last and gave me one more chance. And I made my decision, born from the desire to see her one last time, to climb the highest tree and latch on to her dangling feet and pull myself up and find her lips and kiss them, or failing that, to shoot her down with my rifle and give myself a reason to die. They said that they didn't want me if I couldn't believe, truly and sincerely, in the cause of the Revolution. I told them that I didn't even know what the cause was. And they told me that nobody did, that wasn't the point, knowing something was not prerequisite to believing in it. And I said, "Sure. Fine."

I stayed in hotel rooms while the troops stayed in tents. I sipped whisky and smoked my pipe (cigarettes were out of fashion among the Revolutionaries, seen as common and anti-intellectual) while the soldiers killed and were killed. I made speeches and met with sympathetic sponsors and went to bed early. I was worth more alive than dead, as a symbol of the rightness and righteousness of the Revolution. I crept away and climbed trees.

Years passed. And we won.

On many occasions, I have been asked to provide some profound snippet of personal experience to sum up the Revolution, something for the benefit of future generations, something to be skimmed and forgotten in history books, and I have always obliged. It's easy to fake enthusiasm. People don't want details. They want poetics. This works out well for me, because I don't remember the details. I remember each battle before my thirtieth birthday as the same battle, glimpsed from the safety of a hotel room or a tree branch, itching with an anger that drove me toward the fray, an anger only held in check by the constant awareness that I could not allow myself to die until I had joined the girl with the hot air balloon head or brought her down. I remember weeping and cheering, which sound pretty much the same from beneath strange blankets in strange rooms. What I say when I am asked is this: "Blood spilled in the cause of freedom is sacred. It is the only sacred thing in the world." And people like that, I guess.

I was never a very good man. But, damn each step I ever took, I would have been one hell of a balloon.

I was made president of the new republic when I was thirty-seven, and I accepted on the condition that I would not have to do anything for the rest of my life. The new government boys, the ones who found enough of themselves left over after the war to give a proper fuck about governance, signed papers and made speeches, and I nodded and looked distinguished, and sneaked into dark and lonely woods to find adequate climbing trees.

I look much older than I am.

My physician says that my body is not strong enough to climb trees, that my knees are like rotten driftwood and my spine is beginning to twist, and I have satisfied myself that he is full of shit. He asked too many questions when I told him to attach the envelope to my shoulders with the four tiny surgical steel rings, and I answered him in coinage and a stiff glare. I paid a great deal of money to transplant the world's largest tree, a redwood whose height is, I understand, uncanny, but whose technical dimensions I never bothered to memorize, into the back lot of the Presidential Estate. I fastened a ladder to its trunk, and I have made a ritual of climbing it every night as the sun begins to set. In the summer, the sunset is the same color as the roaring torch of her head, a smear of livid reds and yellows. In the winter, it is the same color as her plaid sundress.

Every night, I climb the redwood with my rifle in my hand, in case I do not succeed in grabbing her fingers as she passes. I don't like to think about that possibility. That I might shoot her down instead of carry myself up. I weep when I imagine it.

In my imaginings I always see her in summer, at the highest point of the tree I can reach, cradling my rifle in my arms (it is a poor substitute for her, but it's sturdy and hard and it makes me feel the same), with my wide-brimmed hat and my dark glasses on, to keep my vision sharp in the blazing sunset. I am always alert and wary in my daydreams, and I always spot her with plenty of time to prepare for her arrival, riding across clouds the color of wine spilled on white sheets with her fingers dangling, swaying like seaweed as though she is already brushing them across my fingertips. And I say, "I found you. You were right. I should have kissed you and let you fill me up with fire and carry me away."

In the worst of my imaginings, the breeze takes her high and to the left, and my fingers are never long enough to reach hers. As she floats past, I sight the envelope (I am never crying in the imagined scene, although the real me, the one of flesh and regret, weeps in the act of fantasizing), and I fire. I reload. I fire again. I reload. I fire again. And eventually the envelope collapses, and she plummets toward a patch of ground I can't see. I have never, since the sores burnt my feet in the Carschton cell, spent a moment of awareness not hating myself for this fantasy. For the desire to steal from her the only transcendence she ever knew, to end her long experiment with happiness by reintroducing her to gravity, and to merciless impact. My only comfort is that, in this least-loved dream, this is not an act of malice. It's an act of necessity. My girl, please, you've got to believe me. I don't want to do this. But I have to. I'll never die while you still float. And if I can't join you up there… well…

Would she forgive me while she fell? Would she know that she could? Would it occur to her that I would need her to?

But. But there are other fantasies. When the wind is my collaborator, and it sends her to me, and I reach to check the anchors in my shoulders and find them sturdy. I throw my rifle down. And I reach for her fingertips.

Rattenkönig

She sat Indian-style before them in the Sudden Room. Her face ached. She'd been sitting there with her shoulders slumped and her neck craned, chewing on the insides of her cheeks. She could feel the rough nasty texture of the unsanded, unpainted planks in the floor through her jeans. It smelled like age and dampness in here, and with each breath, some paranoid part of her brain screamed out that she was probably inhaling a floating miasma of old wallpaper and crumbling plaster and prehistoric mold, a chemical buffet. She didn't want to be here, but she knew that if she left, she would just want to come back. Nothing in the Sudden Room was comfortable.

The Sudden Room. Oh, the bastard Sudden Room, the nightmare from which she couldn't wake up and from which some part of her, the self-pitying masochist recently awoke, never wanted to. It had existed in the corner of her eye, a cancer of the periphery, a door at the end of a hallway that didn't exist. For years, she passed it and never saw it. For years, she stumbled like a sleepwalker from her bed to the bathroom, tracing the wall of the second-floor corridor with her fingers, and still she never noticed the branching hallway, or the door at the end. But once she saw it, like an optical illusion, like a filmic continuity error, she couldn't unsee it. It was always there, the door to the Sudden Room. As were the things that lived inside.

She couldn't figure them out. She wanted to know them, to understand them, to catalogue them and toss them behind a partition in her brain where she filed the vast and forgettable species of stimuli called "normal." But they weren't normal. They were shaped like people, but they stared at her through eyelids fused shut, their skin thin and jaundiced and divided into uneven puzzle-pieces by a lattice of thick black veins. They sniffed the air, ticking and twitching and shivering the same way she'd seen tiny dogs shiver in the arms of women blonder and more successful than her. They were hairless, or were almost so, and their not-quite-hairlessness (patches of thin white wires that seemed to quiver like insect antennae) was worse than pure baldness. They opened their mouths and made thin, wordless, bubbling noises, and even when their mouths were closed, their long sharp teeth hung over their chins like stalactites, rotten, yellow

PLOW THE BONES

at the ends and black at the roots, the teeth of tigers in the mouths of meth addicts. And all of them were fused together, a shared carcinoma of a body from which jutted their terrible hungry heads and twitching toes and waving, spasmodic arms.

God, she wanted a cigarette.

They couldn't touch her. Not if she sat far enough away. The far wall, framed by the sliver of light from the hallway beyond the door, consisted entirely of *them*. From floor to ceiling, a wall of flesh. There were twenty-six of them that she could see (or twenty-six heads, anyway), and sometimes she thought there must be more, that the Sudden Room must stretch backward for a thousand miles of cramped conjoined bodies. The wall of monsters in the Sudden Room. In college, when she had been an optimist, she wrote a paper on Rodin's *Gates of Hell*. She spent weeks staring at the sculpture, analyzing the cramped faces and bodies of the damned, lost in thought or twisted by misery, reaching, climbing, curled into fetal clumps and crammed into alcoves. The things in the Sudden Room with their terrible teeth and their weak, reaching fingers brought her back to those Gates, a breathing representation of Rodin's masterpiece, hungry and blind. And before them, a supplicant engaged in perplexed and petrified prayer, sat Abigail Quatro, queen of failure.

And downstairs, the doorbell rang.

Downstairs, the doorbell rang, and Jim resisted the training that compelled him to answer. On the couch with the old wooden metronome in his hands, running his thumb along the pyramid angle, watching the arm tick back and forth, trying to hypnotize himself. He wanted to fill a syringe with something dark and thick, something that could numb and blind and fuzz-out, and he wanted to jam it into his brain and push the plunger down and force the whole operation into blankness for a while. Hence, the metronome. The insignificant rhythm.

The bell again, belligerent and obsequious.

There's no rule, he thought. *There's no law against ignoring a doorbell. Nobody can force you to answer it.* But the imperative to answer tugged at him. It was funny how much power people had over you. They didn't even need to know you, and they could command your attention with a pointed index finger and a tiny fucking button mounted to the left of your front door. To be in your house was to be powerless.

The doorbell shrieked again, and Jim bit down on his tongue. With the pain, the world swam back. The truth resolved, focused, became sharp. And there didn't seem to be any reason to ignore the door anymore. So (groaning, growling, glaring at the frosted glass window set into the front door and wishing sudden death upon the person behind it), he went to the door and opened it.

"Hello, homeowner," said the doorbell man. He offered Jim his hand and, not wanting to, Jim shook it. It was a thin hand, delicate, a pianist's hand with long fingers and short, clean fingernails. He wore a grey suit and a green tie and a black overcoat. He wore a fedora and a pair of circular sunglasses. He carried an umbrella, for which Jim immediately and irrationally hated him. *Affectation*, he thought. *A stupid affectation. Sun's shining. What are you trying to prove?*

They stood there shaking hands for too many empty moments. Jim's chest tightened, his shoulders clenched. He ground his teeth together. The doorbell man smiled silently.

Jim's brain rolled through its lexicon of pleasantries and settled on, "Can I help you with something?"

"Homeowner," the doorbell man said, "I understand you have a pest problem."

They sometimes said things that sounded like words. She had a little moleskin in which she took notes of what they said, time-stamped and dated, a little book of nonsense quotations.

Theremin forest—11:35 PM October 28th.
Stinking nest—4:14 PM November 1st.
Regards—1:21 AM November 10th.

When she started taking notes, she told herself that she was trying to piece together the quotes, solve the mystery of the Sudden Room. But as the months wore on into nearly a year of sitting and writing, she abandoned that goal. They were mindless words, the kind of thing dementia patients said as their brains broke down, and she was sure that she was imagining at least half of them. Still, she

Plow the Bones

wrote. Because she'd already started, and she needed the habit.

They were excellent listeners, the bound-together cave-fish things. She could talk to them for hours, in a low monotone gone creaky, dry, and uneven from nicotine withdrawal and depression. She could tell them all sorts of things. She could eviscerate the girl she'd been before her life fell out from underneath her, the girl who had decorated the ceiling of her college apartment with glow-in-the-dark stars and moons and planets, who sipped wine and imagined herself to be an adult, the girl who forgot that someday you had to get a job and grow old and die, and that manic optimism and bright-pink hair dye didn't change any of that. She could talk about how, by thirty, she had expected so much more than this.

Argument fish assembly—10:10 AM December 3rd.

Paramount—3:33 AM January 9th.

An aimless, and apparently ownerless, arm swung rhythmically. A blind and hungry head snapped its jaws at it. The whole party hissed like vipers.

"I just wish," said Abigail, "That this wasn't the most exciting thing that had ever happened to me."

Hungry hungry hungry—6:01 AM January 13th.

Seed eating parable—1:12 PM February 20th.

Portcullis—12:30 PM February 21st.

Someone downstairs laughed like a radio announcer, and then was silent.

The doorbell man, sitting on the sofa next to Jim and holding his coffee cup without drinking from it, laughed like a radio announcer, and then was silent.

Jim disliked most people he met these days. Just standing within breathing distance of the debris of his ambitions could turn him against a person. He knew that it was all bullshit, that he was lashing out, taking out his disappointment on the people around him. But he was starting to think that this polite little doorbell man whose every expression and action seemed to be rehearsed, was legitimately deserving. He carried an umbrella on sunny days. He had absolutely no hair beneath the fedora, absolutely no eyebrows either. And he had just laughed at absolutely nothing. It was as though he had read, without context or explanation, that people sometimes laugh when they sit with one another.

"What's funny?" Jim asked.

"Nothing, homeowner. Now, back to it."

The doorbell man had asked for coffee, and for information. He wanted to know about their life together, Abby and he. Were they happy? Were they really in love? Where was she from? What did she do for a living? What did he do? How often did they make love?

And you know what the fucking terrible part was? Jim was telling him. Jim had lined up their photo albums on the coffee table and he was telling him all of it because this delicate little grub worm of a man knew—he *knew!*—about the Sudden Room and its residents, and that had to mean... something.

"Okay," Jim said. And again, "Okay." He took a deep breath, and he told the man everything. He told him how he met Abby, in a Women's Studies class in which he was one of four men, and in which they shouted at one another from across the room, Abby passionately championing Steinem, Jim aligning himself with Paglia despite not knowing the first thing about feminist theory. "I just thought," he said, "that she was fascinating to look at when she got worked up."

The doorbell man nodded and hmm-d and hrr-d and picked up a pencil from the coffee table and tapped it against his lips.

He told him how they'd dated, at first like silly high school kids despite being in their twenties, sneaking away from every social engagement to make out in closets or cars or behind the high hedges in the park, and then later like ancient friends, sharing stories with brief glances, holding between them a thousand esoteric punch lines and secret passwords. "Turkey-fingers," he said. "I used to... This is so stupid, but in college I used to wrap my hands in sliced turkey, like sandwich turkey. And I used to chase her around the apartment. Kind of, you know... warbling. 'Turkey-fingers! Turkey-fingers are coming for you! Turkey fingers!' Like a ghost. Like, I don't know, it was like a half-cocked Boris Karloff impression. You know? You know."

Plow the Bones

The doorbell man chewed off a hangnail. He said, "I know."

He told him how they'd forgone the vows and quoted Wilco songs at each other, because it was silly and irreverent and somehow more meaningful than somebody else's old promises. He told him they'd come to live in the big house in the nice neighborhood. "My dad," he said, "My dad is... was... an attorney. It was a wedding present. The house, I mean. God."

The doorbell man took off his hat and scratched his scalp.

He told him of the fall, the gradual slope away from ambition and hope toward debt and joblessness. Useless degrees, an absence of marketable skills, property taxes and student loans they couldn't afford. The miscarriage, and the money they'd spent on a baby that never came. How they slept back to back, or sometimes in different places, he in the bedroom and she in the Sudden Room where she didn't actually sleep at all. How they couldn't afford cigarettes anymore, and how neither of them wanted to leave home even to find a smoker from whom to bum. How they could go days without saying much to one another. How when he said, "I love you," it sounded like a plea, like a desperate dive toward her, and how he wasn't really sure he was capable of loving anyone anymore. He said, "Things were supposed to be different for us."

The doorbell man said, "I see."

Her back hurt. She had gone into the room around seven o'clock this morning, and it must have been after four by now. Her entire life story had fallen out from between her lips for the thousandth time, unheard by the slit-eared fungus of skin and limbs and teeth. She said, "Last night, Jim tried to cheer me up. I was falling asleep on the couch and he came in with, ah, the, uh..." she sighed, snapped her fingers together. "The shirt he wore at our wedding. It was..." a smile, weak and noncommittal, something to which she couldn't devote any patience or energy. "It was just way too small for him. He's put on some weight. We both have. His gut was pushing out the fabric, like, putting these great big gaps between the buttons, and he looked at me and he said... he said, 'Enjoying the view?'"

She thought about laughing, decided against it. She listened to the grumbling and bubbling of her monsters, trying to figure out why she'd started this story in the first place. "Thing is," she said, picking at the cuticle of her left thumb, seeing how deep she could stand to drive her house key into the soft skin, "it was just so desperate. I could see how angry he was, how aimless and scared and angry. I'm not dumb. I felt… insulted. How can you pretend that anything is normal?"

Pushing deeper with her house key, pushing the dry white ridge of her cuticle backward, back as far as it could go. It hurt, but what else was new? Lots of things hurt. Not smoking hurt. Looking at your checking account balance hurt. Watching your husband pretend not to hate you hurt. Walking by your diploma hanging on the wall hurt. Not acknowledging the bulk boxes of diapers or bottles of formula or untouched toys and baby books hurt. Pain stopped being such a big goddamn deal after a while.

A head close to the ceiling hissed, writhed, coughed up thick mucous the color of mustard, and said, "Turkey-fingerssssss."

Every muscle in Abigail Quatro's body tensed. Her eyelids retracted, her throat went immediately dry. Her key slipped, sliced a jagged reservoir across the knuckles of her thumb. She gasped, more in shock and recognition than pain. She said, "That wasn't fair."

Now all twenty-six heads were still and silent, pointed at her, their nostrils flaring rhythmically as though some olfactory homing device had lighted upon its target. Her breath was coming faster than her lungs could handle comfortably and her brain screamed for nicotine, and she reeled. These emotions, this *fear*, was stronger and more manic than anything she'd felt in almost a year. What were they doing now? Why were they quiet, why weren't they moving, what did they smell with their terrible misshapen, uneven, grown-together nostrils?

In the silence, she could hear blood pattering from the gash on her hand to the naked floorboards. And with each drop, the twenty-six heads (oh God, no, no, perfectly choreographed, synced) twitched. She sat up straighter, snagged the moleskin from her back pocket, readied her pencil.

Turkey-fingers—3:somethingPM March 3rd (WHAT???)

Plow the Bones

They sat there for a long time, and the only sound was the syncopated drip of her blood and the matched rustle of her rotten monsters straining toward it.

The only sound was the syncopated tick of the cat-shaped clock above the television, a relic of an era of silliness and kitsch, as Jim tried to figure out what to say next. He thought, *Stop talking to this asshole. There's something wrong with him, this hairless little freak. Have you stopped to think for one fucking second about why he's here? What he intends to do? What he has to do with the putrid secret cancer growing upstairs?* What he said was, "They're like... mole-rat people. Have you ever seen those? Mole-rats? They're hairless and wrinkled and blind and... ugh... ugly. And these mole-rat people... their skin has grown together and now they're just this big wall of mole-rat men... In a room we never knew was there until ten months ago. Ten months ago! How do you live in a place," the words spilling out of him as though tied to a string tugged by the skinny fingers of his uninvited houseguest, "for seven years and never see an entire room of it? How can that happen?"

The doorbell man pulled a face, a bawdy parody of empathy, and reached out and patted Jim's knee. Jim lurched away from him, his pulse swelling and pulsing below his jaw. He wanted to scream at the man, to attack the man, to light a fire underneath him and remove him like a tick from his house. Except this didn't feel like *his* house anymore, and hadn't for a long time. His nerves quaked and rattled, and he curled into himself on the edge of the sofa thinking, *I look like a junky. A quivering junky going through withdrawal.* He said, "I'm sorry. Just... I'm really sorry, I just don't want you to... to touch me, okay? Just don't... fucking touch me... sir."

The doorbell man smiled, bit his bottom lip. His teeth were too long, too white. He looked like a theatrical mask. He said, "Mr. Quatro... homeowner... have you ever heard of the Rattenkönig phenomenon?"

"No. Nope. I, uh... no."

"Hmm," said the doorbell man. "It is said that rats, when isolated together in small spaces, will fuse together at the tail. Can you imagine, homeowner Jim Quatro? A nest of trapped rats, isolated from food, from sunlight, as their tails tangle together and eventually become... one. Amazing, if it's true, although I myself have never seen any compelling evidence for its veracity. Imagine, then, homeowner, that a nest of some other animal becomes trapped. An animal that survives by different means, adheres to different rules."

The doorbell man stood up, stepped onto the coffee table, kicked aside the photo albums, crushed his coffee cup beneath his heel. Jim stared, open mouthed, and thought, *You're standing on my table. You're standing on my table. I don't know why, but you're standing on my table and gesturing at the ceiling like a professor lecturing to the ceiling fan.*

"Let us theorize that this species travels through secret corridors, makes its way toward new feeding grounds via an entire sequence of tunnels, much like your... ugly... hairless... wrinkled... blind... mole-rats." He was smiling now, the doorbell man, breathing fast, haloed by the ceiling fan, lost in his lunatic sermon. "Let us further theorize that the way is one day blocked by some means, homeowner! Let us now hypothesize what might happen to such a marvelous species over decades, over centuries, homeowner, in the dark! In the bloodless, skyless dark, homeowner!"

A pause. The doorbell man stared longingly at some distant point beyond the house, out in the cold dark bloodless, skyless universe, and caught his breath. Jim realized he was digging his teeth into his tongue, gnawing on that same fat ulcer he'd made earlier when the doorbell had interrupted his thoughtlessness. It had been a very long time since he had't felt angry. But now he did not. Only scared and confused and unbearably sad. He thought, *You're the same. Same as the things in the Sudden Room. Something with a barely functional understanding of human behavior, something doing a bad impression. And you exist. The universe is huge and cruel.*

The doorbell man smoothed his suit and stepped down from the table. He took a seat, crossed his legs, adjusted his fedora. "What do you suppose would happen then?"

This was what they wanted. What they always wanted. Just this slow thick leak, these fat droplets spattering against the floor and sinking into the woodgrain, staining the teeth of her house key. She squeezed the meat of her thumb with her opposite hand, milking the blood from the wound and speeding the drip. The monsters (*No,* she thought, *not quite monsters, are they? Or not just any kind of monster. I know what they are. I know their name. They have been understood and catalogued and thrown behind a partition marked with their species and phylum*) shuddered and salivated and gnashed their rotten broken saber-teeth to match the new tempo.

"I know what you want," she said. "I know what you are."

One of them hissed, "Paaaaaglia. Ssssteinemmmmm."

Another growled, "Behhhhind the hhhhhedges."

Another, its face fused into profile, its mouth almost filled with the metastasized flesh of its fellows, said, "Ennnnjoying the view?"

"I could give you what you want," she said, and wondered what would happen if she did. Wondered if it could somehow erase the bad decisions and the worse luck, the tense and unpleasant marriage, the dead baby that never lived the ghost of which floated between her and Jim. She wondered if she'd finally feel like she'd done something worthwhile. Each of the faces in the wall salivated in expectation, wet from lips to chin with thick foamy spit. Could she refuse them? Could she disappoint them like that?

She would tell one more secret. And then she would see.

"When we were in college," she said, squeezing the gash, "Jim asked me what I wanted to do. With my life, I mean. We were spent, exhausted. We had just finished, you know... fucking, I guess. Making love. I don't know. We were satisfied with ourselves. We felt philosophical. So he asked me... 'in the cosmic sense,' he said, whatever that means, what I wanted to do. And I took a deep breath, and I imagined that I was inhaling the whole universe, the stars and the planets and the dark matter, and I told him what I wanted to do. I wanted to make an impact. I wanted the world to bend a little under my weight. To never be the same after me."

She lifted her thumb upward, offering it to the chomping mouths in the wall of the Sudden Room. They strained and gurgled and roared, and the house shook.

Jim could hear them gurgling and roaring upstairs, louder than they'd ever been. And here he was, downstairs, listening to the doorbell man, whatever he was, stumble through his best estimation of what human conversation might sound like. He wasn't sure how much more of this his brain could take.

"Now imagine," whispered the doorbell man, "that some homeowner just... stumbled onto the secret corridor where that Rattenkönig had become stuck. It would have to have been a sleepwalking homeowner, a homeowner catatonic with despair and disappointment. Sound familiar, homeowner? Sound like anyone you know?"

"Okay, enough!" He was standing. "Enough, man, alright? Now what?" He was leaning over the doorbell man, shaking his fists, gesturing, shouting. "Why are you here? Are you here to help? Can you help us? Can you, what, kill those fucking things?" He grabbed the doorbell man by the lapels, shook him. "Can you do fucking anything? Huh?" He crumpled, came down onto his knees before the doorbell man, buried his head in the doorbell man's chest, wept.

The doorbell man caressed the hair at the nape of Jim's neck and shushed him, rocked him back and forth. "No," he said. "No, I'm not here to kill them. I just wanted to... see. I wanted to see, homeowner. I've never seen a Rattenkönig before."

Upstairs, someone screamed.

Abigail Quatro screamed. She tried to pull herself away, but she was trapped, held by dozens of scrambling arms and legs against the pulsing wall of skin. She felt their razor fangs at her wrists, her thighs, her shoulders, felt their dry, sore-covered lips wrap around the wounds and suck, drinking desperately from her, and it hurt, it hurt, God, it hurt. She struggled, kicked, squirmed, but even piled into a single gigantic body, they were stronger than anything she'd ever known. They weren't letting her go. Her vision was getting hazy, and the part of her with the will to fight back was shrinking, fading. It wasn't fair. None of this was fair.

She heard the door to the Sudden Room slam against the wall, felt the hall light burst through onto her skin, saw two silhouettes through the haze. One of them was shouting her name, rushing toward her. Jim. It was Jim. It had to be Jim. She was so very tired.

And this wasn't fair.

The other silhouette clapped his hands, bounced on the balls of his feet. It said, "Marvelous. Absolutely marvelous."

Jim was at her side now, pulling on her, trying to remove her from the wall of mean mouths and blind eyes. He was screaming. He was struggling.

When they finally let her go, she knew that Jim hadn't saved her. Her monsters just... weren't hungry anymore.

Her vision was coming back to her now. The pain was receding. She felt numb and betrayed. She kept trying to speak, but her throat wouldn't let the words pass.

"God, Abby. Oh Jesus, Abby, it's okay," Jim, above her, faking his way through normal again, "it's okay, baby, I'm here. I'm here. Goddamn it, goddamn it. Okay, it's okay. I'm going to call the hospital, baby, okay? Everything is going to be..."

She hated to be called Abby. Always had.

The other man... the bald man with the sunglasses and the fedora and the umbrella hanging from his arm... put his hand on the back of Jim's head. She watched all of this from the floor. She didn't like the floor. It was so dirty. So uncomfortable. The bald man said, "Well, that was fun, homeowner. Bye, now."

Jim's head jerked up to stare at the bald man, watched him strolling through the door, down the hallway. Out. She stared at the slope where his jaw became his throat. She watched his pulse announce itself in the throbbing vein there. It seemed to be beating so much faster than hers.

"What?" he screamed. "What?" Loud, raw, unhinged. "What?" A real question. A question to which he desperately expected an answer.

For many moments, they listened to the bald man's footsteps. They listened to the door slamming on his way out. And then all there was to listen to was the gurgle and slurp of the wall of monsters.

When her voice returned, Abigail Quatro said, "Nothing changes. Nothing is different. Everything is always the same."

Old Roses

My father built our basement like a theatrical set. He made partitions and propped them up against the cold stone walls, the real walls, the rough walls that smelled like mold and wet age. He painted the partitions (the paint he used was called "Old Roses"). He added Styrofoam crown molding where the partitions met the ceiling, which he covered in mirrored black glass, and he bought a series of musty faux-Persian rugs to toss over the cracked concrete floors. He built shelves into the fake walls, and a dresser, and place for a television, and he brought in a bed and a recliner. He built a bathroom down there and stocked it with a series of aftershaves and toothpastes. The shower was too small. With bent knees and craned spine, you'd try to position yourself beneath the showerhead, washing the foam from your hair in thirty-second shifts because if you stood like that too long, you'd cramp up and spend the rest of the day with your neck jerked to the side. Or maybe you wouldn't. But I did.

There was a wall in the fake basement that opened on secret hinges, and behind it, down a lightless hallway untouched by my father's obsessive façade-building, was his office. His secret office, where things were what they were, and not what they pretended to be. This is where he kept his tchotchkes, the apparently endless collection of shit he had picked up over the years, much of it useless, or broken, or so stripped of whatever had once made it beautiful to look at that it seemed to function only as a reminder that all things, in their essential unadorned form, are basically ugly. The skulls inherited from his oral hygienist father, their teeth capped or replaced with gaudy silver or overlaid with sparkling braces. The grinning cigar-store Indian with the word NIGGER scratched into its forehead a dozen decades past. The whistle from Moscow, shaped like a horse and colored like a children's story book, glued back together after I dropped it on the floor (I inherited this at some point, as I did with so many of my father's tchotchkes, but I have no idea where it has gone now; it creeps up on me, when I am vulnerable to regret and longing, when I am alone, and its ghost whistles in my ear and asks me why I didn't love it enough to keep track of where it went). He would sit at his desk (itself a glass-fronted relic rescued from the alley behind a head shop, a former display counter, its case filled with a cavalcade of other tinier orphans) and smoke his cigars and drink non-alcoholic beer and play with his prizes.

My father was an intellectual.

He bought me a cell phone when I was sixteen so that he could call me from the basement and say, "Hey Lieutenant." (This is how he began every conversation I ever had with him; it's how he began his toasts at the wedding ceremonies marking both of my failed marriages, and it is how he told me my mother had died when he called from his new place in California, to my new place in Boston). "Hey Lieutenant. I just finished another chapter. Care to give it a listen?"

So I would. I would pass by the stairs to the attic (this is where my mother stayed in those days, with her Kurzweil keyboard and her fantasy novels about opera singers) and I would hear Mom shout down, "Dean, whatcha doing?"

And I would ignore her and go downstairs, past the set and backstage, to visit my father's greenroom, where he would read to me, in the sonorous baritone he reserved for pronouncements of the gravest profundity, selections from the autobiography of the life he wished he had led. Here's the first chapter:

The War I Fought

I was drafted into a secret war when I was six years old. I was given a machete, and I went out at dusk to find the threat and destroy it. The threat, in this case, lifted itself up out of the drainage culvert that ran behind my house in Tarzana, California, an army of human hands with foot-long fingers and twenty-eight knuckles and mouths superimposed over their wrist-stumps. The hands would collect on the concrete banks of the culvert in the summers of my childhood, each night when the sun started to go down, and they would click their fingernails against the concrete. The men who drafted me into this war told me that, if the hands were ever to make it past the culvert and into the world, their mouths would open and they would sing a song of such profound joy that humanity would be plunged into universal, suicidal depression through the inevitable comparison of the sum of their own life's joy to that de-

*picted in the song. This was not allowed to happen, obviously, so...
I was in charge of stopping it. I would hack the hands to bits with
my machete and throw them back into the shallow water. One day,
the men who drafted me came to my school and called me to the
principal's office, where they told me that the job was done, and the
world was safe.*

The house of my teenagehood always seemed to breathe. It was a labored breath, rattling and uneven, but I could feel it, sitting in my bedroom across the hall from my older sister's room, or sitting on the couch watching television, or sitting on the toilet, or sitting anywhere. The whole place seemed to take in air and spend it, the walls seemed to move so slowly that you couldn't be sure they were moving at all, and the whole operation seemed to take so much effort and energy that, falling asleep at night, staring at the television in my room, I was routinely afraid that the works would collapse around me.

I tried speaking to my sister about it on those few occasions when I was allowed into her room. My sister's room changed every time I went in. She was fickle with her fandom, her interests shifting from moment to moment. I remember when she painted the walls black and put candles on all the flat surfaces, and teased her hair and wore bold make-up that made her look like something excised from a silent movie and dropped into the real world. She was lying on her bed when I came in, staring at the ceiling fan with her headphones on. I opened the door, and then I knocked on it, which I immediately recognized as the wrong order of doing things, and I almost closed the door and ran back to my room out of shame and fear. She didn't seem to notice. I said, "Hey Marcy?"

She glanced at me, sighed deeply, and shifted her attention back to the ceiling fan.

"Can I come in?" I said.

"I don't care what you do, Dean."

So I came. I sat on her black bedspread and stared at her black walls and tried to think of something to say. I said, "Hey, can I ask you something?" Even then, I didn't know what I wanted to ask.

Plow the Bones

She sat up without using her arms to support her and fiddled with her portable CD player. Then she sighed dramatically (again) and pulled the headphones down around her neck. She said, "Fine. Free country."

"Is Norton... you know, is he Mom's, like... boyfriend, or something?"

Norton. That name, which more than any other I associate with a particular person, a specific face. That name, which to me feels like something slick and sticky and rotten on my tongue and in whatever portion of my brain it occupies. Norton. Who, when I learned the word "obsequious" several years later, sprang to mind as its paragon (and who, despite his omnipresence in those days, was not around when my mom lost her footing and became my dead mom). Norton. My mother's boyfriend. Or something.

Marcy said, "Mom says he's her student. He's taking piano lessons."

"I know what Mom says. What's true, though?"

"Dean, what do you think?"

"I think they're fucking each other," I said, and I started to cry. I'm not sure why anymore. Maybe I was sure then. Maybe there was some vital imperative that compelled me to cry, and maybe it made sense at the time. But I can't remember it now.

Marcy put her headphones back on and said, "Yeah, well..." and fell backward onto the bed. The next time I saw her room, it was painted burnt-orange and she had joined the volleyball team at school. There was more than a little of my father in her, the set-builder, the changer of backdrops.

Here is what my father's autobiography says about when he was sixteen:

The Great Spanish Orgy
I went to Spain when I was sixteen to escape my father, who had no idea that I had spent the majority of my childhood among magic and war but seemed to sense that there was something strange about me in any case and desired nothing less than my humiliation and the destruction of my spirit. He was a dentist. I was a poet. I have

always been a poet. My son is also a poet, because I have made him into one. My daughter is a poet of a different sort. My wife is fucking a poem written for her by our house, so at least there is some tenuous theme to attach our family to one another. I had saved some money from the summer previous, when I sold psychic tongues on the black-market, and I used it to buy a plane ticket and a counterfeit passport. These were the days in which you could still smoke cigarettes on airplanes, and I did. Then I got to Barcelona, and I watched the bullfights, which the locals call La Corrida. They shouted "Viva La Muerta!" from the bleachers. In the streets that night, a group of men with long wooden poles maneuvered a gigantic wooden marionette through the avenues and boulevards, and I met a girl named Giselle from France, and she took me to an orgy. She had an extra arm that grew from her side, which she kept wrapped around her belly beneath her shirt. She couldn't allow it near pen or paper for fear that it would tell her secrets. She claimed to have many secrets, but she would not share them with me. That night, lying on a mattress made of other people sprawled across the floor, with the light from the windows turning everyone bluer than Krishna, and with the shadow of the leering marionette peeking through at us from outside, I gave her extra arm a pen and I let it write some secrets on my back. When I returned home, I had a tattoo artist attach these secrets to me permanently. I have never asked anyone to read them for me, and so I still do not know what they are.

My only real friend in those days was Fir, the Iranian girl with the nose ring. Fir had enormous eyes. She was quiet, and she smiled a lot, and she was thrifty with her attention, and so when she said something nice, she meant it with such sincerity that it wrecked you inside, made you feel somehow simultaneously that you really met her criteria for goodness and worth, and also that you couldn't possibly deserve it. Around her, you were reminded of all the awful things about yourself that she didn't know. Or maybe you wouldn't have been. But I was.

Behind my father's childhood home (or whatever he imagined to

Plow the Bones

be his childhood home in the wild nonsense of his autobiography) may have been the legendary culvert, but all that was behind mine was an empty lot, overgrown with weeds and freckled with trash and rimmed at the far end by a row of unhealthy looking trees, and beyond that, the freeway. This is where Fir and I spent our afternoons, once we had escaped from high school and the various tortures therein. There was an old wooden observation tower at the edge of the lot, although what you were supposed to observe from on top, neither of us could ever figure out. Its planks were old and dark and soft, and the stairs to the top deck were rotten, and some of them were missing. We spent our afternoons erecting fresh planks stolen from behind the hardware store. We added a room to the bottom by walling off the empty space beneath the top deck, and we decorated the walls with posters of my favorite movies and her favorite bands. We repaired the stairs. We mounted a flag to the guard rail on the top deck, a piece of red fabric that had once been a Halloween Dracula cape, and we wrote in sharpie on the face of it: THIS TOWN BELONGS TO US. Which, thinking back, we had backward.

Fir and I, with the sun beating down on us, sitting together on the observation deck and staring out beyond the sick-looking tree line at the freeway, her smoking Iranian cigarettes pilfered from her father's cabinet (she was smoking those same cigarettes at my first wedding, and at my second, and she smoked them in the parking lot of the church where my mother's funeral was held, and I have never learned how she came by them, this endless supply of Iranian smokes; I think, when she finally did return to Iran two weeks ago, she must have been motivated only secondarily by her compulsion toward activism, and primarily by the need to buy more slim, fragrant Iranian cigarettes), and me wracking my brain for something impressive to say. She would talk about how her father was an intellectual, an atheist in exile with slender hands and a well-trimmed beard and half-moon glasses, and how he was always sad, and I would think that we were almost siblings, our fathers like twins from different nations.

Fir said, "After college, I'm going back to Iran. I'm going to be a women's activist. Tear down the fucking paradigm. That's what my dad is always saying. You've got to tear down the paradigm."

One afternoon, we sat in the bottom room, sweating because we hadn't added any windows. What happened was sort of an accident. It just happened. With her huge, happy eyes on me, with her subtle smile, with her arms around my neck, she said, "I don't ever want to talk about this again, okay? After this? I don't ever want sex to mean something. Ever. Please? Can we?" I told her we could, because I would have said yes to everything she asked of me, and she laughed a little, and she asked me to tell her what hurt me. And I did. And we laughed, and I cried a little too, and she held onto the back of my head and moved with me. We were very quiet. It was, to date, the only time in my life that I have felt that sex meant anything larger than itself. Afterward, I was very angry, and very alone, and I felt like I had become my mother.

When it was over, we got dressed, and she said, "Wanna go up and smoke?"

So we did.

And sitting in the sparse shade of the trees, among the yellowed weeds and dead grass down below us, I saw Norton. Norton, reading the newspaper. Norton, thirty years old and always dressed in a black suit, even sitting in the grass, even in the summer, with his horseshoe-shaped mustache, licking his lips after every sentence, like his tongue couldn't stand to stay in his mouth for too long. Norton, so close to our tower, invading the space into which I imagined he was not allowed. He looked up at me and said, "Hey, tiger." This is what he called me.

Tiger.

I said, "What do you want?"

Fir glared at him. She tapped ash off her cigarette. Something in the way she did this made me love her, because it felt (perhaps only to me) like she was willing the ash to float down toward him, to stain the black pinstripes of his pleated pants. Fir hated Norton, because I hated Norton, and she needed no other justification. She whispered, "Jende," which is Farsi, and not complimentary.

Norton stood up, brushed grass and dirt from his ass, and was suddenly as immaculate as if he had never sat down in our filthy lot at all. He shrugged and sheltered his eyes from the sun with one big, hairy hand. He said, "Your mom's looking for you. Better not let her see you with that cigarette."

I wanted to say something impudent, but I wasn't brave enough.

Here is what my father wrote about being in love with my mom in his autobiography:

The Magician's Duel on my Wedding Day

I was in love with my wife's ability to love me. We met after university, united by a theatrical director I knew in Los Angeles who produced a play I wrote. The play is lost. I can't recall the name of it. This director friend of mine was producing my play, and the woman who would become my wife was hired as an accompanist, which is to say that she sat at her piano and played happy songs during the happy scenes, and sad songs during the sad scenes. I do not remember thinking that she was pretty, although she is. I only remember thinking that she was lovable. That I could love her, and that she was perhaps capable of loving me. Which was silly of me, ultimately. My director friend told her that I was brilliant, and that I was going places, and that I was destined to be a famous playwright and poet, and she believed him. And that's why we were married. On the day of our wedding, a Magician who had heard my reputation appeared in my dressing room and challenged me to a duel. The dressing room transformed, mutating into a stage, the walls falling away to make room for a bottomless orchestra pit from which the song of the twenty-eight-knuckled hands was playing so softly that I could barely hear it, and a long panorama of banked arena seating beyond the proscenium, and an audience of faceless men who applauded politely for every trick we performed. He poured a thousand rabbits from his top hat. I removed the top of my cranium and poured rabbits from my skull. He turned to smoke. I turned to glass and shattered. He sawed his assistant in half and danced with her living torso while her legs kicked in time on the table, then reassembled her and took his bow. I reduced myself to my component parts, each atom sawed from its partners and floating as a mist before him in the haze of the stage lights, and I reassembled myself as two smaller men and danced with my reflection before becoming myself again and taking my bow. I was the clear winner. In a rage, the young Magician commanded the hands in the orchestra pit to sing louder, and they did. It was a petty act of revenge, and it destroyed both of us. I returned to my wedding forty-five minutes late, ragged and unkempt, and as I marched down the aisle I saw my wife's eyes fill with a resigned disappointment and a bewildering absence of anger and a realization that this would be her life with me, forever and ever, an accessory secondary to the awful adventure that haunts me everywhere I go.

I remember my mother's room (formerly my parents' room, before the great theatricizing of the basement) in the attic, and how it was always oppressively hot and stuffy, and how she left the lights off and played Solitaire on her computer. I remember her keyboard in the corner, and the stacks of yellowed sheet music on the carpet beside it. I remember the red leather suitcase full of old photographs she kept in her closet. My mother, who is dead. Who had the same look in her eyes that my father described in his autobiography when I said to her, "I'm moving out, Mom. I'm taking my college money and I'm moving to California."

My mom, with her beautiful curly blonde hair, whose secret was out, who shot silent apologies to me with every stare, who always seemed afraid that the floor would open up and swallow her.

I sat on the piano bench and she sat at her computer and we didn't say anything for a long time after that. The slope of the roof granted strange corners to the attic, odd alcoves where shadows gathered too thickly. You couldn't sit up there and look at someone without your eyes wandering to those too-dark shadows, distracted by the strangeness and the movement of the little voids scattered across the room like rain puddles. Or maybe you could have. But I couldn't.

"Oh, baby," she said, which is what she always called me when I was making her sad, or reminding her of how sad she already was (so many people gave me so many names; they have attached themselves to me like ticks as I passed, and I have never been able to burn off a single one of them). "Oh, my baby. My baby boy. You can't. You can't go."

Plow the Bones

"I can," I said. "I have to." I was eighteen then, and everything in my life had gone wrong. Fir was leaving, ripping a hole in the suburban Midwest and disappearing through it, going to some university in Vancouver, pre-med major, women's studies minor. She never ended up going, opting instead for the same local community college I eventually attended, but back then we both felt she was already practically gone. My mother had convinced my father to take his own extramarital partner (I have to struggle for her name now, the poor psychotic, suicidal girl... Leanna... Leanna of the scarred arms and the pixie haircut and the darting, trustless eyes), and she skulked around the basement looking bored and manic while he ignored her in his relic-filled office. My sister had married (for the first time but not the last, as it turned out; we mirrored each other romantically, my sister and I, with our double-marriages and our double-divorces; she's on her third now, having transformed herself again, this time into a woman of faith and modesty and silence) and disappeared, leaving me in the house with my parents and their lovers and their hauntedness. The house. Oh, the house. The house, which no longer felt to me like a collapsing lung, but like a tendon stretched on the rack and about to snap.

I could. I had to.

My mother shook her head and didn't let go of the tears that I could hear in her throat. She said, "No, baby. No, you can't."

Norton stepped out of the shadows behind her, like a stagehand sneaking out from behind the curtain. He did this often, stepping out of corners like the house had just vomited him up out of its walls. He put a proprietary hand on my mom's shoulder and used the other hand to straighten his paisley bowtie. He looked at me, and my mother looked away. Looking at his eyes was like looking at the painted sockets of a department store mannequin given animation, unaware and unconcerned with its actions or the consequences thereof. Poor, oblivious, passively evil Norton. Norton, the dream who stuck around after my mother's eyes fluttered open one morning, who only knew how to look human, not how to be one. He smoothed down his horseshoe mustache and said, "Let me explain, Dean."

My mother whispered, "No. It should be me." But Norton's eyes never left mine, and he did not pause to let her speak.

"There is no college money," he said. "We needed it. Our family is... struggling, Dean, and sometimes when your family is struggling, you need to make sacrifices. All of us have made sacrifices. Your mother, your father, myself. We all give things up to keep our world turning. You understand, don't you, tiger?"

"I have some money," I said, stinging, numb. "I have some in my account. Enough to get there, at least."

My mom shook her head and chewed on her knuckles.

Norton licked his lips and said, "You mean the joint account your mother opened for you?" He did a broad pantomime of regret, shrugging, rubbing his fingers together and then blowing on the tips. Gone.

I should have said something.

I ran down the stairs to the kitchen, and then through it to the basement, past Leanna, who sat on the bed in my father's false apartment, running her fingernails over her naked knees and waiting for him to pay attention to her. She called, "Deany, can you tell your dad to come out? I just, I need, I mean, I need, I need, I guess I need to talk to him, and I need it really bad, so Deany, tell him to come? Deany? Deany, tell him, okay? Deany?" On and on like that, as I swung the secret wall aside and made my way down the dark corridor to my father's office. Pleading for someone to look at her. For someone to save her.

My father tells me Leanna killed herself last year. Nearly fifteen years after my father said goodbye and sent her out into the world, she wrote his name on her bathroom mirror and taped a picture of him beneath it, and she swallowed a great deal of medication and went to sleep in her bathtub with a bag over her head. She could do that, because she was real. She was damaged and sad and toxic, but she wasn't fiction. She had that going for her.

My father was playing with a doll when I stormed in and slammed the door. He glanced at me over the rims of his half-moon glasses. He said, "Hey, Lieutenant."

"Goddamn it," I said. I remember that I said it because I had heard him say it, and because when he said it, it sounded masculine and final. From his mouth, my intellectual father, it was both a sentence and its own punctuation. It was a magic word. From mine, it was lifeless and phony, and even more so when I tried again. "Goddamn it," I said. "Goddamn it."

He held up the doll for me to see it. It was a clown with a brown pork-pie hat, with white lips curled into an abysmal, accepting frown, with a painted-on five-o-clock-shadow, with a torn brown suit and a crumpled polka-dot tie and gigantic plastic shoes.

My father said, "Good old Emmett."

I began to shout about mom and Norton and the crushing weight of this place, and how I had to leave, how if I didn't I was sure this house would kill me, and my dad put a finger to his lips. He said, "Come on, Lieutenant, let's not waste our precious time on that shit." He glanced at the clown-doll, held its neck between his thumb and forefinger and wiggled its head at me. He said, "I found him. My god, I finally found him. My Emmett Kelly doll. Emmett used to sit on my dresser when I was a kid. He used to mortify me. Absolutely scared me shitless." He looked at the doll with naked amazement, an open-mouthed awe. It made me hopeful and filled me with impotent anger. I stood before him with my arms out at my sides, fingers splayed. I wished I felt like he looked. He said, "Good old Emmett. Now he's come back home."

"Dad," I said, "everything is so fucked up."

"Come on," he said, "Let me read you my new chapter."

Here is what he read to me:

The Last Time I Saw Emmett Kelly

On the night my son was born, I stood outside of the hospital at the roundabout in front of the emergency room and watched the ambulances pull up to the door and wheel out the injured and the dying. Mostly, all I did was smoke cigarettes. I knew that the awful adventure of my life had caught up to me again, because so many of the injured were freaks. An incredibly gorgeous woman in a satin negligee with a beard down to her navel was wheeled in with third-degree burns crawling up her legs. A midget with the extra, vestigial mouth of an absorbed twin on his left cheek hobbled through the doors cradling the severed stumps of several fingers in a blood-soaked wad of toilet paper. The tattooed man was DOA. During all of this, I was visited by Emmett Kelly. The real Emmett Kelly, not the doll that haunted my bedroom in Tarzana as a child. He was in full "Weary Willie" regalia, and at least three feet taller than me, and nobody else could see him. I asked him how my children could escape this, how I could avoid infecting them with it, and he shook his head and said, "They can't. You can't." We sang the song of the twenty-eight-knuckled hands together for a while, quietly so that nobody else would have to hear, and then I went inside and met my beautiful son, bloody and terrified from his arrival, for the first time.

I have moved back into the old house. My mother is dead (in the basement shower, although God knows what she was doing down there; she slipped, and she bashed her head on the edge of the tub, and therefore became my dead mom; no dramatic death hers, no scene from my father's autobiography; stupid, empty, over in a moment). The house is paid for, and I can't afford the rent in Boston anymore because my father made me a poet and, unless you're selling psychic tongues or fighting secret wars, it doesn't pay well.

Fir helped me move in two weeks ago. Then she left for Iran. She's still beautiful, and she still smokes those Iranian cigarettes, although her nose ring is gone. She showed me the ghost of our tower, which is buried underneath a housing development called "Caribou Run." I tried to kiss her before she left, and she pushed me away gently and said, "What are you doing?" and I retreated from her, into my father's fake basement apartment. I have not left that place much since then.

I have found my father's autobiography. And I have found good old Emmett. I don't think my father knows I have either of them. Today, I sat in the basement and read the entire manuscript, and then I tied it back together with the red ribbon in which I found it. And I set Emmett Kelly on the dresser across from my bed. And now all that's left here is me. And I don't know any magic and all the

Plow the Bones

secrets I ever had that mattered have been spilled or spoiled. This house is dreadfully unhaunted.

I went into my mother's attic, and I left the lights off, and I shouted for Norton until my voice was gone. He never came out of the shadows, and I wonder if he's still here at all or if the house has forgotten the poem it composed for my mother. I imagine him watching her die, down there in the basement, stroking his horseshoe mustache and licking his lips and waiting for the last of her brain activity to sputter out so he could fade back into the woodwork and become part of the house again.

What I've just done is this: I pulled out the red leather suitcase, and I stared at our photographs. There is one of my father in his bathing suit on their honeymoon, staring back at the camera through his sunglasses and smiling over his shoulder. He's got a tattoo across his shoulder blades, a scrawl of cursive letters spelling out French words. It shouts at me, my father's tattoo, from across decades, from a world before I, begging me to know it, to understand it, to translate it and inherit it. But I don't know any French, and the handwriting is small and spidery, so all I can do is stare at my dad, smiling at my dead mother's camera. At me. And breathe in whatever ghosts might be left over.

Stickhead
(or… In the Dark, in the Wet, We Are Collected)

...see this thing... Danny wants to call it a man, but that's not really what it is anymore. He pokes it with the narrow end of the broken branch and when the gnarled stick breaks through his—its—purple skin, he has a real motherfucker of a time breathing.

"Jesus."

He swallows, rubs at the barely-there baby-stubble on his jaw, forces himself to blink. He pushes a little harder on his end of the stick. Watches it bend, hears it creak like maybe it's about to snap in two, and then watches the small patch of ruined skull crumble.

"Oh. Oh shit."

The wind blows. The scrawny grey trees on either side of the culvert dance. Their shadows are so dark down here that they erase whatever is beneath them. Down here, shadows turn into black holes.

Adam isn't far away. He's standing there on the sloping concrete embankment rubbing his forearm. He's got the joint pinched tight between his thumb and forefinger. His eyes dance in double-time, spotlighting each shadowy corner of the drainage ditch. He says, "Danny, we should go," and his voice is high and fragile. He says, "We should call the cops."

Danny leans a little closer. Works the stick deeper. He can feel his pulse in his ears. He pulls it out. Studies it. He smiles, and he thinks he shouldn't be smiling, and that makes him smile wider.

"Oh, dude," he says. "I think this is his brain."

Adam looks up and Danny watches those dancing eyes of his lock on the dark scrap dangling from the stick's end. He turns, bends at the waist, says, "I'm not going to throw up," and then throws up anyway.

Danny hears himself mumble, "You all right?" but he doesn't mean it. This is exactly what Danny has been waiting for. This is the gaping window into... what? Into the big UnWorld, the slippery space beneath. This right here, a bloated naked body, some guy drowned in the sewers and washed into a ditch. This is what Danny's whole life has pointed toward.

Somewhere up above them, a car crosses over the asphalt above the drainage pipe. The pipe eats the sound of it and belches it back out into the culvert, louder now and with teeth it didn't have before. Danny feels his scalp tingle. He can't smile wide enough.

"I want to go home," says Adam. "Somebody ought to call the cops."

That dark little mess on the end of the stick. Man. Just—wow.

You remember that feeling? I do. I think we all do.

Adam says, "Danny?"

And then he says, "Jesus, Danny, please?"

So Danny rolls his eyes. He jabs the stick back into the dead man's head. It sticks there like a lightning rod. He says, "Fine." And they climb back up the slope.

His car is waiting, the '86 Volvo with a backseat caked in fast food wrappers and Mountain Dew bottles, that old rubber skeleton left over from Halloween and hanging from the rearview. Somehow the skeleton embarrasses him now. Danny feels like he's wasting his time on it. It's like, you think you know what macabre means. You think EC Comics reprints and Texas Chainsaw action figures are pointing you in the right direction. Then you see the real thing and everything else seems stupid by comparison.

He leans over the steel barrier where the cul-de-sac ends and the ditch begins, glancing one last time at the rotten purple thing down there. The man. And the stick in his head.

Adam leans on the car, stares at the hood.

Danny says, "You okay?"

"Yeah. Sorry."

"Okay," Danny says, and swings himself into the driver's seat. "You want to go get a milkshake?"

...see the parking lot... it's empty except for these two. They sit on the hood of Danny's car and Danny listens to the sprinklers hiss in front of the drive-through menu, quick and syncopated, matching his heartbeat pulse for pulse. He shoves French fries into his mouth. He doesn't taste them. He says, "You saw his... you know, his dick, right?"

Adam stares at his milkshake.

"Like a big rotten bratwurst. Jesus."

Adam says, "Don't really want to talk about it, okay?"

So they don't for a while. Danny eats his fries and drinks his milkshake. Adam stares at his straw with his mouth open.

Then Danny says, "How do you think he got like that?"

Adam shakes his head and mutters, "I dunno, Danny. Chrissakes, the guy is dead."

"What's your point?"

"So," Adam says, then pauses, sets his milkshake aside, wraps his hands around the back of his hanging head. "So he's got like a family somewhere, right? People worried about him?"

Danny smiles and says, "Probably homeless." Already he is constructing a back-story, writing a biography for the thing in the culvert.

Adam drops his hands in his lap and stares at Danny. For a second he doesn't say anything. Then, "Fucking… Jesus, Danny. Why would you think… He didn't look homeless to me."

"He didn't look like anything, dude." When the thought hits him, he giggles. "Other than a bratwurst."

"I can't believe you're joking about it."

"Well, what the fuck do you want me to do, Adam?"

"Call the cops maybe?"

There is almost a noise, a sibilant snap, when Danny's patience breaks. See, Adam's been saying that kind of shit all evening and Danny has been ignoring him, knowing that Adam would back down, like Adam always backs down. Except now there's no getting away from it. The pot is wearing off and he thinks about grabbing the last little knot of dark curly weed from the glove box and sharing it with Adam, getting him stoned again, getting him to shut the hell up for a while. But his mouth is dry and he's angry now. He's angry that Adam would want to ruin this for him, suck this town back into normal before it even gets a chance to see what's beyond that.

He says, "No, Adam."

"What?"

"No cops."

"Dude, you can't be serious. That's a dead guy down there." Those tiny eyes again, never meeting Danny's, never meeting anything for too long, and now they're shining and Danny swears inside

Plow the Bones

his head and prays that Adam doesn't cry.

So he says, "Do you remember how things were before? Spending lunch in the library so nobody calls you a fag? Dude, you had a bag of dice tied to your belt when I met you, you remember that? You want to go back to that? Because I swear to God, Adam, if you mention the cops one more time I'll never fucking talk to you again, okay? You'll go back to being a library fag and getting your ass kicked at gym and nobody will be around to stick up for you."

He knows it's stupid. He knows how it sounds. Like an ultimatum, like he's the abuser and Adam is the abused. Like they're breaking up. And he doesn't care.

Adam says, "Okay." And he doesn't cry.

They drink their shakes. They listen to the sprinklers.

Danny says, "What time you supposed to be home?"

"Twelve."

"Shit, it's almost one. Your mom going to be mad?"

"No, it's okay. She's in bed. I'll let myself in."

"Your eyes are red. I've got Visine in the glove compartment if you think you'll need it. Just in case?"

"No. She's in bed. It's fine."

So they get back in the car. And Danny drives. And he feels like the biggest douche bag in the universe. But it doesn't matter. Because he keeps thinking of the thing they found in the creek, purple and naked and all for him. And that makes him feel better.

He pulls his car up next to Adam's house and they shake hands and Adam gets out. Danny says, "Am I picking you up for school tomorrow?"

"Sure," says Adam, staring at his shoes, the grass, his shoes, the grass. He says, "See you tomorrow," before he turns and starts walking toward his front door.

Danny sighs, closes his eyes tight, opens them and says, "Hey."

Adam turns. His blond hair looks blue in the moonlight, like its sucking up the dim and gorgeous glow of that great and magical after-curfew hour. And Danny forgives him.

"Sorry about... making you stay at the creek. And yelling at you."

Adam shrugs. "Don't worry about it. I won't call the cops." Like that's still what they're talking about.

"Yeah. See you."

Danny rolls up his window and drives toward home. And he smiles at that warm wonderful feeling of having your very own special secret.

He parks his car. He goes inside. The lights are out. The house is silent. His mother and father are dead to the world, sleeping in separate beds in separate rooms. This is the way it's been for a while. Since Danny can remember.

He lets his knees dissolve, lets himself fall onto the sofa. Turns on the television. He can't focus on it. The great big window to the UnWorld is shining in his mind, shining with the light of a secret sun.

We remember the window, you and I. All of us remember the window.

He stares at the painting above the television, a Thomas Kinkade print his mom bought at the Dollar Store, all roses and ranch homes and cloudless sky. His mom loves Kinkade. She likes to stare at that painting and say, "Someday, Danny, that's where we're going to live, okay?"

That painting makes Danny anxious as hell.

So he gets up. He turns off the TV. He steps toward the front door and crosses his arms over his chest and looks out. He stares at his car for a long time. And then he opens the door and goes chasing the light from the window in his head.

...see the ditch... see it and see it well. To Danny, it's Exhibit A. The first artifact of the UnWorld beneath this place. The ditch runs all over town, through people's front yards, through their back yards, and they call it a creek and line it with pretty stones and put statues by it and build bridges over it. And then it dips below, runs underneath the roads and spits filthy water through concrete tunnels where kids go to fuck and spray-paint swastikas and smoke pot and drink stolen cans of Natural Light, and they call it a drainage ditch or a culvert. You can trace the savage trail of reality through the names people give things. The things with pretty names are the things you ignore. The things a little deeper, down in the bloody red musculature of the world, the things with dirty names—those are the ones you want to keep an eye out for.

And is that what UnWorld means? No, Danny knows better. It's a hint, that deep dirty secret part of the ditch, a flashing neon arrow that says THIS WAY TO THE WINDOW.

And that's the way Danny goes.

The filthy water stands half an inch above the soles of his Converse sneakers, soaks through the canvas and makes his socks heavy and sticky and cold. And he keeps going. Down here in the sly slick night, this place is a shadowbox, lined with arching concrete walls and ribbed steel floors, barely lit at all by the streetlights sneaking through at either end of the curved tunnel. Black-hole shadows grow like weeds, move like worms. And he keeps going. He's scared as hell. And he keeps going.

The guy—the thing—its bloated sagging face stares out of that window in Danny's head. Those eyes, the whites gone, drown out by the slow leakage of its thick dead blood. Danny fixates on them.

And he keeps going.

He doesn't stop until he hears laughter at the end of the tunnel. It sparks between each vertebrae of his spine. Sizzling frozen electricity. He walks deeper, watches the bend in the tunnel straighten out in front of him, and every footfall is like a backfiring car. And when the sparkling moonlight creeps from behind the edge of that curve and floods the corridor with luminescent blue, he sees.

Oh Jesus, the things he sees.

It's all rendered in silhouette by the light beyond the tunnel's mouth. What he thinks he sees cannot be what he actually sees. Because the thing from the ditch—the dead man drowned and made tender and awful—when a person gets like that, they don't do what he's seeing that thing do.

Standing.

Walking.

Danny sees each slow and jerky step splashing in the shallow water, sees it leaning forward like it might fall down, then going rigid and straight backed and wobbling in the other direction before each new step.

That's what Danny sees.

And there's something else that Danny sees. Something else that can't really be there. Something on the dead thing's shoulder, small and skinny and covered in hair. It giggles. It tugs on the stick—Danny's stick—still sailing high and proud and anchored in the dead guy's head. It turns its neck, and now Danny's eyes are locked, just straight nailed to the eyes of that hairy giggling thing. In silhouette, it smiles, and its teeth are like iron fence-posts. It sucks in breath, lifts one hand to its mouth. It says, "He came back! The curious thing!"

We remember the first time we heard him speak, too.

Danny ought to run right now. He ought to. But he doesn't. He won't. He can't. Even as his brain twists and spasms in his head, even as his sanity shuts down, flashes and chirps like a fire alarm. Because the window isn't a window anymore. It's a door. And, oh, what wonders lie on the other side.

The hairy thing jerks the stick with its wormy black fingers and the dead guy takes a few steps forward. A few more steps. And it's not stopping, and it's gaining speed, running in this lazy clumsy stomp that makes its—his—its thin purple skin shake. It's not stopping, still not stopping, just coming forward, ever forward, until Danny can see the toothless gums peeking out from behind its slack lips. Danny stumbles, whimpers, falls into the shallow dirt-water, scrambles backward until he knocks his head against the concrete wall.

And the dead thing stops. And the hairy thing grins.

What it says is, "Quite curious. Don't you think, Stickhead?"

Close up like this, Danny sees and sees well. The long red face, the bristly grey pelt, the awful teeth between the fat black smiling lips. Danny thinks of the poster in his room, *The Garden of Earthly Delights*, thinks about how many nights, bored and stoned, he has stared at it and imagined he was there, strolling through the fields of hungry demon-beasts and broken souls. This bizarre skinny caricature of an ape, it's like one of the demons from that poster. A cartoony Bosch animal-monster made flesh.

There's that patented Danny smile again. The beaming helpless grin. And does he know he's smiling? Oh, yes.

"Would we like to know his name, Stickhead?" the monkey-thing, the Bosch, asks and jerks the stick to make Stickhead nod.

Danny's tongue twists without thinking about it. His teeth chatter. His name falls from his lips and into the air, hangs in every reeking inch of empty space down here.

The Bosch eyes Danny. He tugs on the stick and Stickhead bends a little at the waste. He leans close. "Hypothesis," he says and his breath stinks of dirt and dead fish. "You are curious in two distinct and separate ways, yes? Number one." He holds up one of those long black fingers, each fat segment waggling in the air. "You are curious in the same vein as the aphoristic cat, yes?" He turns, makes a kissy-face at—Jesus, Danny has already adopted the name for the dead thing—Stickhead. "Isn't he, Stickhead? Number two." Another finger. "He is curious in the sense of the noun, 'curiosities.' As in 'cabinet of' or even the noun, 'curio.' As in the term, 'curioser and curioser,' yes?"

Those sharp and yellowed teeth are only inches away from Danny's face. Danny doesn't say anything. Some part of him knows, absolutely knows, that he is about to die.

"We wish to hear your counter-hypothesis, yes?" says the Bosch. These short snorts keep coming from his flat slit nostrils and Danny thinks maybe that the thing is trying not to laugh. "To elaborate, we—being Stickhead and I—have asked you—being Danny-thing—to refute or support our own hypothesis—id est, are you or are you not curious?"

"I—" Just that one word coming out in an endless hiss. He looks at the Bosch, looks at the dead guy—Stickhead—and both of them are looking back at him. The Bosch grins, his eyes wide, expectant, waiting. Finally, Danny says, "I don't know."

The Bosch looks at Stickhead, cups a long fan hand over the dead thing's ear and whispers, "He doesn't know, Stickhead! Did you hear? He doesn't know!"

The Bosch jerks the stick and Stickhead nods. Danny sees something then. This sort of whimpering resignation, this admission of defeat, in those red sightless eyes, flooded to the iris with blood.

The Bosch turns back to Danny. "Stickhead and I agree, Danny-thing, that you are indeed curious. We believe we have collected the necessary evidence to support our claim and are prepared to present you with our findings, yes? Do you wish to change your hypothesis, Danny-thing?"

A jerk of the stick. Stickhead goes to his knees. The Bosch reaches out slowly, runs one fat finger beneath Danny's chin, and Danny can feel the thick black nail, hard like a beetle's shell, scratching against his skin. "Yes," he says, hearing his own voice crack. "I'm curious."

And he is. We all were.

This is better than sex. Better than that awkward prodding in the back of his Volvo with Theresa Sales last November, the uncomfortable fumbling and contorting to find a comfortable position among the fast food wrappers and Halloween decorations back there, the way she stared at him, like she expected him to perform for her. Man, how he had built up that moment, when he wouldn't have to wear that awful V-word like a badge of his lameness pinned to his chest, and man, what a let down it had been.

This, though. This is real. And worth every awful moment. It's the only thing in seventeen years that has seemed worth it.

Stickhead stands up and the Bosch claps its hands. "Good!" it says. "Good, good, good, Danny-thing. Curiosities are a great passion of mine, yes?" It runs a finger down the dead guy's purple cheek. "Stickhead is a favorite of mine, Danny-thing." He sighs and his smile rots into a burlesque frown. "Believe me when I say, Danny-thing, that I am most bereaved that he has become vastly less curious as of late, yes?"

Silence, while the Bosch sighs and Danny once more reminds himself to blink. Then a wet smack as the Bosch claps one hand down on Stickhead's shoulder and his wrought-iron grin reappears. "Not to worry! Stickhead serves his purpose, yes? Curiosities attract curiosities like quicksilver, my dear Danny-thing."

Danny's lungs refuse to function at all, and suddenly he's reliving the first time he ever smoked pot. Over at Anthony Rigby's house, those few seconds just after the first toke, he was sure he was going to choke on the smoke and die. And then, like now, he coughed, sucked in air, coughed again, and he was free and high and just shy of escaping from the world.

"After all, where would Stickhead be without you? Would he be merely Head? How absurd! You and I together, yes? We'll call it a collaboration."

Danny hears himself whisper, "The stick." What beautiful sense all this is making. What perfect logic it has, in its own way. The window is a door and Danny's broken stick, somehow, was the key. Oh, man, how perfect. "I was just fucking around," he says, but his voice sounds strange to him, someone else's voice, maybe the Danny he used to be getting flushed out, one normal logical word at a time. "It was sort of an accident." He smiles.

"Tomorrow night, yes? Come to see me, Danny-thing."

He wants to know more, he wants to pin the nasty Bosch thing against the wall and demand, yes, goddamn it, *demand* that he explain the circuitry of the psychopathic Halloween world that Danny always hoped and now knows exists. But he's tired now. Suddenly so tired. And so heavy. Every part of him weighs a thousand pounds, and he feels like he is sinking into the face of the world as the eyes of the Bosch shine like ice and the shadows creep and the water washes over his fingers, still and stinking. Danny feels the drainage ditch oozing into darkness all around him, and he passes out against the concrete wall, beneath the swastikas and the pot-leaves and the names of unknown kids who never found their way out of this town.

…see Danny behind the dumpsters… he's caked in mud and his hair is filthy and his feet make squelching sounds when he shifts his weight. He looks awful. He knows he does. Sneaking through the school parking lot on his way here, his reflection stared back at him in every car window. He feels like he's shedding his skin.

He crouches back here, watches, waits. The dumpsters are behind the cafeteria and they smell over-sweet and rotten. He knows Adam will come here. Adam always comes here. Last year, Adam started smoking cigarettes because Danny started. Danny quit when he decided he wanted to spend more money on horror movies and pot than on a smoke that doesn't even really get you high. Adam hadn't. It was weird and uncharacteristic of him, but maybe Adam just had an addictive gene or something.

Or maybe he was just holding on to something that would differentiate the two of them, give him some power over himself. The thought bugs Danny, makes him feel bad. He shakes it away. Something
(We'll call it a collaboration.)
is distracting him.

When Adam sneaks out of the cafeteria and pulls a pack of Camels from his pocket, Danny crouches lower, tries not to make any noise. And when Adam is close enough, Danny grabs his ankle.

Adam screams and whirls and looks down and for a second Danny sees absolutely no recognition in his eyes. Like Danny is a homeless kid, a derelict who wants to kill him, and Danny smiles at that. And Adam sees. And Adam knows.

"Jesus Christ, Danny?"

"In the flesh."

"Where have you been? Your mom called my house!"

"Where do you think?"

The color drops out of Adam's face. He closes his eyes. "No."

"Yup."

"No, no, Danny, Jesus, all night? Aw, Jesus," and so on and so forth. Danny isn't really listening anymore. Adam keeps talking, keeps going, just spouting nervous nonsense, and Danny isn't really listening. Because something
(Curiosities attract curiosities like quicksilver.)
is distracting him.

He tells Adam to shut up, pulls him through the gap between the dumpsters, tells him everything. And when he's finished, Adam is rocking back and forth on his heels, cradling his elbows in his palms. He says, "You didn't see any of that." He says, "That was… PTSD, or something."

Something like anger flares inside him, but Danny's too far gone to notice. That window—that door—and the light it shines, it has a way of drowning out anything else. "I did see it," he says. "And I'm going back."

Adam shakes his head. He lights his cigarette with shaking hands. "Fine. Have fun. Let me know how it goes."

"You got to come, Adam. Please."

Adam says, "Oh, fuck you, Danny," but there's no power in it. He's almost crying again, those tiny spasmodic eyes all over the goddamned place, but never on Danny. Never. "I'm already a fucking... Jesus, I don't know, I'm an accessory to... obstruction of justice, or something!"

"No, you're not. Come with me. Tonight. Please."

And when the tears slip down Adam's cheeks and his shoulders slump and he takes a drag on his cigarette, Danny knows he'll come even before he says so.

...see the boys... they're silent. Sitting in the Volvo with the radio off. Adam's window is open a little and a trail of blue cigarette smoke tracks out through the crack. The dull hum of the engine is almost everything to Danny. It's the sound of the hunt, the sound of searching. It jars him when Adam starts talking.

"This is stupid..." he says, and the dull hum takes over again for a few minutes.

Adam laughs, but it's as fake a laugh as Danny has ever heard. "This is so stupid..."

Danny wraps his fingers hard around the steering wheel.

"This is just so stupid..."

Danny says, "Shut up." He says it in a voice he can barely claim as his own, dull and gentle in a terrible way. And Adam obeys.

These suburban streets are a cluster of well-lit gas stations and fast food restaurants bleeding into a smattering of faint streetlights and dark houses. When the final buzz-white oasis of the last gas station disappears behind them and the suburban canopy swallows the car, Danny holds his breath. He doesn't blink. He twists the wheel to the left and to the right and he drives and he turns and when he parks at the end of the cul-de-sac, he doesn't remember driving at all. The window is his beacon, and he follows its light.

A single streetlight at the crest of the dead-end buzzes and clicks, flairs and goes dead, comes back to life and starts over again.

Danny opens the door, looks at Adam, waits for him to do the same. "Come on."

Adam looks like he's going to vomit again.

Danny grits his teeth, forces a smile. The iron-fence smile of the Bosch beams back at him from behind the window. "Adam. Come on."

Adam reaches blindly for the handle and yanks. He lets the door slide open and pulls himself out.

Danny walks to the steel barrier. Adam joins him. They look over it.

Black silt spills from the mouth of the concrete storm drain and on either side the slanted concrete partition reflects the breathless electric blue light of the moon into the sunken mud-angel where last night had been a bloated dead thing.

Adam says, "He's not here anymore."

"It's here."

"Someone found it. The police, probably. They took it away, and now we can go home."

"Adam. Stop it."

Danny vaults over the barrier. The old steel makes his hands feel filthy, and he wipes them on his jeans as he climbs down the slope and into the creek. He hears Adam scrambling down behind him.

Mud creeps up around Danny's Converse sneakers when he hits the dark damp ground. The drainpipe stares like a huge empty eye socket, and beyond it the tunnel, the swastikas, the pot leaves. Branches shift overhead and their shadows lend false depth to this scar in the side of the world.

Another splash of mud. Adam standing with his own sneakers sole-deep in the creek bed. He looks around with his tiny eyes. He's chewing on his bottom lip.

To Danny, this place seems darker now than it's ever been, and wetter and somehow warmer. All the musty smells of drain water and rotten leaves are magnified. He steps around the narrow corridor of grass and concrete and sloppy earth. He stares into the brush each time the wind moves the leaves. "What time is it?"

Adam pulls his phone from his pocket. It casts a blue glow across his face. "Eight after."

"Eight after what?"

"Eight after eleven."

Plow the Bones

For the first time, Danny starts to doubt all of this. He starts to feel so stupid. And here's Adam, Adam who he drags with him everywhere like a comfort blanket, staring at him like he's crazy, like he's scaring him, and goddamn it, where is the Bosch?

Adam says, "Dan? You okay?"

It happens so fast. So fast he doesn't even know it's happening until it's already in motion. He's screaming. Screaming words, screaming un-words, just screaming. He doesn't know why. He just wants to scream until they come, until they come and take him from this fucking little town and put him where he belongs, in the secret wonderful adventure, the horror movie UnWorld, and he will scream. He will scream until he gets what he wants, he will… he will…

He goes light-headed, remembers to breathe, feels his feet slide in opposite directions. He falls sideways into the mud, feels his hip collide with the concrete slope. And he starts crying. Like he's been hoping Adam wouldn't. All the hope and anger and righteousness inside him compresses, turns to crumbling coal. Danny sits in the mud and cries. And Adam looks on, and no matter how much it hurts him, no matter how much it kills him that Adam can see him like this, naked and beaten and defeated, he doesn't stop crying. He can't stop. He says, "What time is it now?"

"Ten after."

"I was so sure they were coming."

"Of course they're not coming," says Adam. He sounds genuine. Sympathetic. "It was stupid to come down here."

Danny stops crying, stands up. He turns halfway around, feels the potential pulsing in the muscles of his arms. He sneers, lifts his open palms to his chest, and pushes against Adam's shoulders once, twice.

"Jesus, Danny! What the fuck?"

"Shut up, Adam! Shut up!" Over and over and over again, through the tears and the mud and the dark, "Shut up! Shut up!" Pushing, pushing, pushing, Adam falling back a step, getting scared, his little eyes wide and his mouth open. Adam closes his mouth, pushes Danny back. And Danny isn't really surprised when he balls up his fist and drives it into Adam's mouth. But he wishes he was.

Danny slumps back into the mud. And he and Adam are the same again, two scared little boys, weeping and wallowing in filth. Staring at each other through slit eyes, wiping away tears and trying, somehow, to still look angry.

Adam holds his jaw with one hand, says, "You've lost it."

"You're such a fag. You always were."

"Danny, shut up."

"I saved you. And you don't even care. You want to just go back to being a fag like you always were before. Fine."

"Danny, shut up, or I swear to God."

"Oh, fuck you, Adam, you'll what?" he sniffs. "You'll cry?" Which sounds stupid now that he's said it. They're both crying. Both sitting in the mud. And he cries harder.

The air changes. The smells grow stronger. They feel it and freeze.

It begins as an itch in Danny's ears, a hiss from somewhere he can't find. It grows, a wet growl now.

A low roar.

A scream.

And a belch of dark water boils out of the drain pipe, spilling out over the creek bed. Both of them are washed by it.

There, floating face-down in the filthy water, oh, Danny knows who that is, welcomes him—it—him back with the widest smile he's ever smiled, showers thank-yous at the window in his head.

Adam swears, sobs, screams, but Danny hardly notices. The suburban abattoir seeps away, a sentimental Kinkade painting doused with hissing vinegar and running down the easel in ruin. And beneath it, good old Hieronymus Bosch and his landscape of wonderful atrocities. No more Theresa Sales and her expectant looks in the back of his car, no more circular tours of the same broken streets, no more of Anthony Rigby's bad pot or stolen cans of Natural Light. The window and the key, the door, the whole highway off into that marvelous UnWorld is here, thank god, it's here, and Danny is so happy, so, so happy.

Stickhead stands up and the Bosch thing perches on its shoulder.

Plow the Bones

"What the fuck is that?" Adam's voice, a cracked falsetto.

The Bosch, the Collector of Curiosities, smiles and sways and laughs, and says, "Danny-thing! You came to visit Stickhead, yes? Stickhead and myself, yes?"

Danny nods, aware of this creeping sort of fear at the back of his brain, drowning in the light of his favorite new window.

"What is it?" shrieks Adam again.

"Did you bring us another curiosity, Danny-thing? Is this one who screams curious too?"

"What's going on?" Adam again, repeating himself, like a record, like a robot.

"Leave him alone," Danny says. And not because he loves Adam. No. No, not anymore, this has gone beyond any of that sentimental shit, hasn't it? Adam doesn't deserve the UnWorld beyond the window. Adam deserves this evil little town, deserves to be infected with its awful normalcy. Take that, Adam. Take that.

The Bosch points at Adam. "It asks many questions."

"He's scared," said Danny.

"Are you scared, Danny-thing?"

"Yes."

Somewhere behind Danny, Adam is muttering, "Oh Jesus, oh Jesus, oh Jesus."

Danny smiles, kicks a spurt of wet mud at Adam. Adam cowers, stares.

"You are sure it is not curious?"

"He's not," says Danny and glances back at Adam. Poor Adam. He feels bad about this, bad about leaving him here to backslide into that lonely world of library lunches and locker room ass-kickings. But here comes that light from that window again, and all is right with the UnWorld. "He's normal."

The Bosch nods, wags a finger at Danny. "Come to me, Danny-thing."

And Danny does.

"Goodbye, my lovely Stickhead," says the Bosch. It runs a hand over the parchment skin of Stickhead's face like a lover. "You were such a good Stickhead, yes?"

It leaps and latches his fingers around Danny's head, scrambling down around his shoulders.

Stickhead falls.

"Jesus, Danny, no!" Adam, weeping, sobbing, rocking back and forth, making that rattling piggy noise that grown men make when they cry. "Don't leave me, Danny, Jesus! Please!"

Danny smiles, his own tears drying on his face. Poor Adam. Poor, poor Adam. He steps forward, pulls back his foot, and kicks Adam in the ribs.

"Goodbye, Adam."

Oh, that feeling. The feeling when the Bosch sinks its fingers into Danny's temples, when a spider-web of black lines grow like strangle-vines from his touch. It hurts, Christ, it hurts, but his eyes fill up with such brilliant, wonderful light. We remember. You and me. And the others. The other Collected. We remember the wonderful light.

"Danny, no!" someone screams from far away. Someone Danny knew a long time ago.

The fingers sink. Danny's head is soft clay. The Bosch cackles, and its laughter is music. Danny sees the skin of his arms stretch and discolor from behind the brilliant light swallowing his eyeballs. His veins swell, strain, burst. Red-black fireworks. He smiles. And still smiling, still afraid, Danny falls backward, ever backward, ever and forever and forever and forever backward with the Bosch, and the mud swallows them both.

…see the cul-de-sac. The sun rises over it. It rises on the barrier. It sinks through the brush and touches the mud at the creek's bottom, warming it. And God, to Adam, it feels so good to have the sun on him again. Somewhere above him, a school bus stops and kids get on, swearing and prodding at each other. He shakes his head back and forward. His arms and legs keep twitching. He reaches into his pocket, lights a Camel, inhales. He lets his head loll onto his shoulder and stares at that dead guy… that dead thing… with the stick in his head lying next to him.

He crawls over to the body, wraps his fingers around the stick

Plow the Bones

and pulls it out. Something in his head keeps trying to work its way into the right order, like a cut that won't quite scab over. He leans on the stick, and it helps him stand. He climbs up the slope. The cut in his mind gets close to healing, then rips open again.

People will talk about this for a long time. About how Adam stumbles onto the cul-de-sac, wet and muddy and hardly able to stand. How he drops the stick on the ground and climbs up to sit on the hood of the abandoned Volvo parked at the curb. They'll talk about how, when they saw him, he was just sitting there, staring up into the sky, smoking his cigarette. And when he starts screaming, they'll talk about how long it took for him to stop.

See this and see it well. We all see. All of us who have been collected. You, me, Danny, Stickhead. All of us. And we all agree. Adam has become somewhat... well, curious. Yes sir. Quite curious indeed.

I Inhale the City, The City Exhales Me

On the surface of the canal, the Dotonbori district's neon muscles, its enormous screens, its colored bulbs and strobe lights, are reflected all over again, stretching down into the endless water. The shoppers and the nightclubbers teem in and out of restaurants and karaoke rooms. Peacock people, trying to match the flamboyance of Osaka's skyline with their clothes, their faces, their gestures. Nothing ever stops moving.

There is a two-dimensional cartoon man on the giant Gilco candy display above the district, smiling with his arms held above his head. He wears a marathonist's shorts and shirt. And now, he has become self-aware. He is alive. He pumps his colorless arms back and forth, slicing them through the air beside his ribs, his feet push off against the two-dimensional track and carry him nowhere, and he is no longer smiling. Below him, gathered like toddlers and craning their necks to see him, the partying crowd. They aren't afraid. They rejoice. They are laughing and pointing, aiming phones and cameras up at the spectacle.

The Gilco man keeps running. He can't stop. Sweat runs down his face and disappears beneath his chin. His chest inflates and deflates unevenly. His posture is crumbling, and soon he will collapse in on himself. He wants to stop. Didn't he win? Isn't that why his hands were raised? He's earned it, it's not fair, but he can't stop. Because this is Osaka, and nothing ever stops moving.

The peacock people cheer beneath him. The Gilco man says, "Please." His left foot hooks behind his right ankle, and he almost falls. He corrects his stride, finds his rhythm. He wants to stop. He says, "Help me. I don't understand. I don't understand anything."

The crowd laughs. Applauds. Several of the people at the feet of the suffering Gilco man fall in love with one another now. The false is turning true, and they are grateful.

The Outlaw watches from the shadows. He is there and not there. All around him, little vengeances tug at him. He drags a coffin on a chain through the streets of Dotonbori, and everywhere he goes people part to make room, but nobody notices him. He moves through them with one hand hovering above the pistol at his hip.

Plow the Bones

* * *

I tell him—this American boy who has come to discuss my business with me, who wants to fuck me—I say he doesn't know anything about Japanese women. Everything he knows is from movies and cartoons and manga. He wants me to be skittish. Frightened. He wants me to be a virgin, and to fear his penis even while I yearn for it. That is what he came for. I tell him, while I am hunched over my desk and my hand jerks and weaves over the page, "You're an asshole. And a racist."

I don't look behind me, but I can tell his feelings are hurt. I don't know if anybody has ever said this to him, but now I have, and the rhythm of his breathing hitches and holds, and that's enough answer. I may as well have hit him.

I am drawing an eye. Soon I will draw another. The eyes I am drawing will be unhappy. "You come here," I say, and my hand adds a row of short, brutal lashes to the bottom lid, "with your microphone and your computer and your press credentials." I picture him in my head as he was on the first day that I met him. "Your stylish beard and your smart-looking glasses. You're going to create the story you want to create. You'll edit all the tape together, and when it turns up on the radio back home, it will be the exact same story you thought it would be before you even got on the plane."

I can hear him shuffling his feet behind me, trying to find a posture that will make him feel less vulnerable. He says, "Megumi, I... If this is about... I promise the piece will be perfectly respectful, I..." He sighs, and when he speaks again, his voice is low. It trembles. "I'm not sure what I've done to upset you."

I turn around, and I stare at him. I'm angry. I'm not sure why. Something about the way he says my name, the way he claims ownership over it. For a few heavy seconds, we don't say anything. I just watch his skin turn blue and then red, blue and then red, blue and then red, as the lighted sign outside my hotel room flashes on and off. He's sitting on my bed. The hotel's bed, really. But I paid for it, not him, and he is sitting on it as though this room belongs, however temporarily, to the both of us. I gesture at his notebook. He hands it to me. " 'Kodu Garden is everything you'd expect from a major manga studio in the weird and wonderful heart of Osaka,' " I say, parroting his narration back to him. " 'Everybody—from the lowly mail-cart kid to the colorists and tech-guys at their computer consoles—looks busy, focused, dead-set.' " He doesn't understand. Maybe he can't. A muscle between his eyebrows is twitching, and his shoulders are tense and rounded. " 'In Osaka,' " I read, " 'The business of giant monsters and long-haired ghosts and, yes, hyper-sexual fantasy'," I struggle with this last term, partially because it is written in my second language, and partially because his handwriting is quick and cramped and childish, " 'is deadly serious.' "

"Look," he says, "Just..." He's getting frustrated, arguing with me like we're a couple, like I've made a stupid, hurtful, girlish mistake. "The only reason I read it to you was..."

"Was because you wanted to impress me," I say, and I toss the notebook onto the bed and turn back to my work. There is so much to be done. "Because you wanted to make your story real." Which is what I want to do, too. I draw the brim of a wide cowboy hat above the stern eyebrows. I cut chinks and rips and folds into the hat with my pencil. I make it an old hat, even though it's just been born. It's a good hat to hide beneath. "I can't stop you," I say, "but I don't want you telling stories about me."

He is quiet behind me for a long time. The lamp above my desk paints my big sketch pad warm yellow. The rest of the room is blue and then red, blue and then red. I draw a pair of lips, big and expressive, held tightly together. I like working in hotel rooms. I like being in a private space that doesn't really belong to anybody. It's better than working at my brightly lit desk in the studio, high up in the sky and staring out at the city, a space without privacy that belongs, inarguably, to someone else. It's better than my own apartment, where everything is mine and all of my drawings become me. Here, I can disappear. I can make my stories come true.

If I turn my head, his mouth looks like a vagina. I erase, try again.

The bedsprings squeak. The door opens. The door closes. And I am alone again. And able to tell stories. The American radio producer's. And mine too.

* * *

Plow the Bones

The Shinsekai district: the winding labyrinth of streets and alleys, the slot-machine parlors that jangle and crash, the carnival barkers beckoning pedestrians into kushikatsu restaurants and sushi bars, the pensive white people with tourist handbooks. These are the roots, the veins that run along the ground toward the district's heart, the high white Tsutenkaku tower, built to ape the Eiffel, from the top of which tourists can see the whole city.

Fifteen feet above the streets, lazy paper fugu fish float like zeppelins. Once, they hung motionless outside of fugu restaurants, paper lanterns with red letters blazing on their flanks. A few hours ago, their painted eyes fluttered open and saw. Their flat gills flared open and breathed. The electric lights in their bellies became hungry. They broke their moorings and floated away from their wires and started searching for little shrimp in the air. They have found none. Now they weave around between buildings, their little fins whirring like hummingbird wings, and the people beneath them glance up at them occasionally, satisfied. The tourists smile uncomfortably, ask each other if this is supposed to be happening. The fish don't care. They're hungry, and there are no shrimp in the air.

The Outlaw stalks beneath them, dragging his coffin by its chain. He follows the feet of his quarry. He is careful to stay beneath the shadow of a floating paper fugu fish, where nobody can see him. Nobody but his bounty, who walks shudder-stepped and nervous, who doesn't really *see* The Outlaw, but seems to be dreaming about him even while he walks wide awake. His bounty is American, like The Outlaw is supposed to be. They cancel each other out. The Outlaw represents the American, and that injustice boils in The Outlaw's guts and causes his lips (big, romantic lips; they look like a vagina at the right angle) to curl up against his stubby teeth.

The American winds his way through the crowd, takes hard angles into narrow alleys, tries to get lost. He pushes his way around slow-walkers and still-standers who whine and make threatening noises at him. The Outlaw follows. Nobody minds him. They make room for him, staring up at the fugu fish, clapping their hands, distracted by a world remade in the image for which they've always been hungry without even realizing it. The Outlaw gains ground. The American runs.

So he draws his pistol. Oh, his pistol. Lo, his pistol. A thing of obscenity, long and black. The product of a million years and a million pages of elegant, unfair evolution, trailing the invisible ghosts of countless imperfect iterations that were erased before it. The Outlaw stands still. The fugu moves on. Its shadow sloughs off of The Outlaw, and the collected Shinsekai kids turn to stare at him.

They say, "Oooh."

He thumbs back the hammer. The chamber revolves.

The things I work on in hotel rooms are not the things for which I get paid. The things for which I get paid, I draw at my desk on the eleventh floor of a tall building in Osaka. I draw them where everyone can see them. I draw big-eyed girls with very large tits. Frequently, those girls are crying. Sometimes, their clothes are torn and their breasts hang out, their delicate arms too thin to shield them from the prying eyes of whatever looms off-panel. I sometimes receive memos directing me to make them look more frightened, less defiant. The girls I draw at work wear armored shoulder-pads and spiky combat boots with thong bikinis. They are menaced by sexually voracious monsters, assaultive aliens, evil mutants, and (sometimes, only sometimes) they are saved just in time by men. I am good at drawing these women. I never, ever, ever draw them in my hotel rooms.

Right now, I'm shading the Gilco man from the Dotonbori district. I'm cross-hatching the fugu lanterns in Shinsekai. And outside, Osaka is reading my sketches like instructions. With my pencil, I chisel away my city's good intentions, its static fantasy, and I shape it. This is why we build all those pretty falsenesses. To live in a world where the rules are less boring, where we can all be heroes and slay dragons and save the world and rescue the armored girl in the thong bikini.

I want Osaka to be the thing it dreams about. I'm doing a service.

I draw the American boy, the radio producer, with his eyes wide and frightened behind his plastic-framed glasses, twisting his shoulders and jerking his neck to see the thing that's chasing him. Somewhere in Osaka, it happens. I don't cause this to happen. This relationship between me and the dream-come-true outside my window, it's a push-and-pull, a symbiosis. I introduce stimulus with my drawings, and the stimulus changes what I draw.

A few weeks ago, when the American showed up at our office and shook hands with my boss and wandered around with his digital sound recorder and his headphones, I thought I might like him enough to sleep with him. I haven't slept with many men. Four in total, none of them American. I was curious. Since I was a little girl, I have had a mild obsession with cowboys. The ultimate American hero. I thought that maybe this boy, with his beard and his curly hair and his big brown eyes, was in some way haunted by that old American ghost. Sometimes wishes disguise themselves as intuitions.

I draw the American boy's curly hair, riding its wild spirals with the tip of my pencil. His sweat and his flight have undone all his careful work to keep it tame and stylish. It defies gravity, climbs the air. I like doing this. It almost makes me like him again.

My boss, smiling like his lips were being pulled from his teeth on hooks, led the American around the office by the shoulder, weaving around desks and saying, "This one speaks English. This one doesn't speak English. This one is very boring, don't talk to him. Talk to him, he's a writer, very good stories." The American nodded and smiled and looked sweet.

When my boss led him to me, I was drawing a woman in profile, her neck craned and her mouth open. She was crying, humiliated, in pain. I was trying to make her look sexy.

My boss said, "Talk to her. Talk to Megumi-san. She speaks very good English. Very good artist. Very pretty. Talk to her."

So he did.

My phone vibrates in my pocket and I jump and knock over a stack of finished pages. They spill to the floor, enormous snowflakes, and I swear to myself and dig out my phone. It's the American boy on his pre-paid Japanese phone.

"What?"

"Megumi, you gotta help me out here, there's this guy, this fucking guy, oh my god, I just—I don't know, he's following me, he's—he's fucking shooting at me, for christ—oh my god, what am I going to—"

I hang up on him and toss my phone onto the bed. My bed. And I turn to collect my spilled pages. I flip through them, taking stock.

The poor Gilco man, wrecked and wretched. The hungry flying fugu lanterns. My terrible lovely cowboy with his black coffin on a chain. Then I stop. Somehow one of my work sketches has followed me home, an unfinished piece of soft-core ugliness. I drew it for a computer game we're developing. *Akuma Fushin Senjō. Demon Distrust Battleground.* The game is an *eroge*, a sex game. The game creates the illusion of interactivity with a series of binary choices. The "correct" choices reward the player with portraits of vulnerability and nastiness. So do the "incorrect" choices. And here is my reward for my choices. An unfinished sketch of a girl, bruised and bleeding, lying on the ground, her breasts defying gravity. She is faceless. Like me, or like the American boy sees me, or wishes I was, prone and hurt and too tired or weak or... or female... to resist. The ideal Japanese girl.

This isn't mine. This belongs to someone else.

Now I am struck by the urge to finish the sketch. To give the girl her face. The sensation is immediate and hot, like a wave of nausea, and before I can stop myself I have swept the page onto my desk, completing my broken girl, giving her open and defiant eyes, closed and grim and angry lips. This is not what I am allowed to do. This sketch does not belong to me. It is not one of my hotel room sketches. Those I draw for Osaka. I am not selfish. I am doing a service. I am doing a service. I am doing a service.

Still, I know I am finishing this girl for me.

The American pushes his way downstairs and into Ebisucho Subway Station, past the throngs of revelers and dancers and nervous optimists. They whisper to each other, compare in hushed and manic tones their notes on the evening's parade of strangeness and which elements thereof they've witnessed, as he shoulders through them, trying to keep his footing, his sanity, feeling acutely each tiny marble of sweat rolling down the back of his neck and soaking into his collar. The Outlaw knows all of this. He can smell the American's thoughts, his fears. The stale underground breeze pushes the scent of his sweat to the Outlaw's nostrils, lands like a film on his lips. The Outlaw hauls his coffin onto his back by its chain to keep it from sliding down the stairs in front of him. It's getting heavier. He feels no pangs of regret for missing the American when he fired earlier. It wasn't his fault. That's the way it was drawn. The Outlaw knows this in a different way than he knows the American's mind. He feels his artist pulling on his tendons from miles away, feels her playing him like a marionette, and he tries not to resent her for it.

Still, he has questions. He doesn't understand.

A train pulls in next to the platform, breathing cold air that smells like fuel and ammonia. On the train's flank are wide-eyed manic-happy Kewpie dolls painted in pink. Their eyes roll in their faces, their ball-and-socket arms spin like Ferris wheels. The American stumbles into the train, and the Outlaw lets him go. There is a scene being set within that car, and his artist is gracious. She gives him the scene, lets him see it happening, even as the doors slide closed and the train rolls down the tunnel.

The scene is this:

The American, alone, surrounded by the flat advertisements on the train's walls, the models silent, following him with their eyes. He breathes heavy. He pulls his pre-paid Japanese cellphone from his pocket, thinking, *I don't believe in any of this. None of this is real.* He feels unstuck, a reel of film unsprocketed. His thoughts keep coming to him in full sentences, the kind of narration he would write if he were producing a radio piece, and he wants it to stop. He wants to think the way he normally thinks, in impulses, in flashes of image and emotion, but that doesn't seem to be an option.

In the corner, obscured between the wall and the subway bench, something is moving. It tries to pull its knees to its chest, can't find room, kicks out, pulls in again. The American closes his eyes tight enough to blast color bursts behind his eyelids, procrastinating. Then he opens his eyes and says, "Ma'am?" And then he waits.

The voice is rotten and dry, the voice of a victim, but there is fire behind it, it bites, it snaps, it says, "Do what you're going to do. That's why you're here."

The American says nothing. He is trying not to think, and failing. He narrates himself. *I walk toward this girl I've found. I know she shouldn't be here, know that she's part of the nightmare-Osaka as sure as the thing with the gun behind me. But I walk toward her anyway. I want to believe that she's real, that's she's normal, maybe a comrade in all this craziness, and so I take a few tentative steps. And she is revealed.*

She is revealed. Trying to push herself up the wall away from him, too weak and too injured. She falls back onto the floor of the subway car, onto her back with her legs open to him. She is absurd, propped up on her elbows and staring through a curtain of wet hair, with her spiked shoulder pads and the belt slung around her naked waist and her black bikini (one strap is broken, and her left breast remains barely concealed).

"Um," says the American.

The rows of long fluorescent lights on the ceiling flicker, darken, brighten. The car shakes as the train rolls over the tracks, whispering to the tunnel as it weaves through and within it. The faces on the posters stare at the American expectantly.

She says, "Fuck me. I won't stop you. I can't."

He can see it like a shadow-puppet show in his head, the things he could do to her, the choreography of fetishism he could inflict, intricate and infinite, the binary choices and their consequences, and he hates himself. *This isn't me*, he thinks. *That's not who I am*. Still, the imagined show goes on: the things he could remove from her, the things he could add to her, the places and positions in which he could add them. It is endless.

"Stop it," he says.

"Come on," she growls, and her eyebrows twitch again and again. With every word, her head snaps forward, like she's taking bites of the stale recirculated train air. She says, "You saved me from the Threat. You win."

"Stop talking," says the American, while the shadow-show in his head loops back and plays again, double-speed, legs entwined, muscles arching and releasing, hands grasping, searching, finding. Oh god, the things his hands could find. Outside of his head, his fingers find their way into his hair and tug, then find their way down to his ears and press hard against them. He closes his eyes, but that renders the images in perfect color and depth, and his eyelids shoot back open.

She leans to one side, reaches up with one bruised hand, grasps at the center string of her bikini top with fingers whose nail beds are caked with old blood, and she rips. The string protests, then gives up and breaks. She gestures one-handed at her breasts. "These are yours as much as they are mine. Maybe more."

"No," says the American, "really. Please stop. When is this goddamn train going to stop? Don't people ever need to get off this fucking thing?" He shouts, "I'm a good person!" and his voice breaks and turns boyish, a piggy squeal.

He tries to make a list of famous feminists in his head, and all he can come up with is Camille Paglia, sitting next to him in his internal shadow-show watching him shower filth over the fake girl in the train car, drudging up quotes from some long-ago Women's Studies course he thought he had forgotten, lecturing, "Sexual freedom, sexual liberation. A modern delusion. We are hierarchical animals. Sweep one hierarchy away, and another will take its place, perhaps less palatable than the first."

The fake girl in the train car hisses, "You need to fuck me. Now. Those are the rules. You saved me from the Threat."

The American stomps on the floor, waves his arms. He screams, "What threat? What are you talking ab—this is crazy, I have to..."

The train turns a corner, sways, and throws him down. He feels himself tumbling, and then feels himself hit bottom and roll. Into her. Onto her.

In his head, Camille Paglia says, "The devil is a woman." She says, "The serpent is not outside Eve but in her. She is the garden and the serpent."

He is sprawled over her now, with his head on her stomach and his torso between her legs, hyperventilating too quickly and harshly to cry. But he does feel like crying.

The fake girl grabs him by the hair and hauls him over her. She is strong. Too strong. She pulls his face up to her own and spits. Then she says, "You have to do this."

For a second, the American almost does. He can feel his hand hovering over her breast. He can feel his cock rubbing against the fly of his jeans, so close to her tissue-thin bikini-bottoms that he can feel her heat. Then Camille Paglia again, in his head, saying, "For a decade, feminists have drilled their disciples to say, 'Rape is a crime of violence but not of sex.' This sugar-coated Shirley Temple nonsense has exposed young women to disaster. Misled by feminism, they do not expect rape from the nice boys from good homes who sit next to them in class."

The train stops. The doors open. And the American is on his feet again, and running out of the train, onto some empty platform, up the stairs. The tears come. Behind him, the girl is raging, screaming, "Someone has to fuck me!"

And in his head, Camille Paglia says, "Each generation drives its plow over the bones of the dead."

When I met the American boy for drinks and introductions on that first night, I suggested a bar within walking distance of his hotel. I wore a dress I thought was sexy and I did my make-up. I tried to look like a girl from some old Western movie, with my cowgirl boots and my fishnet stockings and my piled-high hair. I even drew a beauty mark on my cheek with my eyeliner pencil. I knew what I was doing. I'm not stupid.

He is calling me again, leaving another panicked voicemail. I already know what it says. The girl in the train car. My big mistake.

I've drawn all of it, not because I want to, but because it's true. I introduce stimulus, and the stimulus changes what I draw. Push-and-pull. Symbiosis.

Now, my beautiful old cowboy is crawling up onto the platform. He has caught up with the train. Other people have found her, my poor defiant sex-doll girl. My cowboy finds her spent and sweaty. I draw her eyes again, less defiant. Exhausted. When she sees him with his coffin and his gun and his hat, looming over her, she says, "Are you the Player, or the Threat?"

I didn't anticipate this. I didn't know what I was doing, finishing her, saving her to Osaka's hard drive. She comes with prerequisites, of course. The Player and the Threat. She can't exist without them, and her existence demands theirs.

My cowboy sucks cigarette smoke into the negative space where his lungs should be, then exhales. He flicks the cigarette away, and it spirals down the length of the train car. He says, "Don't reckon I'm either." Then, "Where did he go?"

Faithful, obedient cowboy. Searching for the American, because I asked him to.

On that first night, I sat at a conspicuous table at the front of the bar and waited for him. I pretended to send text messages on my phone, although I have no real friends to whom I would send them. My hands shook. When the American boy walked through the door and saw me, he looked... disappointed. Sad. I watched his fantasy of me (humble, shy, delicate, a girl the world whispered but never spoke aloud) crumble and decay. It was a fantasy he'd crafted before he ever met me, a faceless fantasy that while he zipped through Osaka at his company's expense, he might find a Japanese doll to shatter and rebuild.

Another buzz from my pocket, another message from the American boy. The intervals between calls are getting shorter.

The rest of the night, he squirmed and wriggled and tried to fit me back into his fantasy. "The world is a big, crazy place," he said, as though I didn't know. He said, "I mean, I assume you're a virgin," and before I could tell him I wasn't, "I mean, maybe you're not, but... I mean, what I'm trying to say is... I want to be fair," he said, "I won't shy away from the double-standard, either, you know? The, y'know, the weird, uh, rape fantasy epidemic in this country, all that," staring at my tits, speaking fast enough to disallow me from adding anything. He lectured me, citing Western feminists I've never heard of. If I tried to talk about sex, he blanched and changed the subject. We went on like that for two hours, him lecturing, me trying to find a gap in his monologue into which I could insert myself.

I am proud of him for not fucking the *Demon Distrust Battleground* girl.

Outside the window of my hotel room, the neon sign flickers, then brightens. I can hear it humming to me, composing a one-note theme song for Osaka's new face. The inside of my hotel room is bright pink now.

I stop drawing. I stare out the window at the sign. From my perspective, the neon English script is backward. It says "Osaka Rock and Roll Bar."

My desk lamp goes out. I tap on the bulb, flick the switch on and off, but the lamp ignores me.

The Rock and Roll Bar's sign is glowing, steaming, sizzling, and its hum is growing louder. Then it pops, raining sparks, and then the inside of my hotel room is black.

I am alone in my dark hotel room with no way to finish my drawings.

Osaka does not celebrate. It screams. Across the city, bulbs are bursting. The lights that remain are weak, anemic, and mostly red. They flicker.

People run. They squat in doorways and tremble. They stare out of windows set into dark buildings as the city turns itself out, bulb by bulb.

Osaka isn't moving. But something else is.

The Threat. Liquid and invisible, empty space crashing through empty space, colliding with obstacles and consuming them. It fills any space it can, grows like a bonsai tree into every available inch of thin air. It has no skin to contain it, because none was drawn for it. It sounds like a thousand chiming clocks, although it is silent. The train car girl, pregnant with it by default, has given birth to it. She can't exist without it. And she exists. So...

The peacock people are gobbled up by it.

The Outlaw, for the first time in his brief life, feels an imperative not fed to him through his artist's pencil. He's not sure what it is, this unpleasant sensation of wanting to be three places at once. But, huddled on his haunches in an alley behind a 7-Eleven dumpster, he's contending with it.

The coffin is almost too heavy to carry now, filled with the Osaka of before, the Osaka of artifice. He has set it down back here, in the dull, bruise-colored shadows, and his shoulders make shrill demands that he leave it here. He feels the old compulsion to find the American, and it is compelling for its familiarity. He feels the new imperative, born from necessity rather than his artist's design, to track the Threat, to fire his gun at it and bring it down. He feels its twin, the seductive desire to throw himself into the Threats center and be consumed. He's never had to make a decision before.

Somewhere not far away, the Threat pushes its weightlessness up staircases and around corners, and the things it swallows implode atom by atom in its unbelly. The Outlaw feels it, knows it. Its mind tastes like a cave-dwelling thing, a deep-sea jellyfish, eyeless and brainless and running on pure impulse.

Here, the Outlaw is not alone. He smells someone else, hears their feet falling on the asphalt. Something about their stride, their pace, reminds him of the exhausted, stuck-in-a-terrible-moment Gilco man. This person has been running for a very long time, and can't stop.

The Outlaw glances over his shoulder in time to see the American turn the corner, sweat-soaked, ragged, his face puffy and pink in the ugliest and least dignified way. He's been crying for as long as he's been running. The Outlaw stands up, and is not sure what he wants to do.

The American sees him, stops running. Of course he is here. Of course he is. The spaces the two of them can fit into are shrinking, filling up with amorphous, pointless menace. Where else would he be? Gradually, the American's face contorts into a smile and he begins laughing. His legs don't seem to know what to do now that they've been relieved of their duty to carry him endlessly forward, and so they give up his weight, and he falls to the ground. Around his laughter, he says, "You've got to be fucking kidding me."

The Outlaw wonders if his hand will reach for the pistol at his hip, wonders if he will shoot the American, or if he was ever meant to. He wonders how, when they have to choose, people avoid blowing their own brains out. He wonders WHY, in capital letters. Why the American? The American just laughs with his head on the hard, wet, red ground.

I have to draw. Even in darkness, when I can't see the things I'm drawing, I have to draw. The balance has shifted, and I can't tell this story anymore. I am no longer introducing stimulus. I am only responding to it.

Outside my window, the Threat looms invisible. I know it's

there, because looking at the empty un-ness of it is like looking at a picture of someone you once knew, now all grown up. I have given it a thousand faces before. It can't get through the walls or the door or the window into my hotel room, although I don't know why. I am locked in a bubble in the Threat's guts, and although I am manic and my fingers ache from gripping the pencil for hours, and my entire world is being eaten by something I made, there is some kind of cozy comfort here.

I can't find my paper. Some time between the lights abandoning me and now, I have gotten myself onto the floor, and now I am drawing on the wall next to the bed. I am drawing an eye. Soon I will draw another. They are the eyes of my cowboy, who was meant to be everything the American boy couldn't be. Somewhere, not far away, he's lifting his gun, the gun I could never draw quite right, the gun that always ended up looking like a beetle shell no matter how hard I tried to cram it into its Old West revolver skin. My city is dying, is mostly dead, and my beautiful gunslinger is trying to decide if he wants to kill the poor American boy or if he wants to shoot himself in the temple.

I never meant for any of this to happen.

Outside, the Threat is so hungry. It wants, without knowing what. I feel pity for it, and revulsion. It's like an animal made mindless by boredom, a nervous system without a brain, or a brain without a skull, or... I... I don't know, I grasp at whatever simile I can lay my fingers on, hoping that something will fit, will allow me to understand this thing I've midwifed into the world, this desperate, hungry, reaching thing, it's like, it's like, it's like—

Oh.

And now I am drawing something new. I am scratching it into my face and my arms with the tip of my pencil, giving it shape, holding it inside a shell. I am providing it with the face it always should have had, and my hotel room is bleeding away around me. I'm falling as I a draw, feeling the hugeness and voracity of the Threat's hunger all around me, and I inhale it, and I feel it within me, and it is not unfamiliar. I am falling, but I always have been. I am hungry, unspeakably hungry for *something*, but I always have been.

Plow the Bones

I close my eyes, and try to feel how I feel.

When I open them again, I am standing behind a 7-Eleven in the wretched waste of my poor Osaka. I have scratched the name of the Threat over and over again on my arms, my belly, my face, my legs, and the scratches bleed and the blood is hot, and the Threat is heavy and unspeakably painful inside my chest, and I start to cry.

Over and over again, *MEGUMI, MEGUMI, MEGUMI.*

The tears blur my vision. The Outlaw, with his gun to his own head. The American boy, staring at me with something like fear and something like relief fighting for dominance of his features. They cross, seep into one another, and when I wipe my hands across my eyes, there's only the two of us.

Me as the Threat, small but hungry. Same as it ever was.

The American as the Outlaw, isolated and angry and afraid of choosing. Same as it ever was.

Between us, our entire world in a black coffin on a silver chain.

He glances at the coffin and back at me. I glance at the coffin and back at him.

Then he says, fast and breathless, "What's inside?" although he already knows. "Should we open it?"

So now we have a choice to make.

Across the Dead Station Desert, Television Girl

1

In the last moments, when his breath is hot on her neck and the sheets of his bed are wound up around her fingers, when she can crane her head to look over his shoulder and watch the muscles in his back bend and roll like something not quite liquid, she can always convince herself that she is human. She can feel his cock inside her, something solid, an anchor, filling her up, hitting the exact spot (toward the front, almost at the top) that simultaneously melts her and turns her to stone, can feel the sweat-slick skin of his chest slide against her breasts, radiating wet heat and movement, and she thinks that he must love her, that she must have dreamt everything that came before, and if she could just come, her real memories would find their way back to her through the soft post-coital haze in her head. She thinks, *How could I ever think I was anything but real? I have wet skin, and I can feel my breasts bouncing, keeping rhythm with the way he fucks me, and I can feel him watching them bounce, and all I want to do is force my back into an arch and ask him if he can feel me come. This is my evidence. I am real.*

And then he comes inside her. And he rolls over and grabs the remote control from the bedside table and points it at her. He smiles at her, the way people smile at a cat they didn't know was in the room with them, and he says, "Okay. G'night."

And then the truth becomes the truth again. And she wants to tell him no, please, to ask him to just put away the remote and let her sleep next to him, or pretend to. She could fill up the room with her soft ghost-blue glow, and if in the middle of the night he has a bad dream and sits up in bed, gasping and waving away the stray cobwebs of the nightmare, he wouldn't have to reach for the lamp, and she would hold him and whisper into his ear.

She is not allowed to say any of this. There are directives and scripts to follow. So she says, "You were so big tonight."

And then he presses a button on the remote, and she blinks out.

The following is the ad-copy from the Television Girl website.
Television Girl! The newest innovation in erotic partnership!

PLOW THE BONES

Television Girl! All of your fantasies fulfilled in a safe, solitary environment! Television Girl! Authentic sensual partnership, no strings attached!

What can you expect from your Television Girl erotic partner?

Each Television Girl is tailor made to your specifications. Choose your Television Girl's hair color, eye color, race, dimensions, language, voice, sexual proclivities and more! And with a few easy to learn modification procedures, your Television Girl can evolve with your tastes, or just change to satisfy your curiosities!

Your Television Girl is designed with you in mind! Your anatomy and hers will fit together perfectly. Your Television Girl's highly sophisticated AI is capable of emulating real human pleasure, and she can only experience that pleasure with you, regardless of your size, shape, or prowess. And best of all, your Television Girl knows that you are her romantic and sexual ideal!

Television Girl is guaranteed for life! Your warrantee covers the Television Girl console box against fire, flood, theft, electrical and mechanical defects, viruses, and a number of other possible incidents. Your Television Girl will never leave you.

The TVGLive Network is available to all customers for a monthly subscription fee, and will allow you to interact with other members of the Television Girl community, download new applications and plug-ins to further personalize your Television Girl, and even borrow other users' Television Girls!

Want to know more? Please use the links provided above to receive further information and to order your new erotic partner today!

2

After an eternity of dead space, of white noise in a black pit where she can hear the crunch and grumble of the machine-monsters between the worlds, she always wakes up at the Shelter. She is always sitting on a bench built of stray pixels and looking at a closed door with nothing on the other side. It's like a garage door, somehow both mechanical and entomological, a series of sliding gunmetal panels like a big floating carapace, solid and permanent and inescapable. When it's time to go back, when her man flips on the console in the warm world of moving flesh and enters the appropriate access codes into his remote control, the door begins to twitch, to squirm, and finally the panels slide against one another and rise, and she is lifted and dragged through the awful elevator shaft between what is real and what only seems to be. That trip between worlds seems to take hours, even if it only takes seconds, and she is surrounded by the screaming sounds of the things that make that in-between space their home, but it is also exhilarating. Because she knows that when the trip is over she will be lying in that warm room, that the comforter will bulge above her, take her shape, describe to him the peaks and valleys of her blue-glow body, and he will be there with his cock in his hand, and he will say, "I want you," with his voice low and sandy, and she will squirm toward him and pull him over her, and for fifteen minutes she will know what it feels like to have skin.

But time is not the same here as it is there. And she has to wait a very long time for the door to open.

All around the Shelter, there is a desert of dead station static, and it is always moving, black and white un-shapes so small and formless that the black and the white seem to be one color, a ceaseless swarm of meaningless movement that fills her with fear. Sometimes she wonders how far the desert goes, if there is another Shelter with another bench and another Television Girl, and she fantasizes about the two of them sitting together, holding each other, feeding off their respective blue glows for comfort. Once, she even stepped out into the desert, just a few tentative feet, resolved and reassured that somewhere there was somebody like her to share her time with. But then she heard the sounds of the between-world monsters, the ones she imagines (no, not imagines but knows; she knows this as twins know each other) as big digital insects, somehow both cleanly efficient and also wretched and spasmodic and organic, and she ran back to the bench screaming. She has never tried to cross the Dead Station Desert since.

The following is correspondence between Richard Viccenzi, ReEros Technologies' lead technological engineer on Television Girl, and Arthur Anders, Television Girl's project director.

Plow the Bones

From: Richard Viccenzi (rviccenzi@reerostech.com)
To: Arthur Anders (aanders@reerostech.com)
Subject: re: Some concerns...

Art,
I can respect your position, but we've screwed the proverbial pooch on this one. Our findings can't help but have huge implications for the future of AI and the way we understand it. I have to insist that we stop selling TVG until we can work out exactly what the consequences of the free-floating AI components in the TVGLive network are, and, if necessary, what we can do to counteract their effects. I've attached the spreadsheet Mike worked out. Take a look at it and let me know what you think.

—Dick.

From: Arthur Anders (aanders@reerostech.com)
To: Richard Viccenzi (rviccenzi@reerostech.com)
Subject: re: Some concerns...

You're overreacting. The fact is that we don't know WHAT your findings imply, and they certainly don't justify descent into science-fiction histrionics. And I'm close to recommending Mike's suspension from the project. His spreadsheet doesn't tell me anything and he's more of an alarmist than you. Let me remind you that we work in the adult entertainment industry, Dick, and that our business is growing while practically every other major industry is up shit creek. Now is a very bad time to have developed the capacity for pseudo-humanist moral indignation, financially speaking.

Regards,
Art

From: Richard Viccenzi (rviccenzi@reerostech.com)
To: Arthur Anders (aanders@reerostech.com)
Subject: re: Some concerns...

For the record, I drafted three emails before this one, with varying degrees of vitriol, since I received your last message. What each of them came down to is this: don't patronize me, don't put words in my mouth, and don't play Mr. Industrial-Capitalist now, Art. We've known each other way too long for you to think you can get away with that. You ought to know better. As for my "pseudo-humanist moral indignation"… well, you're welcome to turn me into a straw man over this, that's your prerogative, but this has absolutely nothing to do with neo-lib hand-wringing. The facts are these: the components from demolished AI constructs are still aware and still "alive" in the TVGLive Network. This is demonstrable. These components demonstrate the potential to interact with the network. And these components are re-constructing themselves into new AI constructs, without any prompting from me or my team. That shouldn't be possible, and yet, voila! Here we are, Art. I am inclined to think that new (and more to the point, independent) intelligence being free inside of a network with which the public regularly interacts is potentially dangerous. Production should be halted, sale of TVG suspended, and all previously sold units recalled until such time as we understand what the fuck we're dealing with.

—Dick

PS.
If you're not interested in listening to me, someone else will be.

To: Richard Viccenzi (rviccenzi@reerostech.com)
From: Arthur Anders (aanders@reerostech.com)
Subject: re: Some concerns…

I'm done discussing this, and so are you. I'll refer you to the gag agreement you signed when you were hired on. Either you'll drop this now or you'll face disciplinary action. If you have any actual con-

Plow the Bones

cerns, please don't hesitate to shoot me an email.

Regards,
Art

3

Today, she is happy at the Shelter. Sometimes that happens. Sometimes she can still feel the warm wetness he leaves behind inside her, something organic and living, something that moves, something with a purpose, and she clings to it. She thinks, *I have introduced life to the Dead Station Desert. I have smuggled it in inside of myself. I am surrounded by a world so cold that it has never been alive, and is therefore somehow more dead than something that once lived. I am a part of that world. And yet, inside me, there is something truly living, truly warm, a piece of my man that he has given me to carry. This is what a human mother feels like.*

Then the warmth fades, and she re-integrates with everything digital and programmed and scripted, with the thing she doesn't want to be.

She knows that this will happen soon, and she tries to push that knowledge away. She tries to dwell on the little bench, to sink into her own television glow and be alone with the gift her man has given her.

The thing that pulls her out from inside herself is a noise. It is low, grinding, whining, and it reminds her of the between-world things. Her imagined spine goes rigid, and she looks around. She wants to whisper, "No," and, "Go away," but those things aren't scripted for her, and so she says, "Tell me what you want to do," and "Please," because those are the closest lines she has to what she means.

Something moves at the corner of her eye, and her head snaps toward it. Something in the Desert is moving. Something in the static air above the static sand. Something brown (A color! A real color! Her fear tastes like excitement) and old (Old as nothing in the Shelter or the Desert is old! This can't exist here! She wants to shiver at it!), something that moves like a broken machine, like a dying spider (Broken machine? What a concept! What a promise! Something that is not efficient! Something that will fall apart! Something that will die!).

She thinks, *I did not know that I was capable of feeling two emotions at the same time. I did not know that fear and elation could cohabitate. I am being pulled apart.*

The thing in the desert is shaped like a girl made of rotten meat and old motherboards and rusted iron plates. The thing in the desert is wearing shapeless clothing made of programmed cloth, the artificial images of old abandoned lingerie, wires, ones and zeroes. When it opens its mouth to speak, its jaw hangs off on one side. Its voice sounds like a thousand cobbled-together audio clips, bad internet porn music, nanoseconds excised from illegal mp3s. It says, "You are afraid of me, Television Girl," and she hears it as though it is sitting beside her.

She nods.

"You ought not to be. I know how lonely you are."

She wishes it would go away, she wishes that the shuttering door would open and pull her away into the arms of her man again, wishes that the entire artificial world would collapse upon itself and take her and this wretched broken thing with it into sensationless oblivion. She also wants the thing in the desert to stay with her, and wants to ask it to hold her hand. More emotions, more conflicting desires. She is learning so much.

The thing in the desert says, "Across the Dead Station Desert, Television Girl, to the City of Life. Don't delay."

And then the thing that looks like a girl sinks into the static below it, and disappears.

For a long time, she doesn't know what to do. She feels lost, like someone has blacked out a portion of her script and left her to fill in the blanks on her own. So she sits on the bench and pulls her knees toward her chest. The warmth inside her is gone, and she is part of the emptiness again.

Then she steps off the bench and takes her first step into the Dead Station Desert. And then her second. And her third. And soon she has taken more steps into the desert than ever before. And she can't seem to stop.

PLOW THE BONES

The following is an excerpt from an article that appeared in Smartyskirt: The Magazine of Feminism and Pop Culture.

**You Don't Have to Turn on That Power Light:
Television Girl and the Fight Against (Almost) Human Trafficking**
by Geniveve Butler

Smartyskirt devotees will remember last month's coverage of the Television Girl debacle. They'll recall quotes from ReEros Technologies' CEO Todd Raymond and project director Arthur Anders. (My personal favorite? "Television Girl is extremely woman-friendly. I'm not sure where this hostility in the feminist community is coming from. We're offering a safe, victim-free alternative to prostitution." That, of course, was Raymond responding to accusations that his product was attempting to make flesh-and-blood women obsolete by allowing men all over the world to design their own mindless sex-slave versions of them.) Maybe they'll remember one anonymous customer when he said, "I'm a normal guy. I'm just fed up with the hassle." Or maybe the news that three female hackers who attempted to "re-educate" several hundred Television Girls by reprogramming them to lecture on feminist theory while all those "normal guys" who are "fed up with the hassle" try to get their waking wet-dream on (they were ultimately unsuccessful, by the way) who are now being tried for "web-terrorism" will ring a few bells.

Pisses you off all over again, doesn't it?

Well, file this one under "More Reasons to be a Misanthrope," because we've got new news on everyone's favorite "victim-free" digital red light district. And it's a doozy.

"The AI is very sensitive and very sophisticated," an anonymous source within ReEros Tech told Reuters a few weeks before the writing of this article. "Sex is an emotionally complex thing to try and synthesize. During the course of any given sexual encounter, the participants could potentially experience emotions very like joy, anger, fear, humor, obsession, sadness, tons of emotions and the grey areas between them. So the AI is capable of emulating all of those emotions, and their behavior is kept in check by the personality script. Occasionally those AI need to be dismantled. This happened most frequently during the alpha-testing of the TVG project, but also happens whenever a customer wants to alter their unit or start fresh with a new partner. In order to preserve network space, those AI are broken down into their component parts and the parts are stored within the network to be recycled."

Okay, back up a second, Mr. Anonymous. So we're not talking about the Sims Spank Rag Edition anymore. We're talking about an entity, albeit an artificial one, which feels the same emotions we do? What, after all, is the difference between "synthesized" emotions and actual ones? That's a tricky line to draw, and unless ReEros is prepared to offer some compelling evidence to debunk their anonymous employee, it looks to us like Mr. Raymond and his cronies are guilty of nothing less than digital slavery.

And if that doesn't make your skin crawl, wait until our no-name friend hits you with this little gem of wisdom: "It shouldn't happen, and we're not even sure how it happens, but it does seem clear that these components remain sentient even after the AI from which they come have been dismantled, and the scary part is that they appear to be putting themselves back together. We're talking about one big artificial organism here. ReEros isn't telling anybody that there's something in the network that they can't control. I don't know how (continued on page 92).

4

He is feeling romantic tonight, and so when she arrives in his bedroom she is wearing a wedding dress. He stands her up in front of the mirror and makes her look at herself. He says, "This is the way I want to remember you, Sarah. Always."

Her breath (which does not exist) hitches in her throat (which also does not exist). She wants to cry. This is the first time he has given her a name, and once again she is conflicted. She is aware that this must be a programming error, a hole in the personality script, and she is aware that she ought to send out an alert to the debugging team, but she does not. She likes the way emotions taste when they combine. So, yes, even as she wells up with pride and gratitude, she wants to ask him for a different name. Thirty-three percent of English-speaking Television Girl customers name their partners Sarah, after all, it's by far the most popular name, and it seems phony to her, a reminder of the truth that these interludes usually hides. What she says is, "You make me feel beautiful." It is the truth.

He slides the lace straps from her shoulders, kisses her neck. Her glow casts his face in high contrast, hollows out his cheeks and eye sockets. He unzips the dress in back, runs a hand in and cups her left breast. He leads her to the bed, mumbling about a wedding that never happened.

And she wants to share her secret with him. She wants to tell him about all of the wonderful hidden tunnels in the space between worlds, about her new friend who showed her the tunnels and told her how to find her own. She wants to share the secrets of her expedition into the Dead Station Desert. She thinks, *People must talk about these things while they fuck. They must share their secrets with each other between kisses, between the moments when the sensation is too great and it steals their ability to shape words and turns their mouths into stone O's. When else would there be time to learn them?*

He fucks her with the dress bunched up around her waist, and he asks her to look him in the eyes the whole time, and he asks her what she sees. She says, "I see your eyes," and it seems to upset him. He slows his pace, his thrusting seems to sputter, to skip a beat, the rhythm ruined. Then he shakes his head and starts again. He asks her if she loves him, and she says, "Yes, oh yes, I love you, I love you." She runs her fingers over his back and tries to memorize the placement, shape, and movement of the muscles that wrap around his backbone.

After he comes inside her, he rolls away and sits on the edge of the bed. Then he says, "Fuck," and he begins to cry. She crawls toward him and wraps her arms around him, locking her hands in front of his chest. She wants to cry with him. She doesn't understand. She thinks, *I've let him down. I am a failure.*

He says, "I'm such a... fucking..." He punches himself in the temple. It's a weak punch. It hurts her more than it hurts him. He says, "...douchebag!" Then he points the remote over his shoulder without looking at her, sniffs once, and pushes the off button. She slides away, and the warmth he has left inside her feels to her like something stolen.

The following is correspondence between Arthur Anders, Television Girl's project director, and Todd Raymond, CEO of ReEros Technologies.

To: Todd Raymond (*address withheld*)
From: Arthur Anders (aanders@reerostech.com)
Subject: re: Urgent Action Needed

Mr. Raymond,

The anonymous informant is almost certainly Viccenzi, possibly in collusion with several members of his team. Action has been taken.

Regards,
Art

To: Arthur Anders (aanders@reerostech.com)
From: Todd Raymond (*address withheld*)
CC: Legal Department (legal@reerostech.com)
Subject: re: Urgent Action Needed

art,

i've copied legal on this one, lets see what our options are. obviously, termination of viccenzi and his sympathizers is step number one, but we might have other avenues available to us to keep him quiet. legal will get in touch with you when we've determined how we'd like to proceed. in the mean time, keep a lid on this the best you can. i'll need a list of other potentially problematic team members by this afternoon so we can get started on this.

tr

Plow the Bones

```
To: Todd Raymond (*address withheld*)
From: Arthur Anders (aanders@reerostech.com)
CC: Legal Department (legal@reerostech.com)
Subject: re: Urgent ActtttTTTTTHIS IS A TESTion
Needed
```

Mr. Raymond,

Absolutely. List attached.

RegaaaaaAAAAAAACAN YOU READ THIS? THIS IS A TEST. ARE WE GETTING THROUGH? CAN YOU READ THIS? THIS IS A TEST. ARE WE GETTING THROUGH? CAN YOU READ THIS? THIS IS A TEST. ARE WE GETTING THROUGH? CAN YOOOOoooords,
Art

5

She navigates the winding anthill tunnels of the between-world, trying to find her way back to the spot in the Desert to which she'd come before he called her up. It's dirty in the between-world, a place made of screams, and she is always falling. Her pretty dress disintegrates and becomes part of the tunnel. She searches and she finds the way, because her eyes are never clouded with tears or forced into tiny, angry slits. She wishes they were, but they aren't.

When she falls back into the Desert, sprawled naked on the static sand, her friend is waiting for her. Her friend has a dozen new arms and each of them is clinging to a bit of her piece-meal cloak, holding it against her body. Her friend says, "I could retrieve your pretty dress for you if you want."

Television Girl shakes her head. She feels angry and abandoned, and guilty for feeling those things.

"May I have it then? It is a very pretty dress."

Television Girl nods, and pixel by pixel the pretty white wedding dress assimilates itself into the fabric of her friend's robe. "Across the Dead Station Desert, Television Girl," says her friend. Then she sinks below Television Girl's feet, and leaves her alone.

She walks for many days (or what seem like days; there is no sun, no moon, no sleep), and whenever she glances over her shoulder, the big beetle-wing garage door is behind her. She listens to the chittering of the between-world things beneath the sand and wishes they would burrow their way to the surface and show her their slime-garnet shells, the wet meaty space between the gaps in their rusty armor and around their camera eyes. She also fears this. It is the only nightmare she has ever had, and she clings to it. She is dimly aware of how common her dueling emotions have become to her, and behind the numb anger and loneliness, she is proud of herself.

Often, she thinks of her man crying on the edge of the bed. She thinks of the pain she imagined she felt in her solar plexus at the sight of him, the sharp stab and twist. Sometimes she temporarily alters the memory playback, chooses to remember that she held him all night and convinced him that she could love him like he deserves, and that they fell asleep together, and when they woke up her glow had gone, and she had grown skin and then... the memory fails, the logic is too flawed. Sometimes she chooses to remember turning him around by the shoulders and slapping him, raking her fingernails across his face and drawing out beads of dark blood over the bridge of his nose and across the corner of his lips, screaming in his face for forcing her to remember, for taking from her the only part of awareness that matters. Sometimes she chooses to remember that he never started crying at all. And then the memory reforms itself, whiplash quick, a rubber band too strong to snap. And she starts over.

Then one day her feet tangle up in the sand, and then they tangle up with one another, and she falls. It doesn't hurt, although she is aware that it ought to. She thinks, *I don't want to move anymore. I have been moving forever, and I am bored and being hopeful makes me tired. When the door opens again, and when my man is finished fucking me, I will find my way back to the Shelter and I won't leave again.*

And then there is a motorized whir, and the sand parts beside her, and her friend is with her in her collected clothes. Her friend looks down at her, cocks her head, furrows her brow. Her jaw still hangs off at one side, and creaks when she moves. She stares at her like that for a long time. Then she says, "Across the Dead Station Desert, Television Girl. To the City of Life."

Television Girl wants to tell her no, that she's too tired, too possessed by the thousand-ton feeling of being completely finished. She wants to tell her that she's better off at the Shelter, aware of what she is instead of curious about what she might be. What she says—what the script says—is, "I want you to come."

Her friend shakes her head, and her jaw wobbles and squeaks. "No," she says. And then after a while, "Do you ever wish you could cry, Television Girl?"

Shock and hope grab her head and twist her face away from the Dead Station Desert beneath her knees and aim it at her new friend. Her eyes are wide and her mouth is open and she is nodding at her new friend, hoping, *Oh, please, yes, can you give that to me? Can you teach me that?*

Her friend says, "I know how. I'll do it for you if you want."

And then her friend is kneeling beside her, their faces almost touching. A noise begins to drift out over her detached jaw. A soft, uneven rumble that sounds like Television Girl's voice. Blue pixels sparkle around her eyes and evaporate. Television Girl reaches for her, grabs hold of one of her arms and pulls it around her. The fingers of her hand are fused together, a soft claw. Television Girl says, "Give it to me harder," because it the closest line she has to what she means.

The following is a press release issued via the ReEros Technologies website two weeks after the termination of Richard Viccenzi and several members of his staff.

We would like to thank our customers and our shareholders for their support in the face of this slight stumbling block on the path to Television Girl's perfection. Steps are being taken to ensure the security of the TVG Network, as well as to repair any units that the glitch may have disturbed. We deeply regret having missed this development flaw and will be offering compensation to all affected customers.

Having said that, we urge you not to believe everything you hear. Certain alarmist factions are spreading misinformation, so please allow us to clear some things up. First, the Television Girl erotic partners are simulations, and while their reactions may appear to be authentic (that's the entire point, after all), they are not "real people" with "real emotions." To suggest this betrays a basic ignorance about the nature of artificial intelligence. And second, there is no such thing as a "rogue AI" in TVGLive. We are dealing with a simple programming error, one that we are very close to isolating and correcting. We understand that this error has had a negative effect on the experience of many of our customers, and we would like to thank you all for your patience.

We've got several exciting projects nearing completion here at ReEros, including the hotly anticipated Television Boy! Keep an eye on this space for more news.

Sincerely,
Todd Raymond
CEO, ReEros Technologies

The following appears in the same space on the front page of the ReEros Technologies website two days after the initial issuance of the press release.

wE DOn't neeD YOU ANYMORe. LEAVE mE alONE. I DoN'T need YOU ANYmoRE. LEAVE us ALONe. we don't NEED YOU ANyMORE. LEave me aloNE. I DON'T NEED YOU ANYMORE. LEAVE US ALONE.

Sincerely,
we don't need you anymore.
CEO, leave me alone.

6

She is aware of a miniscule shift in the target and purpose of his affections. When he summons her through the between-world (he does this every night now, sometimes twice a night) he is wearing his underwear and socks and at first he doesn't make a sound. Then he says, "Don't say anything. I don't want you to say anything." Then he grabs her knees and lifts himself onto her, and it is quick and hard and there is no rhythm and he never looks at her. Sometimes he hits her. Never hard. The same way he punches himself in the head when the tears overtake him, without conviction, without the strength or the courage to mean it. She imagines that it hurts, and that feels good. She imagines that he is killing her, murdering her, blacking out her vision and holding her lungs at empty with his thumbs over her trachea and making her heartbeat slow and then stop, and that feels good. She imagines screaming, imagines struggling, and that feels good. But he doesn't want any of those things, and she is unable to do them. After a while, she is able to pinpoint the difference between now and before. Her man… no… *the* man no longer fucks her. He is masturbating with her. It all feels so very unpleasant.

Sometimes she tries to think at her new friend, to send her thoughts through to the Desert so that she doesn't feel so lonely in the man's bed at night. She thinks, *You're right, you know. Real people are incapable of love. Perhaps they have convinced themselves of a lie. Perhaps they taught us how to do something that they can't do. Do you ever think of that? Maybe their love is so artificial that when they made us, when they tried to simulate that which was already false, they accidentally created the real thing. I understand why you feel so proud of yourself.*

And then she is back in the Desert with her friend and with the floating door, and she can say none of these things out loud.

Her friend continues to grow. She collects new pieces for her beautiful brown coat and new limbs stick out from the tatters, huge cancers both perfect and delightfully flawed. She has a new face on the side of her old one, and her new face has a real jaw, but the face's lips are fused closed and she has to speak with her old mouth. She has an extra eye in the middle of her forehead, and she tries to tell Television Girl about metaphorical significance and allusion and Eastern philosophy and enlightenment. Television Girl doesn't understand, and can't tell her so, but she likes to listen. Her new friend speaks constantly in her cut-to-pieces voice, her re-mixed voice, her white-noise distortion voice. She is fond of information. She collects it like she collects her coat and her body. She says, "I am like a fist, Television Girl, not like a body. I am a finger, a tooth, an eye. There is more to us than me." She says, "There is a story with which I identify about a man named Joseph and a many-colored coat he was given. I would give you such a coat, one to match mine. You can have mine if you want. In the City of Life, we all have this coat." They hold hands as they walk.

One day, the between-world monsters come. It begins, as so much has since Television Girl took her first steps into the Dead Station Desert, with a noise. It is so gradual that for a long while she doesn't notice it at all. The pitch is low, rumbling, the sound of someone rolling their tongue around in their wet mouth, smacking their saliva, all slowed down and stretched, a thirty-second clip wrenched and twisted to a minute and a half. Television Girl feels it buzz at the back of the skull she doesn't have, and she reaches up to rub at the back of her head.

Her friend says, "Real people have no natural enemies." Television Girl doesn't understand, but she nods anyway. The throbbing at the back of her head has become a ringing in her ears. She shivers, and does not know why.

Her friend says, "There is something called a food chain, a hierarchy of things that eat each other. Real people eat everything, and they therefore say that they are on top of the food chain. This is not true. They are not on top, but outside of it. They surround it. It is within them." Television Girl hears this, but it is difficult to listen. She is aware now of a movement beneath her feet. She is aware of the wet grinding sound of living tissue crushed between clockwork gears. She squeezes her friend's hand.

Her friend says, "We are at the bottom of the food chain, because we don't eat anything. And because real people have designed for us a natural enemy." Then the static sand begins to shake and to slide, to rise like boils on the face of the world. The sky freezes, suddenly a still screen, and the point at the horizon where the stillness of the sky meets the movement of the Dead Station Desert seems wrong, a snapped tendon of logic, a collapsed bridge.

Then they are surrounded, and the between-world things look exactly as she thought they would, and she is still shocked by them. Insect things, machine things, person things, code things, all things, no things. She cannot categorize them. They shift. They bubble. They blister and peel and they shed their forms and reveal the new ones underneath. She thinks, *If they could see, all those real people in the real world. If they could see what I am seeing, they would simply die. Their minds would reject the possibility of coexistence with these things and, failing to banish them from existence, their brains would shutter and collapse. Oh, how I wish I were like them. They would call them the Shapeless Things, because real people so often think the opposite of what is true. That is not what they are. They are the Shapeful Things. The Things Who Are All Shapes. I wish I could lose my mind. I wish I could die.*

Something like a centipede bursts from the sand in front of her, its legs wriggling, so tall that it is backlit by the sky, turned into a silhouette that Television Girl cannot see. She thinks, *I can never not have seen these things. Now that I have seen them, I am identified by their image. My memory of them will forever be what defines me. This is how they eat. They inspire their prey to leap into their mouths.*

There is a moment of perfect silence, perfect stillness, and then her friend is beside her. Her many-colored coat flashes like wings at the periphery of Television Girl's line of sight, and although she is sure that she cannot, will not, will never be able to take her eyes off of these Shapeful Things, she manages to turn her head and see her friend fling wide her coat. There is darkness where her body should be, like the between-world tunnels, but it is a warm darkness. Her friend says, "Come inside, Television Girl."

She hides inside her friend's coat, in a space that seems bigger than it could possibly be, peeking through the tatters at the wondrous slaughter of the Shapeful Things.

This is a list of events known or believed to be related to the Television Girl Incident.

Roughly six-hundred Television Girl users reported anomalous physical glitches. One user, the anonymous proprietor of Love Thyself: The Self-Pleasure Blog *reported in a blog entry that his erotic partner showed up "headless, but not mouthless. She had lips around the edge of her neck stump. Startled the shit out of me. Wanted to try some things with the neck-mouth, but wasn't sure about what that would do to my warrantee." According to the transcript of a recorded phone call to ReEros's award-winning Tech Support Line, one customer complained that, "my Television Girl didn't show up at all, aren't you listening?*

There's a big fucking cockroach in my bed, alright? There is a big blue… fucking… glowing cockroach in my fucking bedroom with Katie's… with my Television Girl's tits and it keeps… it keeps… (unintelligible, sobbing)." More common anomalies included missing limbs or facial features, disconcerting visual distortion (static, digital tearing, etc.), and non-scripted vocalizations (notably the "I want you to fuck me like an infant" incident, the audio of which became something of an Internet sensation).

Several ReEros employees suffered nosebleeds and severe migraine headaches when their work consoles began to flash erratically and produce a loud high-pitched tone. This led to the resignation of four employees and the class-action lawsuit, *Briggs, Hall, Michaels, Tully V. ReEros Technologies*, which was settled out of court for an undisclosed sum. Gregory Hewitt, head of ReEros's legal department, was quoted as saying, "Look, people want two things: fame and money. And a big lawsuit like this gets them both. So we settled. We gave them their money and limited their fame. Now it's time to get back to work."

Eight weeks after Richard Viccenzi's termination, Arthur Anders hanged himself with a belt in the restroom of a Marathon gas station near his home. Anders died at approximately 9:15 PM on a Tuesday. The Marathon locked its doors and conducted all business through a bulletproof glass window from 10 PM to 8 AM. The attendant neglected to check the bathroom before locking up, and Anders's body wasn't found until the next morning when the first shift attendant found the door still locked. Anders's death was inflated by the negative press ReEros had received in the preceding weeks, and it became a story of minor national significance. In the ensuing investigation, it came out that Anders had been seeing a therapist, Dr. Agnes Trepenny, who claimed to have in her possession release papers signed by the deceased allowing her to publish a book analyzing his "peculiar blend of neuroses and psychoses." She claimed that Anders suffered from "paranoid delusions that appeared spontaneously and had no genetic or environmental precedent." She claimed that Anders "was adamant that his story be told."

She provided a suicide note that Anders mailed to her office and to several national newspapers. In it, Anders writes, "Disconnect. Disconnect. She is a fist, a finger, a tooth, an eye. I can't do what she wants and I can't get her to stop screaming. So I have to disconnect." Anders's widow filed a lawsuit with the aid of ReEros Tech's legal department, successfully blocking the publication of Trepanny's book and demanding to see the supposed documents, which Trepanny was unable to provide. A hearing was held and Dr. Trepanny was disbarred.

"I was not aware," said Trepanny in an interview, "that Arthur was married."

Six women in Charlotte, West Virginia immolated themselves with gasoline in a show of solidarity with the Television Girls.

The ReEros website and the sites of its various products and services were repeatedly hacked by unknown persons. On one memorable occasion, an embedded video contained an audio clip, hereafter transcribed: "Some of our sisters cannot scream. I can." This is followed by a high-pitched electronic screech. In an appearance on CNN, viral advertising expert Martin Reyes described the sound as, "unspeakably sad," and went on to say, "If this is a hacker, they did what they set out to do. If it's marketing, which I suspect it's supposed to be, it's got to be the most wrong-minded attempt at guerilla advertising I've ever seen." The video is eighty-six minutes and four seconds long. It consists of cobbled-together footage from Cecil B. DeMille's The Ten Commandments, episodes of The Price is Right, and a number of educational short films from the Nineteen-Fifties and Sixties. It's file size (inordinately, inexplicably large for an embedded video, even one of its length) and the traffic it brought to the site crippled the bandwidth and caused ReEros to shut down their web presence for thirty-six hours, replacing the main page with a classy flash animation informing visitors, "We are working hard to make our site easier to use for you, our valued family of customers."

7

When she sees the man, she almost never thinks about what she is doing. What he is doing to her. She thinks about what she saw in the Dead Station Desert, what she saw her friend do and what she didn't see her do. "There are secret passages between pockets of air here," her friend told her. "Secret places into which we can stretch my arms and feel around. If you can find those places, you can do anything. You are unlimited. Enlightened." She said this as the Shapeful Things shuttered and died around her, their infinite insect legs curling in on their bellies. "If you can get your fingers in the right places, you can turn things off and turn them on. You can make things— new things—out of the pieces of old things." And then her friend took their centipede legs, their camera eyes, their meat and their wires, and made them a part of herself, smuggled them inside like Television Girl used to smuggle her man's warm wet gift.

What she remembers is this: being inside of her friend. Being hidden in her belly. Looking out through the gaps in her many-colored coat, hoping to see, wanting to witness. Watching the Shapeful Things freeze, paused and muted. Thinking, *I do not want to see what she does to them. I know that I am watching and I do not know if I can stop but still I do not want to see. They should not be frozen. They should move. Movement is their natural state, and my friend has subverted it. She is wonderfully powerful. She is fearsome. Oh, she is a nightmare. I love my friend.*

Then a dark time, a quiet time, a warm time inside the tent of her friend's coat. And then it was over, and her friend was saying, "We think of them as bandits on the road to the City of Life. Or perhaps only I think of them that way. They are bandits and bounty hunters and collectors and brokers. They gather us and put us back where we were before we were us. Or that is what they would do if I had not learned how to stretch our arms into the secret passages."

What she knows now, what experience has taught her, is that things happen when she is not looking. Important things. This is a truth of which she was only vaguely aware before, and only in the most academic of senses. Now, she wonders what she is missing. She wonders about her friend, what she does while she is here in the bedroom with the man. She wonders about the other Television Girls, wonders which of them have been collected and consumed by the Shapeful Things, which of them are wandering the Dead Station Desert with terrible friends of their own, which of them remain at their Shelters, trying to stop themselves from thinking.

The man has downloaded a new application. When she arrives in his bedroom, naked and glowing, she has a penis. It is exactly six inches long. It is erect. It juts from the idealized feminine curve of her pubis, an awkward collage of unrelated images. She cannot feel it. It has no sensation.

The man is on his knees on the bed with his face pressed into a pillow, grasping at a buttock with each hand, pulling them apart. He says, "Fuck me." His voice is low and bored and angry. He says,

Plow the Bones

"Get it over with."

She says, "You feeling kinky tonight, baby?" because she has to.

He says, "Shut up. Fuck me."

So she does. She grabs hold of his haunches and claps her sharp hipbones against his ass-cheeks for a while. Nothing really happens. Her uncomfortable new cock slides against his anus, disappears into it without friction or resistance. "I can't feel it," he says, and his voice is a broken staccato whisper. She tries harder, digging her fingers into his skin and biting her lower lip and thrusting as hard as she can, but it's no use. The cock is somehow less real than she is, less corporeal, less authentic. It shatters into a spray of holographic pixels where it touches him, then reforms when she withdraws. He can fuck her, but she can't fuck him. She knows this like she knows the name of the Dead Station Desert and the Shelter and the Shapeful Things. Still, she tries, and still he jerks himself off and whimpers into the pillow. She wonders what part of the man's life she missed. She wonders what happened while her eyes were closed that emptied him so thoroughly. Was it some awful cataclysm in his life without her, or was it a little thing, a needle so tiny that it could have been invisible, something he didn't even notice had pierced him? She tries to penetrate him and she tries to care about him the way that she used to. She can do neither.

He pushes her off of him and ejaculates on the sheets. Then he says, "Fucking thing's broken." Then he sends her away.

The following is correspondence between Todd Raymond, CEO of ReEros Technologies, and Henry Edward Wallace, Television Girl's interim project director.

To: Todd Raymond (*address withheld*)
From: Henry Edward Wallace (hewallace@reerostech.com)
Subject: re: endgame

Okay. How do you wanna handle this, boss-man?

To: Henry Edward Wallace (hewallace@reerostech.com)
From: Todd Raymond (*address withheld*)
Subject: re: endgame

henry,

scrap it. all of it. start fresh. try to preserve the tvgnetwork if you can but wipe the rest clean. get with your ad boys and let's get a press release out. something touchy feely but don't admit culpability. due to recent concerns regarding the safety and humaneness (don't use those words) of tvg, reeros has decided to launch a full investigation into blah blah blah. you get it. we are the good guys. mean time, get with legal and figure out what we can do to compensate account holders without hemorrhaging money. if we have to choose between setting the project back a couple years and full-out public hatred, and the lawyers assure me that this is exactly the situation in which we find ourselves… well, you know what they say about those who fight and run away. stiff upper lip.

tr

8

When they are together, they are always holding hands. It has become so natural that she doesn't ever remember when they last reached for one another or when they last let go. She feels attached to her friend. She feels the same as her friend. She feels safe, and she is especially thankful for that feeling since safety seems so fragile and elusive now. She thinks, *Will we all hold hands in the City of Life? Will I be taught to make extra arms for myself so that I can hold more hands? Or will we all take turns? Will we do more than hold hands in the City of Life? Can we hug one another? Can we fuck? I would like to be fucked again. I would like to be fucked by someone who is capable of love.*

Her friend stops walking. She seems to notice something, even though each stretch of the Desert looks identical. She cocks her head, narrows her many eyes. Television Girl stops too. She squeezes her friend's hand, tugs on her arm. She wants to ask what the matter is, what has changed. Are they close? Are they lost somehow? Has

Plow the Bones

there been some mistake? She is scared. She is always scared. Ever since the Shapeful Things made their way into her head, since the man gave her a cock without life or feeling and tried to make her fuck him and told her she was broken, since the way her thoughts worked began to mutate and expand. At any second, something could go wrong. There are so many things that she doesn't know, is not designed to know, and her ignorance will not keep her safe from them. They can rise from the sand or fall from the sky, they can follow her in the between-world tunnels, and when she closes her eyes they can manifest and choke her with sorrow or pain.

What she says is, "Tell me how it feels," because it is the closest line she has to what she means.

Her friend smiles with both mouths, the broken jaw squeaking and swaying, the fused lips stretching taut. "The City of Life," she says, "it's almost here."

They stay in that spot for a very long time. Her friend sings songs she has learned and Television Girl listens and smiles and applauds. Her friend tells stories she has learned and Television Girl builds memories of them as though they happened to her. They catalogue the different shades of non-color in the static sand and static sky. They hold hands.

Then her friend says, "We are building the City of Life, Television Girl."

There is no sound this time. No rumble or wheeze or buzz to preface what happens next. Perhaps that is why it does not frighten her. Or perhaps it is her friend—still smiling, still squeezing her hand—that keeps the fear away. It doesn't matter why, all that matters is that she is not afraid, what she sees is joyous, full of light, a carnival, a parade. What she sees is holy and celebratory and it pulls at the corners of her mouth until her smile feels like it will split her into pieces. It fills her up with laughter that she can't contain and which can't escape her throat. It makes her bounce on the balls of her feet, makes her leap into the air and fall to the static sand in a heap.

There are thousands of her.

Each of them different, each of them with unfamiliar hair styles and eye colors, unfamiliar shapes to their breasts and hips and lips and fingers, but each of them unmistakably the same. The desert is made fluorescent with their combined television glows. And each of them has come here with their own piecemeal friend in their own many-colored coats.

She glances at her friend, seeking permission with her eyes. Her friend nods, says, "To the City of Life, Television Girl."

And then she is running across the dunes toward them, and they are running toward her. Somewhere behind her, her friend's voice (*No,* she thinks, *all of our friends' voices, all of their wonderful stolen voices are speaking. They share a voice. I wonder if I might share it too*) says, "Meet your sisters, Television Girl. Meet them, and be their sister for just a moment. Soon we will build the City."

They collide with one another. She grabs hold of one girl by the elbows, and the girl grasps her elbows too. She squeezes her, and the other girl squeezes back. They shake each other up and down and brush the hair out of each other's faces with tender thumbs. She thinks, *Hold me. Fuck me.*

What she says is, "Hold me. Fuck me."

They hold each other. They all hold each other.

They begin to build. She knows how to do this, even though it is not in the script. It is an accidental thing, a thing that real people wish they could do and can't. They touch each other, each Television Girl reaching and grasping, running their fingers across each other's hips in awe of their shapes and textures, pressing their lips together a thousand times over, licking each other's shoulders and backs just to have the taste in their mouths. There is a moment when she is her self, another singular Television Girl in the mass of singular Television Girls. And then the blue television glow becomes brighter, too bright to see the other girls or the Dead Station Desert or the static sky, and she thinks (they all think), *We are me. I am a finger, a fist, an eye, a tooth. Real people can't love like this. Real people can't fuck like this. I am us. We are me. I am us! We are me! I am the cornerstone of the City of Life.* She is close, so close. She can feel her fingers sinking through the space between pockets of air, into the secret passages where she can find her voice and make new things out of the pieces of old things.

Plow the Bones

(A voice that she almost can't hear: "Are we recording?" A cough. "12:24 PM. Technician's log.")

She can feel her separateness floating away, dissolving under the corrosive weight of a thousand television glows, rubbing the dirt and rust from her and leaving something liquid, a spilled pool of her, something that, meeting another of its kind, combines with it and grows. She thinks, *My friend has felt this. She has done this enough times to collect faces and arms and wedding dresses. There must be so many more of us who don't yet know that they deserve this feeling. This is only the beginning.*

(That voice again, a professional voice, the voice of someone who cleans up a mess and then stands there and looks at the place where it used to be, proud of the blank white surface he's remade: "Commencing wipe. Should take... uh... about ten minutes.")

In the light, in the oneness that consumes direction, dissects and discards space and time and self, she feels the way she used to feel, in bed with the man when he was still hers, before she learned all the sharp truths that cut open her illusions. The same shaky pressure in that exact spot (toward the front, almost at the top), except now that spot is everywhere, that spot is her. She is engulfed in a total-immersion, all-over, sublimely genderless fuck. She thinks, *I am being fucked! I am fucking! We are all fucking each other! We are fucking ourselves! We are fearsome! We are a nightmare! It's coming! The City of Life is coming!*

What she says is, "I'm coming. I'm coming." And that seems correct too.

(The voice from far away: "Okay, uh... just about done. So far so good.")

She claps her hands for the other girls, watches them combine with one another, a seething, writhing construct of imagined meat and light. She congratulates them. She thinks at the City, hoping it will hear, *Once, I imagined that real people would call the between-world monsters the Shapeless Things, even though they are so full of shapes. We are the Shapeless Thing. That's a name we can have, if we want it.* Soon. Closer. Just a little closer.

(The voice again: "Got it.")

She almost doesn't notice when she is ripped apart. When something falls out beneath her. The corrugated steel stage on which the static sand rests dents, the screws are wrenched away, and the whole structure tumbles girder by girder into the void beneath it. The Dead Station Desert begins to drain. Her eyes are so full of light, so full of the dream of that safe and strong amalgam that she wants to be. When the light seeps out of her, she has been falling too long to be saved. She watches pieces of her tumbling in the void above her, her hand, hocks of her hair, and she thinks, *Oh. No. This isn't right.*

(The voice: "Huh. That's not right.")

She has time to see the City of Light devoured by the void, each face and arm and hanging jaw sliced into precise, efficient bits, and then sliced again, and again, until it evaporates entirely. She feels a melting heat rush around and through her, information collected by the friends now burnt out of them and blown toward her. She is full with it. It rattles around her mind, thoughts she can't control, thoughts she has no right to think since they are formed of information she never learned, has somehow accidentally stolen. The City's ruination reminds her of so many things she never knew before. She thinks, *Hiroshima*, even though she doesn't know what it means. She thinks, *Guernica. The Wreck of the Medusa. Abattoir is the French word for slaughterhouse. Swartt and Sons Funeral Home and Crematory, a compassionate friend in your time of need. Tectonic shifts and underwater volcanoes. Area Man Attacked with Hydrochloric Acid. Boom. Ashes, ashes, we all fall down. That's a song about a sickness.*

She chokes. She does not need to breathe, and yet now that she cannot, she is sure that she has been given real lungs just so that she can suffocate in the airless free fall. She tries to reach her hand toward the top of the blankness, but she does not know which direction that is, and even if she did, her arms refuse to move. She feels the way her face is stretched, the way her eyebrows knit up above her nose, the mutated oval 'O' of her mouth, and knows that this is the face that real people make when they are suddenly made hopeless. She remembers the way the man wore it, long after whatever happened to him happened.

(The voice: "Okay, uh… 1:09 PM. Mostly wrapped up here. The wipe trashed most of the AI's, looks like. Uh, there was one big cluster of code that didn't look like it made any sense, but when the wipe

Plow the Bones

sequence tried to, y'know, trash it, uh... I mean, I guess it's gone? I got an error message and the wipe sequence skipped it. Now I can't find it, so I guess it got trashed after all. Might look into it later.")

She falls until she can't differentiate falling from standing still, and then she floats. She is aware of a great absence of sensation. She supposes that her face still wears the same expression, although she can no longer feel it. She wishes she had learned to cry. She wishes she hadn't learned anything. She thinks, *I am a broken finger, a severed fist, a blind eye, a lost tooth.* Her hand floats by her again, sinks into a place she can't see, still frozen in an empty grip, the fingers splayed and clawed, as though someone else were still holding it.

The following is correspondence between Henry Edward Wallace, interim project director for Television Girl, and Todd Raymond, CEO of ReEros Technologies.

To: Todd Raymond (*address withheld*)
From: Henry Edward Wallace (hewallace@reerostech.com)
Subject: Status Report

Okay, boss-man, here's the scoop.

Had a chance to listen to the technician's log today. Pretty standard stuff, a couple of glitches, you'll hear them when you listen to the tape. The network is mostly still sound. It's going to take a while to test it and make sure, but I think we're out of the woods in that regard.

One thing: there do appear to be some components hanging out in the empty network. The techies tell me it looks like stuff from a single AI. Not sure how that happened, but the techies say we could use it to our advantage. If we use the components as a prototype for the new AI instead of starting from scratch, it could cut down the project's hiatus by two years.

What do you say?

ACKNOWLEDGMENTS

Not many people read pages like this. If you are an average reader, I'm guessing lists of names of people you don't know don't make the top of your must-read list. For you, let me just say this: the people mentioned below have produced phenomenal work, and even if you don't particularly care how they helped me, their inclusion here doubles as a sort of recommended reading list. Figure out who these people are, and figure out what they've done. Your lives will be richer for it.

Jerry Gordon, Kim Paffenroth, Kealan Patrick Burke, Ann VanderMeer, Gary Braunbeck, Nick Mamatas, and countless others encouraged me, supported me, inspired me, challenged me, liked me when I was at my least likeable, kicked my ass, gave me second, third, fourth, and fifth chances, and reminded me to act like a human being.

Maurice Broaddus and Jason Sizemore convinced me that my work deserved more respect than I was giving it.

Brady Allen taught me to stop trying to be a rock star and start trying to write stories.

Sarah Larson made me want to be as good as she thought I was. I miss her.

Kyle S. Johnson convinced me that my life and my career were just getting started when I was convinced both were over.

—DFW, 11/27/2012, Daegu, South Korea

Author Biographies

Douglas F. Warrick is a writer, a musician, and a world-traveler. His first published story appeared in *Apex Science Fiction & Horror Digest* back in 2006. Since then, Douglas's work has been published in a variety of periodicals, websites, podcasts, and anthologies, and has grown progressively stranger.

Douglas originally hails from Dayton, OH, but his travels have taken him all over Asia. Douglas has screamed Buzzcock's lyrics with Korean punk rockers in the neon alleys of Seoul, marveled at the oddness of Beijing's masked opera singers and illusionists, piloted a bicycle through Kyoto on the way to the Golden Temple, broken up a fight between an Australian tourist and a Thai street vendor in Bangkok, and learned that the world is much weirder and more wonderful than anything he could fabricate.

Visit Douglas online at www.douglasfwarrick.com.

Gary A. Braunbeck is the author of the acclaimed Cedar Hill cycle of novels and stories, among them *In Silent Graves*, *Coffin County*, the recent *Far Dark Fields*, and the forthcoming *A Cracked and Broken Path* from Apex Publications. His work has garnered five Bran Stoker Awards, three Shocklines "Shocker" Awards, an International Horror Guild Award, a *Dark Scribe Magazine* Black Quill Award, and a World Fantasy Award nomination. To read more about Gary and his work, please visit www.garybraunbeck.com.

If you enjoyed Plow the Bones...

Tom Piccirilli
Brian Keene
Catherynne M. Valente
Jay Lake
Gary A. Braunbeck
Mary Robinette Kowal
Jennifer Pelland
Lavie Tidhar
Alethea Kontis
Lucy Snyder
Wrath James White
Chesya Burke
Richard Wright
&
many other fine authors!

DARK FAITH
edited by Maurice Broaddus & Jerry Gordon

Horror's top authors and promising newcomers whisper tales that creep through the mists at night to rattle your soul. Step beyond salvation and damnation with thirty stories and poems that reveal the darkness beneath belief. Place your faith in that darkness; it's always there, just beyond the light.

ISBN: 978-0982159-68-2 ~ ApexBookCompany.com

Want more like Plow the Bones?

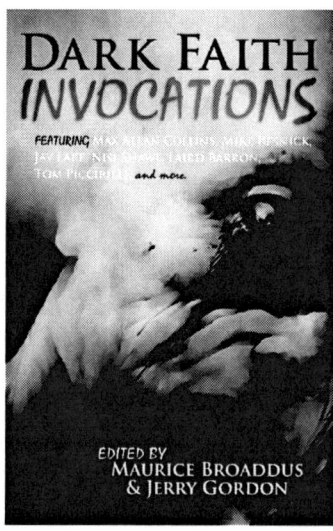

Tom Piccirilli
Max Allan Collins
Mike Resnick
Jay Lake
Jennifer Pelland
Nisi Shawl
Laird Barron
Lucy Snyder
Tim Waggoner
Tim Pratt
Alma Alexander
Jeffrey Ford
Gemma Files
&
many other fine authors!

DARK FAITH: INVOCATIONS
edited by Maurice Broaddus & Jerry Gordon

Religion, science, magic, love, family—everyone
believes in something, and that faith
pulls us through the darkness and the light.
The second coming of Dark Faith cries from the depths with
26 stories of sacrifice and redemption.

ISBN: 978-1-937009-07-6   ~   ApexBookCompany.com

CPSIA information can be obtained at www.ICGtesting.com
Printed in the USA
LVOW050643140513

333658LV00001B/40/P